The
VENICE
MURDERS

BOOKS BY MERRYN ALLINGHAM

FLORA STEELE MYSTERY SERIES

The Bookshop Murder

Murder on the Pier

Murder at Primrose Cottage

Murder at the Priory Hotel

Murder at St Saviour's

Murder at Abbeymead Farm

Murder in a French Village

The Library Murders

Murder at Cleve College

Murder in an English Castle

SUMMERHAYES HOUSE SERIES

The Girl from Summerhayes

The Secrets of Summerhayes

THE TREMAYNE MYSTERIES SERIES

The Dangerous Promise

Venetian Vendetta

Caribbean Evil

Cornish Requiem

Rio Revenge

The London Reckoning

The

VENICE
MURDERS

Merryn Allingham

bookouture

Published by Bookouture in 2025

An imprint of Storyfire Ltd.
Carmelite House
50 Victoria Embankment
London EC4Y 0DZ

www.bookouture.com

The authorised representative in the EEA is Hachette Ireland
8 Castlecourt Centre
Dublin 15 D15 XTP3
Ireland
(email: info@hbgi.ie)

ISBN: 978-1-83618-585-7
eBook ISBN: 978-1-83618-584-0

To a most beautiful city that I've grown to love.

1

VENICE, JUNE 1959

'Happy?' Jack Carrington asked.

His nearly new wife looked up from the risotto she'd been demolishing, her face aglow, and reached across the table to squeeze his hand.

'How could I not be?'

Sitting beneath La Zucca's green-striped awning, baskets of flowers hanging from its iron rails. Flora's gaze drifted across the narrow canal that ran alongside the terrace: to the jumble of pink-painted houses and terracotta roofs opposite and to the landing stage where a solitary gondola danced on the coming tide as it waited for morning.

'Our first evening in Venice, Jack! And only a few hours ago, we were still in Sussex! I find that so hard to believe.'

The journey had been smooth, far smoother than she'd expected. When Jack had first suggested they fly to Venice, she hadn't been at all keen. It had taken him time to persuade her that, if they were to make the most of their honeymoon, this was the way to travel; had taken time to overcome her fear of boarding a plane for the first time in her life. But eventually she'd agreed, swallowing hard when the tickets arrived and she saw how much they had cost. In the event, those tickets had been worth every penny, though Flora couldn't say that she'd actually enjoyed the experience – in her opinion, the plane was flying quite high enough at treetop level – but the pilot had had other ideas and somehow in less than four hours they had arrived at Treviso airport and from there taken a coach to the Piazzale Roma.

Her first sight from the coach, however, of what she'd taken to be Venice, had been a crushing disappointment; a glimpse of a forest of cranes, a spread of smokestacks and clouds of filthy air.

'Mestre,' she'd read aloud from a signpost they were passing 'So not Venice?' She was hopeful.

'Porto Marghera,' Jack told her. 'Mestre is next door. Marghera is the industrial zone. Chemicals are what they manufacture mostly.'

'It looks a wretched place.'

'It looked even more wretched after our bombers got to grips with it,' he said drily.

'I didn't think Venice was bombed in the war.'

'Venice wasn't. Marghera was. In the thirties, there must have been sixty or so working factories here. The place seems gradually to be getting back on its feet, but it's taken a while to recover.'

They had crossed the causeway by then which, together with the railway bridge, ensured that Venice was no longer an island, and arrived at a Piazzale Roma that to Flora had seemed little better. It appeared to be nothing more than a giant car park which, in truth, it was, since from this point travelling by road was impossible.

But then the magic had happened. A private launch sent from the Cipriani was waiting close by, ready to take them on a wondrous journey down the Grand Canal. And how truly grand it was – every bit as magnificent as Flora had expected, palazzo after palazzo standing proud on either side of the broad waterway.

In no time, it seemed, they'd travelled its whole length and were being whisked across a further stretch of water to the hotel she had set her heart on, and to a beautiful balcony room. They'd had time then only for a swift unpacking before they'd caught the same launch back to St Mark's, back to Venice itself, to enjoy this, their first dinner, of what was now a very belated honeymoon.

'That was the best risotto I've eaten in years,' Jack said, pushing his empty plate to one side and easing himself back into the wicker chair. 'Dare I say, even better than Alice's.'

Alice Jenner, head chef at the Priory Hotel, an expensive establishment in their home village of Abbeymead, had charged them with collecting recipes wherever they could on this trip. It would keep them busy, she'd said severely, too busy to get involved in any of 'that pokin' and pryin''. She wanted them home in one piece.

'You can say it, as long as you don't let her hear. She's been trying to achieve the perfect risotto, I think, ever since she read Elizabeth David, but has never quite got there – no one else in England seems to make it better, though. Do you think the restaurant owner would give us the recipe?'

'I doubt he would. It's probably a family secret. In any case, the chap seems too busy to ask.'

Flora glanced from the terrace towards the restaurant door where the proprietor was talking earnestly with another man. More than earnestly, she thought. He had his legs planted astride, almost filling the doorway, his hands were pistons thrusting at the air and his plump cheeks appeared to quiver as he spoke.

'Don't we know that man? The man he's talking to. He's from our hotel, isn't he? The receptionist who checked us in.'

Jack followed her gaze. 'Yes, you're right. Nice chap. Franco – that was the name on his badge.'

Franco Massi had been helpful, offering them all the courtesies expected of a prestigious hotel, but doing so with an engaging friendliness. He'd been happy to suggest several restaurants near St Mark's where they might eat on their first evening in the city. This small restaurant, with its brightly striped awning, had been one of his recommendations.

The quarrel, and it was definitely a quarrel, had now escalated in noise and fury and several of the customers at the surrounding tables had begun to look alarmed. The owner, Silvio Fabbri, according to the legend above the doorway, stopped punching the air and instead jabbed fingers at his antagonist's chest, whereupon Franco grabbed hold of the man's arm and twisted it to one side. A full-scale confrontation was emerging but was saved, to Flora's relief, by the waiter who had served them. He stepped between the two men, muttering something beneath his breath and waving a warning hand towards the sea of customers transfixed by the dispute. It seemed to bring both men to their senses; Fabbri let his hands fall to his sides while the receptionist pulled back, then turned abruptly on his heel and marched away.

'What was that about, do you think?' Flora's eyes were wide. 'Did you understand anything?'

Jack had learnt a little Italian from his war years, but the speech had been too rapid and too idiomatic for him to translate even a sentence. He shook his head. 'They were speaking in dialect, I'm pretty sure.'

'Veneziano? I read about it. My book said it was the local language.'

'It could have been Veneziano. I wouldn't know. But it was a nasty confrontation.'

'Yes,' she said, feeling a little unsettled. 'And strange, too. Franco appeared such an easy-going man. But it's over, and I'm about to eat my first Italian ice cream before a very long sleep in that magnificent bed that's waiting for us.' She pondered the menu. 'But how on earth am I to choose? *Crema, amarena, vaniglia, fragola, pesca*, and on and on... which one, Jack?'

'*Cioccolato* and *crema*,' he said without hesitation. 'Made for you!'

It wasn't until the next morning that the quarrel they'd witnessed was recalled. After a leisurely breakfast on the Cipriani terrace overlooking the lagoon, they again took the hotel's complimentary ferry across the Giudecca Canal to St Mark's Square, and spent most of the morning wandering, stopping only for Flora to browse one or two of the gift shops they saw on the way. Walking was the thing to do. All the guidebooks Flora had read had been adamant. Just walk, they'd advised: along narrow paths, over small bridges, in and out of piazzas. Lose yourself in the atmosphere; in fact, lose yourself quite literally. That would have been easy enough, she thought, but thanks to Jack's map reading, they arrived at the Accademia Gallery as they'd intended, only to decide that it was too beautiful a day to spend indoors.

Now, elbows resting on the plain wood of the Accademia Bridge, an appealing counterpoint to the marble splendours all around, Flora looked along the glinting waters of the Grand Canal. On one side, the dome of Santa Maria della Salute and on the other a quieter bend of the canal which would lead eventually to the Rialto Bridge.

'Shall we keep walking, or is it time to try some lunchtime pasta?' she asked, holding her face up to the sun. Freckles were already making themselves at home, first on the bridge of her nose and later, she knew, they would sprinkle her cheekbones.

Jack came to a halt, appearing to weigh the options. 'My stomach is definitely suggesting pasta, and my legs are saying they've had enough, so let's find a café – there'll be plenty on our way back to St Mark's.'

Arm in arm, they sauntered off the bridge, Jack stopping to buy a newspaper from one of the local sellers they passed. 'Testing my Italian,' he explained.

'And, of course, that's just what you need on a honeymoon!' She gave him a playful nudge, catching hold of the paper as he was tucking it under his arm. 'This photograph on the front page.' She opened the newspaper fully. 'Isn't that... isn't that Franco Massi?'

Jack stopped, spreading the paper wide and fumbled for his reading glasses. Once he had them perched on his nose, he peered down at the image, frowning heavily. 'You're right. It is him. Oh... oh...!' Abruptly, he folded the newspaper in half and went once more to tuck it beneath his arm.

'What?' she asked, half-impatient, half-concerned.

'He's... he's dead,' Jack said reluctantly.

'He can't be.'

Even more reluctantly, he unfolded the paper again and showed it to her. 'The report says that a man was found in the Grand Canal early this morning, a little way from the Rialto – by a worker at the market – and has subsequently been identified. Hence the picture, I imagine.'

'Are you reading it right?'

'I know my Italian is poor, but I can read that. It's there in black and white.' His fingers gave the newspaper a sharp rap.

'He wasn't at reception this morning, was he?' she said slowly. 'I imagined it must be his day off, but...'

Flora fell silent for a moment, adjusting the straps of her sundress several times as though it would help her to think. 'Franco was in such a temper last night when he stormed off, I wonder... do you think he could have been walking blind, not watching where he was going, then tripped and fell into the canal?'

Even as she voiced the explanation, it felt limp. Jack, however, seemed keen to agree. 'Probably,' he said. 'I guess people fall into canals every day.'

To Flora's ears, he sounded hopeful, and she knew why. He'd want nothing to disturb what should be a perfect holiday. It didn't stop him, though, from returning to read the article, his eyes now travelling down the paper. 'There's a sly comment here from the journalist. Not actually accusing the dead man of being a drunkard, but suggesting he wasn't averse to a drink.'

'Massi wasn't drunk,' she objected.

'Not when we saw him, but later? In an alcoholic haze, it wouldn't be difficult to come a cropper in that maze of alleyways and end up in a canal.'

Flora felt the niggle, a lack of conviction. 'Unless it wasn't an accident.'

Jack lowered the paper and stared at her. 'No!' he said at last. 'Definitely no! We are not going there, Flora. This is our honeymoon. Massi's death is being treated as an accident by the authorities and that's how it should stay.'

'Of course it should,' she said airily.

Side by side, they strolled in silence along the narrow alleyway and into a large open square, home to several cafés.

'Shall we find a table here?' he asked.

Eating, though, no longer felt so important to Flora and instead of answering his question, she said quietly, 'I don't think we should forget how many times we've encountered so-called "accidents" – in Abbeymead and beyond – which in the end have turned out not to be so accidental.'

'Flora!' he pleaded.

She gave a little shrug. 'OK. If you insist, it's an accident.' She took his arm again and hugged him close. 'You're probably right. It was a different situation when it was our own village involved and people who were close to us. In any case, Venice is too wonderful to be sidetracked.'

'Good,' he said encouragingly. 'Now for lunch. We could eat here or walk on to the Giardini. There's a lovely café in the gardens, I remember, but it's a bit of a hike.'

'No matter. It means I'll see even more of Venice on the way. And isn't it wonderful being able to eat outdoors all the time? I could really get used to it, though we'll be home before we know it. How are we going to fit everything in? We've less than two weeks and there's so much to see.'

'There is, and we'll have to choose wisely – it's much too hot to rush around. We can decide on a plan over lunch.'

'Will visiting your mother be part of the plan?'

'My mother?' He sounded startled and Flora could understand why.

The last time Jack had seen Sybil Carrington, now Sybil Falconi, had been in the south of France almost two years ago. Since then, communication between mother and son had dribbled to a close, and a familiar silence descended.

'She's living nearby, isn't she?' Flora suggested gently. 'I thought you might want to call on her, or at least telephone.'

She had been unsure whether to mention Sybil. At home, she'd studiously avoided including his mother in any conversation about Venice, but now they were actually in the city it felt uncomfortable not to at least try to make contact.

'I don't particularly want to,' he said. 'And I doubt she's eager to hear from me.'

After a fraught childhood, Jack had managed a kind of accommodation with his mother when he'd acted the dutiful son and rode to her rescue, exposing a very nasty plot against her. But it couldn't be said they were ever likely to have what Flora considered a normal mother and son relationship.

'She wouldn't expect me to call,' he went on, 'and, in any case, the count's estate will be miles away – the Veneto is a large area. And, after what happened in France, I've seen enough of wineries to last me a lifetime. This is *our* time, Flora.'

She couldn't feel completely happy over the situation, but kept her thoughts to herself, wanting nothing to spoil the holiday that had filled her dreams for months.

'Tomorrow, we could take a boat to San Giorgio Maggiore,' Jack was saying, as they walked out of St Mark's and onto the Riva degli Schiavoni, a walkway that bordered the lagoon. 'That's the one you can see from our hotel balcony. Or, if we're up for a "church" day, the Redentore is actually on the Giudecca. And I saw a Vivaldi concert advertised – it was being held in the church where he played. The one we've just passed.' He came to a halt. 'Shall we eat here?'

Despite their decision to head for the Giardini, he'd stopped at a *bacaro*, a tiny neighbourhood bar tucked into an alcove off the Riva. 'What do you think?' He pointed to the display of finger food he'd spied.

Flora looked. 'Too tempting to leave,' she confirmed and, in a very short time, they'd found seats at a table in what was no more than a passageway.

'You're going to love these,' he promised as the waiter brought an array of small plates to the table. 'Almost as much as you loved last night's risotto!'

And she did: a plate of fried meatballs, a variety of *cicchetti*, a dish of breaded shrimp and one of baked zucchini, all washed down with several glasses of cold rosé.

Wiping her fingers on a paper napkin, Flora's sigh breathed content. 'I love eating this way, but it makes you greedy. Because the cicchetti are small, you order far too many.'

'Never too many,' Jack said solemnly, pouring another glass of wine.

2

It was quite late in the afternoon before they strolled back along the Riva to St Mark's Square and found the small telephone cubicle at the corner of the piazza from which they could call for the Cipriani boat. Ten minutes later, the now familiar launch arrived at its berth and soon was skimming them across the Giudecca Canal, heading for the pale pink walls of the hotel. A breeze blowing off the lagoon brought welcome relief from the heat, but sent Flora into a flurry, trying unsuccessfully to prevent a mass of long waves falling into the kind of tangle that would take for ever to brush smooth.

At the steps to the hotel's front garden, a uniformed porter was waiting to greet them, offering his hand and helping her climb gracefully from the boat. So civilised! Such a perfect arrival! Except, for the picture to be complete, she should be wearing silk rather than cotton – even a cotton patterned with the brilliant red poppies she loved. And dark sunglasses, she thought. And a wide-brimmed floppy hat, of course. She mustn't forget the hat.

Once Jack had joined her on dry land, they walked together along the crazy-paved path that ran through the garden to the hotel entrance and into a foyer where whirring ceiling fans and marble tiles underfoot washed them cool.

'I'll get the key,' Jack murmured, making for the reception desk. A solitary clerk was on duty, Flora noticed, the fate of the girl's colleague once more intruding into her thoughts.

Jack had walked only a few yards before he was brought to a halt by a voice he knew. A voice Flora knew, too.

'Jack?' The accent was foreign, the tone agitated. 'And Mrs Carrington, as I must call you now.' Flora had walked quickly to her husband's side.

'Count Falconi, how nice,' she said uncertainly. 'But...'

The count, a wealthy Italian with estates in both Italy and France, had married Jack's mother the previous year after a somewhat tempestuous courtship.

'I am sorry, signora, that I interrupt your holiday.'

'Our honeymoon,' Jack corrected.

The count nodded sadly. 'I would not do this but Sybil, she insists.'

'That sounds like my mother.' Jack said it laughingly, but his tongue held a sharp edge.

'You see...'

They waited.

'I am in trouble,' Massimo Falconi announced.

The count had lost weight, Flora noticed. His silver hair seemed thinner and his face a little more lined. He was still a handsome man, but a less substantial figure than the one she'd known in France.

'I am in trouble,' he repeated, and made a sudden grab at Jack's arm as though to stop him escaping, but then half turned to Flora with the suggestion of a smile.

'And Sybil, she thinks you can help. Both of you.' The count cast a glance around the foyer. 'Please, I need to talk. Is there somewhere...?'

'The garden, maybe,' Jack suggested. 'It's a quiet enough place.'

Except for the ducklings, Flora thought, as they walked from the hotel's rear doors and into the Casanova gardens. A mother duck and her three babies had spluttered their way out of the pond and come quacking towards them but, after a few desultory pecks at their shoelaces, lost interest and waddled away.

Jack shepherded their visitor towards a bench that sat in the shade of one of the cypress trees and that, along with roses, chrysanthemums and thousands of aromatic plants, made the gardens such a delight. Flora had woken early that morning and already explored a little, knowing that beyond the immediate lawn lay a vineyard and a large fruit and vegetable garden which she'd assumed must provide most of the daily produce used by the hotel's restaurants. She remembered reading in her favourite guidebook that years ago the Giudecca had been the market garden for Venice, so maybe the Cipriani's three-acre oasis was what was left of those far-off days.

The count plumped himself squarely down on the bench, but it was a while before he spoke. 'It is the priest,' he began heavily.

Two pairs of eyes looked enquiringly at him, and he started again. 'The priest at Santa Margherita. It is a church in the San Polo district of Venice. You know the area?'

'I don't know Venice very well,' Jack confessed.

'And I don't know it all,' Flora chipped in.

'If you take the *vaporetto*, the number one line, up the Grand Canal, San Polo is just below the Santa Lucia railway station. It is the smallest and oldest of the six *sestieri*. It has always been a working-class district, though now it is changing. But then all of Venice is changing.'

'And the priest?'

'Father Stephano Renzi. He was our local priest for many

years until he made the move to the city. He is a good man, a very good man.' It was said with emphasis.

Flora had assumed that being a good man would surely be a given for a priest but said nothing, hoping they might get to the bottom of this mystery very soon and allow her the time to take a leisurely shower and change for dinner.

'He has lost a painting,' Falconi continued, but then amended, 'The church has lost a painting. It hung in a small side chapel and was attributed to Rastello, I believe, or at least his studio, though there has been some disagreement. But it was valuable, and valuable to Santa Margherita since people would pay a small fee to view. Many made a special journey to the church, art lovers, of course, but also believers, pilgrims, sometimes a journalist from a newspaper or the radio. Without the painting, the church will suffer a large drop in income and it is not a rich area.'

'But... how can you lose a painting?' Flora asked for them both. 'Was it very small?'

'No, no. A large painting. Stolen from its fixings on the wall.'

'It sounds like a professional job,' Jack said quietly. 'It would have needed careful planning. But surely its disappearance is a matter for the Venice police? And isn't there a squad in Rome who deal specifically with art theft?'

'This is not all,' the count said mournfully. 'Father Renzi's housekeeper is also missing.'

'You think she took the painting?' Flora's eyebrows rose sharply.

Falconi gave a small laugh. 'Not at all. Filomena Pretelli is a pious woman, a devoted woman, who has looked after the priest for many years. She is also very small,' he added.

'Are you saying the painting and the housekeeper disappeared together?' Jack stretched his legs which, bunched against the bench, had begun to cramp.

The count nodded. 'It would seem so.'

. 'Then it's even more a case for the police.'

'Stephano Renzi has reported the matter, but the police have said that there is no investigation to be had. The house-keeper must have left of her own free will. There is no sign of a struggle, her overnight bag is missing with some of her clothes – the lady has very few – and they insist it must be that she has gone on a trip somewhere.'

'Would she leave without telling the priest?' If the house-keeper was such a loyal and devoted employee, it seemed the obvious question.

'Of course she would not!' In frustration, the count gave a small tug to his otherwise smooth hair. 'And Stephano is beside himself with worry. But it is easier for the police to think so. As for the painting, they have passed the matter to Rome, as you suggested, Jack.'

'It's distressing, I can see, but how can *we* be of any help?' Jack was echoing Flora's own conclusions.

'Sybil thought, I thought, that maybe if you asked a few of those questions you are so good at, you might discover a clue, maybe more, to who is behind this bad business. Clues we can pass to the police.'

'We're foreigners here, Count. If we start asking questions, I don't think we'll be too well received. And I've no idea, even, who we would speak to.'

Jack was trying to let down his new stepfather gently, Flora could see, but his refusal should have been more definite.

'I know I know.' Count Falconi was agitated. 'It is a desperate request, I realise, but Father Renzi has come to me for help and I must do something. I am the big landowner in the district – people look to me when they are in trouble. Stephano was a good priest, a dedicated man, and does not deserve this in his older years. Not after all the problems he has suffered.'

'What were they?' Flora was alert. Maybe there was more to this mystery than a stolen painting and a missing housekeeper.

Fidgeting in his seat, Massimo crossed his legs. Then uncrossed them. 'Two, three years ago,' he began, 'Stephano was forced to move to Venice from the church he had served for most of his priesthood.'

'In what way forced?' Now, Jack was alert.

Falconi sighed. 'I know only a small part of the story.'

'Then you must tell us what you know. But can we stroll through the garden as we talk? My legs have gradually fallen asleep.'

The count rose to his feet and with Flora on one side and Jack on the other began a slow saunter around the grassed space, circling the duck pond, the rabbit hutches, and onto the paths that criss-crossed the vegetable garden.

'There is a family in his old parish,' the count began again, 'who made trouble for Stephano. It had to do with a son that the priest had in some way harmed. Or, at least, they believed he had.'

'What type of trouble?' Jack asked.

'Vicious gossip, wicked lies. That kind of thing. It made Stephano's life unbearable, so bad that he had no option but to ask the church authorities for a change of post. And they were happy to agree. Over the months, they had become alarmed at the bad feeling in the village and they found him a position as priest at the church in San Polo. His housekeeper, Filomena, went with him.'

Jack stopped walking. 'This trouble, do you think it has anything to do with the painting that's missing from the Venice church?'

The count spread his hands. 'It seems unlikely, but really I have no idea.'

'The village that you mention,' Flora intervened. 'Where is it actually?'

'It is more like a small town than a village, but beautiful. Quite beautiful. My estate is only a few miles distant. It takes me no more than ten minutes to drive there. Asolo, that's the name.'

Back in their room, Jack strode to the long windows and opened them wide to the warmth of the lagoon. After their conversation in the garden, the count had drunk a glass of wine with them, asked them again for any help they could give, then taken the hotel launch to the Piazzale Roma where his saloon car and chauffeur were waiting to drive him to Casa Elena, his estate in the Veneto.

Joining her husband on the balcony, Flora looked across the water at the Renaissance magnificence of San Giorgio Maggiore, the angel atop the campanile a tiny figure against a sky of deepest blue. Below them, a constant stream of every kind of vessel: several small boats – sandalos they were called, Jack had told her; a single gondola, its oarsman facing forwards, on the lookout for a passenger; a *motoscafo* powering past fruit barges loaded high with oranges and bananas.

They turned to look at each other, their faces mirror images, both nonplussed by the count's request.

'What do we do?' Jack asked.

'What can we do? It's impossible.'

Putting his arm around her, he hugged her tightly. 'You're right. It is impossible and my mother had no right to involve us. But that's Sybil all over, impervious to anyone's comfort but her own.'

'The count is very worried, you can see. I imagine she was hoping to take some of the worry off his shoulders.'

'And put it on ours! She's not going to do that.'

Flora pulled away slightly. 'Your last words to the count were that we'd see what we could do.'

'Which is precisely nothing. They were words, Flora, just words. We have to forget it. Hopefully, the housekeeper will turn up safe and well, and the art theft chaps from Rome will soon be on the hunt for the painting, if they aren't already. In a few weeks, there'll be no problem, but in a few days our honeymoon will be over.'

Flora had to agree. They had so little time to enjoy this amazing city and, though she could understand Sybil's concern, it seemed too big an imposition. She would do as Jack suggested and put it out of her mind.

That wasn't too difficult. She had a new frock to wear that evening – they were eating in the hotel's wonderful floating restaurant – a black cocktail dress, the first she'd ever owned, with an hour-glass shape and a ruffled peplum draped from the waist. Its pencil skirt showed a daring three inches of leg and Flora had never felt more grown up.

Dinner was memorable, not so much for the dress or the food, fabulous though they were, but for the sheer beauty of the evening: below them, the gentle sound of lapping waves, while above a moon sliding in and out of small puffs of cloud dusted the lagoon with splashes of light. And across the water, the basilica of St Mark's, now a blaze of illumination, shone from the darkness.

Such a backdrop demanded notice and it was difficult to give their complete attention to what they were eating, but somehow the *linguine rustiche*, followed by the fillet of turbot, disappeared and they were once more perusing the menu.

'I think I can squeeze in a dessert,' Flora said, lowering the leather-bound volume, her eyes sparkling. 'We are so lucky, Jack! To be here, at this table, in this city! Just look at that view – I can't get enough of it.'

Jack looked but pulled a face. 'Tell me, why did I forget to bring a camera? I could have bought a cheap one. It would have done the job and we could have bored everyone to death with the photographs. Now, when we get back, you'll be asked to describe in detail everything you've seen. Sally, for one, will be hanging on your words.'

Out of all their friends, Sally Jenner, Alice's niece and the owner of the Priory Hotel, had shown the greatest enthusiasm for their trip.

'It's a journey she could make herself.' Flora took up the menu again. 'I think I'll settle for a *panna cotta* – I had one once when Alice was feeling particularly daring. Or there's a Sicilian lemon tart. I wonder how that's different from the usual lemon tart? How about you?'

'I shouldn't have either. I'm too full already, except I'm tempted by the *panna cotta*.'

'The Priory is doing so well,' Flora continued her earlier thought, 'Sally could easily afford a decent holiday, and she definitely needs a break, managing the hotel alone as she's done for months. It could help her get over the Hector thing, as well.'

'Really?' He looked sceptical. 'Hector's engagement is a bit more than a "thing".'

'I don't think Sally's heart was truly broken. It was more her pride that was battered. The fact that Hector preferred my assistant – but it was always going to be Rose.'

'I can sympathise.' Some years ago, Jack had also suffered a battering to his pride when, three weeks before his first wedding, his bride-to-be had left him for his best friend. 'I'm not sure that a trip to Venice will be the cure, though.'

'It might be,' Flora said blithely. 'And she could bring Alice! Her aunt could do with a break from the Priory kitchen.'

'That would be a recipe for disaster! Come on, what's it to be? *Panna cotta* or Sicilian lemon tart?'

Some time later, they walked from the restaurant along the path that skirted the garden and through the rear door of the hotel into the foyer. A single receptionist was on duty, the same young woman who had staffed the desk for the entire day. This evening, she was not behind her desk, however, but had her arm around an older woman and seemed to be trying to lead her to one of the large armchairs at one side of the foyer.

Flora quickly took in the situation and, out of respect, looked away: the older woman was crying, sobbing quietly but continuously into a handkerchief. A door opened along the polished corridor that ran to the right and the receptionist, Flora saw, looked relieved. It was the hotel manager, smooth and purposeful, walking swiftly over to them.

'Signora Massi,' he murmured, cupping his hand beneath the woman's elbow, *'per favore, vieni con me.'*

'Did he say Massi?' Flora whispered to Jack, as the manager gently ushered the weeping woman down the corridor and into his office. Then, without waiting for an answer, she walked over to the reception desk. 'The signora?' she asked. 'Was that lady the mother of Signor Massi?'

The girl looked shaken, but nodded her head. 'The poor lady. She has come to Venice for her son. She must identify him. Her husband is too unwell at the moment to travel from Asolo and this business with the police, it has to be done.'

'Asolo? Did you say Asolo?'

'It is Franco's home town, signora. A small town but very beautiful.'

Flora spun round to face her husband, her eyes alight with a new enthusiasm.

3

'Asolo, Jack!' Cheeks flushed, she bounced into the bedroom and turned to face him as he followed her through the door.

'I heard,' Jack said placidly.

'First the priest and now Franco Massi.'

'They come from a small town close to Venice and both ended up in the same city. That's not unlikely. A coincidence.'

'A coincidence they both had bad things happen to them? The priest was chased out of Asolo and Franco is dead.'

'The priest fell foul of what sounds a deeply unpleasant family and the receptionist met with an unfortunate accident.' He tried to speak calmly. 'Nothing too mysterious.'

Walking across to the long windows, he took a last look at the lights of San Giorgio Maggiore before swishing the curtains closed. As soon as the receptionist had mentioned the name of the town, he'd known it would send Flora buzzing, her imagination in overdrive with all kinds of speculation. It was the last thing he wanted, but if he knew Flora – and he should by now – she wouldn't be content to walk away.

He turned and she was standing facing him, bright and determined, the hazel in her eyes almost black with excitement.

'Before he drowned,' she said, 'Franco had a very bad quarrel with the owner of the restaurant we ate at last night. La Zucca. What's the betting the owner comes from Asolo, too?'

'I'm not betting and neither are you.' He took hold of her shoulders and gave her a small shake. 'We agreed, remember. An impossible task, we said. No involvement.'

'That was before I knew Signor Massi came from Asolo. It can't be the coincidence you say it is.'

'Why can't it? Massi's death was an accident and they do happen.' He was being stubborn, he knew, but it mattered greatly that nothing marred their honeymoon.

'An "accident"? Like the one that saw Polly Dakers die, or Percy Milburn, or Alex Vicary a few months ago. Like Kate's father, even, right at the beginning of our detective work.'

'That *was* an accident.'

Flora gave a small *hmph* and turned so that he could unzip the very special cocktail dress. For the moment, she said no more and, after hanging the frock reverently in the wardrobe, made for the bathroom.

At the door, however, she paused. 'I'm not happy, Jack,' she said, the brightness gone from her face.

That was obvious, he thought.

'I need to settle things in my mind. To feel that there really isn't anything we can do. Franco was a decent man, friendly, helpful. If it wasn't an accident...'

'How are you ever likely to discover that? We're foreigners with no idea even how to begin. And this city is built on water. He won't be the first to drown in a Venetian canal.'

'I could talk to some of the staff,' she said doggedly. 'A conversation or two. Find out if there was anything in Franco's life that didn't seem right.' She walked back to him and clasped his hands. 'I have to do it, Jack. Please understand.'

Inwardly, he uttered a long, quiet sigh. But Jack knew when he was beaten.

. . .

Breakfast on the terrace the next morning, beneath blue and white umbrellas, was a leisurely affair, a large buffet of juices, cereals, fruits and cold meats greeting them as they were shown through a sea of crisp white cloths to a table close to the lagoon. Beyond an ornamental ironwork barrier, the water was just yards away, a moving backdrop, boat after boat plying past as they ate. And they could have eaten for most of the morning, a flurry of attentive waiters ensuring their table was never bare.

Flora had finished her last piece of melon – a modest breakfast was all she could ever manage – as Jack was about to tackle his scrambled eggs and smoked salmon.

'I forgot to bring a handkerchief,' she said, patting the handbag that hung at one side of her chair. 'While you finish, I'll pop back to the bedroom. I'll only be a minute.'

She knew Jack was unlikely to be deceived, but she also knew that he had smoked salmon to eat and wouldn't want his eggs to go cold. As she'd anticipated, he pulled a wry face, but picked up his knife and fork without a comment.

Reaching the bedroom, Flora was delighted to find a chambermaid busily changing the linen. She needn't go looking for someone to talk to after all; she had a captive audience.

Hearing Flora's footsteps, the girl looked up from her work, a little startled. '*Mi scusi, signora,*' she murmured, beginning to make for the door, '*tornerò.*'

'Come back?' Flora hazarded and, when the girl nodded, she put out a detaining hand. 'Please don't go. I'm only here to collect a handkerchief. *Un fazzoletto,*' she remembered, feeling pleased with herself. For the last few months, she had been trying hard to memorise at least a little Italian vocabulary and, for some reason or another, *fazzoletto* had stuck in her mind.

Smiling cheerfully at the maid, she walked across the room to the antique walnut chest and began opening one after another of its drawers, making a play of searching through her underwear, before asking, 'Do you speak English?'

'A little.' The girl made a gesture with thumb and finger to show the small extent of her knowledge.

It will have to do, Flora thought, and mime is always useful. 'When we arrived at the hotel,' she said, 'there was a very nice man at reception. His name' – she patted the side of her blouse trying to indicate where a badge might sit – 'was Franco Massi.'

The girl's face clouded.

'Do you know him?'

'Franco not here.'

'Oh!' She hoped her surprise appeared genuine. 'What a shame – he was so helpful. I would have liked to speak to him again. Has he left the Cipriani?'

'*Sì*.' Her voice was so quiet that Flora had to strain to hear.

'But he worked here a long time?'

The maid held up one hand.

'Five years?'

'Yes, five.'

'He was good at his job. *Il suo lavoro – era bravo?*'

The girl gave a small, sad smile. '*Sì, sì*. From London,' she offered.

'Franco worked in London! The Ritz maybe,' Flora suggested, half joking.

To her surprise, the maid nodded enthusiastically at the name. 'The Ritz,' she said, in an awed voice. 'In Venice, he work the Gritti Palace. Very smart. You know?'

'The big hotel on the Grand Canal?'

Again, the girl nodded. 'But Franco come here and the Cipriani best.'

'It's wonderful,' Flora agreed. 'And it must be lovely to live here all the time. Do you have a room at the hotel?'

'*Mi scusi?*'

'A room.' She pointed at the girl. 'For you, *una camera qui.*'

The maid laughed. 'No.' She showed Flora her wedding ring. 'I live in Mestre,' she spelt out slowly.

'And Franco?'

'*Qui, naturalmente. Nell'allegato.* In annexe.'

'Franco was single? *Franco non sposato?*'

Flora once more gave thanks to the Italian primer she'd found tucked into the corner of a top shelf at the All's Well. The time she'd spent with it, between serving customers, was paying off.

'*Non ancora.*'

'Not yet. So, he was getting married? He had a fiancée? *Una fidanzata?*'

The girl spread her hands. The conversation was too tiring to continue, Flora saw, and no doubt she had a dozen more bedrooms to make up.

'I'm sorry,' she apologised. 'I'll go now.'

'*Il suo fazzoletto?*' the maid called after her.

But Flora had gone, handkerchief forgotten. She had an annexe to find.

It wasn't difficult. Avoiding the breakfast terrace, she stepped out of the rear door of the hotel and, instead of turning right into the garden as she'd done previously, she looked left, and there it was. A square block of honey-coloured stone no more than a hundred yards away.

Outside its main entrance a workman was busy resetting paving slabs. '*Buon giorno,*' she greeted him as she came close.

The workman got up from his knees, his apron clanking with the tools that hung from each pocket. '*Buon giorno, signora.*'

She pointed to the building behind him. '*Allegato?*'

'The annexe, yes,' he said in English to Flora's relief.

'I have a message,' she began. 'For Franco Massi. From a friend in London.' She'd cobbled the excuse together on her way down from the bedroom and hoped it would suffice.

The man shook his head. 'Franco is dead, signora.'

'But how dreadful!' Again, she adopted a shocked expression. 'I wonder... this card...' she said slowly, making a pretence of feeling in her skirt pocket for the non-existent message, 'could I leave it somewhere? In Franco's room, maybe. His family will come for his belongings, I imagine, and they might want to write to his friend.'

The excuse was sounding thinner with every word she spoke, but the workman seemed not to think badly of it. 'The room is there.' He pointed through the door at the lower corridor. 'On the left, signora. Room number three.'

Thanking him, she walked into the building and along the corridor he'd indicated to the third room. Thankfully, the door had been left unlocked and very quickly she slipped inside. Flora's first impression was how small the room was and how tidy: a single bed, a small chest of drawers and a wardrobe appeared to be its only furniture.

On top of the chest, a row of toiletries stood in a line – hair oil, talcum powder, a sharp-smelling cologne, when she put her nose to it – and behind the wardrobe doors, another row, this time of very smart suits. An extremely well-groomed young man, she thought, and, casting her mind back, it was an image of quiet polish that she recalled. A book by the bedside, a biography of Giuseppe Garibaldi, hinted at Franco's interest in his country's history, but other than the clothes and the book, there was little to suggest anything of the man who had lived here so recently.

Until she walked over to a tiny desk, pushed into one corner. Its wooden surface was completely bare, clear of any papers or ornaments, and was why she hadn't immediately noticed it. Now, she saw there was a photograph frame sitting to one side. Just one photograph. The fiancée, she decided.

Picking up the frame to get a better look, Flora almost dropped it in surprise. The face – it was familiar! She knew this girl. She would swear it. Starting to pace up and down the small room, she tried to remember. Then she had it. The Priory, that was how she knew her. A year or so ago when Dominic Lister was still Sally's business partner.

She sank onto the bed, still holding the photograph. That's right... she was remembering more now. This was the very girl Sally had mentioned a few months past, asking Flora to get in touch if she had the time when she and Jack were in Venice. She had completely forgotten Sally's request, she realised, the excitement of the trip her only excuse. Sally had been furious, she recalled, when Dominic had hired the girl as a chambermaid. The girl had come with no experience but she had come with a pretty face. That was pure Dominic. But then Sally had relented, hadn't she, and made friends with the girl. Flora had quite often seen them together in Abbeymead, drinking a cup of tea at the Nook, the village café, or shopping for food in the high street. When the village had proved too quiet, the girl had left to work in Brighton, but she had obviously kept in touch with Sally even after her return to Italy.

But what was her name? Flora struggled to remember. Barbara? Belinda? Not Italian enough. Bianca! That was it!

Bianca had been Franco Massi's fiancée! Another coincidence perhaps? Flora doubted it very much.

4

By the time she returned to the breakfast terrace, Jack was finishing his second cup of coffee.

'Did the handkerchief go on holiday, too?' he teased.

Refusing to rise to the bait, Flora sat down opposite. 'I've something to tell you,' she said quietly.

'I thought you might have.'

'Franco Massi had a room in the hotel, in a staff annexe, and I've been there.'

'More breaking and entering?'

'The door was open.'

'Just trespass then. I wonder what the local cells are like?'

'Stop it, Jack. This is important. Franco was engaged to be married and there's a photograph of his fiancée on his desk. Guess who it is?'

'I won't – you know you're longing to tell me.'

'Bianca Benetti.'

When Jack looked blank, Flora gave the table an impatient tap. 'You must remember her.'

'Must I?' He continued to look blank.

'She worked at the Priory for about six months. As a chambermaid. Dominic Lister employed her and it made Sally angry.'

'Oh, that girl. She's here in Venice?'

'This is her home city. Sally asked me to look her up if I had the time. She was a friend of Sally's – *I* never really spoke to her much – but then I forgot about contacting her and left the phone number back at the cottage. But, just think! Bianca was Franco's fiancée!'

'I am thinking. Why does it matter?' Jack remained unmoved. 'He was engaged to a local girl who turns out to be Bianca. Not an impossibility. He could have met her in England, London probably, at some social club or another. There are plenty of Italian clubs in the capital. But poor girl—'

'*I* think it matters.'

'I can't see how,' he said cheerfully. 'If you've left her number behind, you've no way of getting in touch with her and can't pass on Sally's good wishes. Except now it would be condolences. Just be glad you've been spared an uncomfortable conversation. Now...' Scrunching up his napkin and discarding it on the table, he got to his feet. 'We should go. We've a morning at the Scuola Grande di San Rocco – how's that for a name? It has some wonderful Tintorettos and, I promise, you're going to love them.'

Feeling deflated, Flora mumbled a reluctant assent. She'd thought this new discovery would light a flame and persuade Jack there was a mystery to pursue, but evidently his assurance to the count that 'we'll see what we can do' was, in truth, as meaningless as it sounded. She couldn't entirely blame him; this was their honeymoon and he'd waited a long time for it. They both had. But when things didn't add up for Flora, she found it impossible to let go. A terrier digging for a bone was how Jack had once described her, and that still held true. For the moment, though, she would be the tourist he wanted.

Allowing herself to be piloted through the foyer and along

the crazy paving to the lagoon, she found a shady spot beneath a magnolia tree where they could wait for the hotel launch which would ferry them to St Mark's.

'A line one *vaporetto* will take us up the Grand Canal to the San Tomà stop,' Jack said, rescuing his straw hat from the bush where a stiff breeze had blown it. 'The Scuola should be a five-minute walk from there.'

'You've brought the map?'

It was as well to check. A five-minute walk could turn into several hours if you lost your way amid the narrow *calli* – as you were almost bound to.

'I have, but don't worry. There'll be signs to the Scuola. It's a tourist attraction.'

The thrum of an approaching boat had them on their feet, the hotel launch pulling into the landing stage a few minutes later. They stood back for its passengers to disembark, but there was only one. A familiar figure, as it happened. It was Sybil Carrington – Sybil Falconi, Flora corrected herself – who stepped out of the boat and was walking up the steps towards them.

'Jack! Just the man I want to talk to!' was her greeting, to a son she hadn't seen for nearly two years and, as far as Flora knew, had made no attempt to contact since they'd said goodbye in a Provençal village.

But then Jack's relationship with both his parents, now divorced, was hardly smooth, his early life filled with unnecessary drama. Once fully grown, he'd made sure he saw them as little as possible.

Sybil, carefully adjusting her dress, managed to avoid any suggestion of an embrace for Jack, and instead swept on to the girl standing by his side. 'And... Flora, isn't it?'

Faced with this elegant figure in mauve silk shift and matching wide-brimmed hat, Flora felt every inch a scrubby schoolgirl. Suddenly, the daisy-covered cotton skirt she'd earlier thought such fun now seemed horribly tawdry.

'I'm glad you took my advice and finally married the girl,' Sybil continued with a smug glance at her son. 'I told you she'd be a good choice. I must say I take some credit for the way things have turned out.'

Jack's lips clamped shut. Sybil was the last person from whom he'd accept advice, Flora knew. He'd simply been waiting for her to decide that *she* wanted the marriage, too.

'It's always good to see you,' Jack said with heavy irony, 'but we were just leaving for St Mark's, to do some sightseeing, and we should get going – unless you'd care to come with us.'

'Sightseeing? No, of course not. You can put it off for ten minutes, surely. I've travelled all the way from Elena to be here – you might, at least, offer me a drink.'

Flora felt slightly ashamed that they hadn't, though she knew that Jack would be chafing to get away. 'Of course we can wait a while,' she said. 'We can order tea in the garden.'

Her husband's lips had become even more firmly compressed but, refusing to take notice of the signals he was sending, Flora waved a hand at the several comfortable chairs spread at intervals around the lawn. And by the time they were seated and had given their order, he'd recovered his temper sufficiently to say mildly, 'It's not difficult to guess why you've made the journey, Mum, but you do know the count has visited us already?'

'I do, and he came back with nothing – some vague promise that you would do what you could. Meaningless.'

Flora had to agree.

'I knew how it would be if he went alone,' Sybil continued briskly, 'so I'm here to plead for him. I've no idea how good a novelist you are, Jack, or how many books Flora sells each week, but I do know the pair of you are good at finding things out. You uncovered the plot against me when no one else would believe there was a problem, *and* you made certain that I'd suffer no further threat from Massimo's family.'

'How is his family?' Jack asked. 'He didn't mention them.'

A diversionary tactic? Flora wondered. If it was, Sybil took the bait.

'He won't. It's too painful. That whole dreadful business still haunts him – it's not every day you realise you have a killer living beneath your roof. Wherever possible, Massimo loses himself in his work and I do my best to jolly him along – I know he's glad we married. And glad to have that wretched daughter and his ex-wife tucked behind the doors of a convent where they can harm no one.'

'Are you living in Italy permanently now?' Flora asked.

'We're in the Veneto for most of the year – Massimo prefers Elena to the south of France. And so do I. The palazzo is magnificent and the count is very much the grand seigneur of the district.'

In other words, Sybil was enjoying her husband's wealth and status enormously. She had become the queen bee she'd always dreamed of being.

'You're very welcome to visit the estate,' the queen bee said, in what was clearly an afterthought. 'But that's not why I'm here,' she added quickly. 'The count needs help. Not a vague promise to do what you can, but a commitment. At least, to talk to Father Renzi. He speaks English and he speaks it well. He's a decent man, a good priest, but the poor chap is quite distraught. He knows very well his housekeeper wouldn't simply take off, but the police refuse to listen to him.'

Jack poured the tea the waiter had just brought and handed his mother a cup. 'You do realise we're on our honeymoon?'

'Of course I do. You sent us an invitation to the wedding.' An invitation for which Jack had received no reply, Flora remembered. 'But what's a honeymoon? Just a glorified holiday.

You'll spend plenty of time together – you've a lifetime ahead. This is more important.'

'To you,' he pointed out.

'To the count and he's my main concern.' Her voice had softened and she seemed genuinely to care for her husband. Marriage had evidently mellowed Sybil a little. But only a little.

'This business is bothering him hugely,' she continued, 'coming on top of the dreadful stuff in his own family. You know he has a heart condition? I worry about him. As the most influential person in the district, Massimo feels a responsibility; he was the only person of authority the priest could think to ask for help. But he has no idea what to do or where to start. You might, though. And you should.'

There was an awkward silence, Jack refusing to take up the challenge and Flora sensing the unwisdom of intervening between mother and son.

'How much time would it take to go to Santa Margherita and talk to the priest?' Sybil asked abruptly. 'Don't bother with the painting – I never could abide religious art and, in any case, the art theft chaps can deal with that matter – but a woman disappearing. An elderly woman, defenceless, alone. That's too important to ignore.'

'OK.' Jack gave in. 'We'll talk to Father Renzi, but that's all we'll do. We've only days in Venice and we're going to enjoy every one of them. I'm determined they won't be spent sleuthing!'

'Do what you can,' she said, getting to her feet. 'And come to Elena before you leave the city.'

'Before you go... Sybil.' Flora couldn't bring herself to call her by anything closer. 'Have you ever heard of Franco Massi?'

Sybil frowned. 'Who is he?'

'He was a receptionist here at the Cipriani.'

'Oh, staff,' she said indifferently. 'No idea.'

'Still the same mother,' Jack murmured in Flora's ear, as

they escorted her to the launch waiting to ply its way back to St Mark's.

'What about you?' his mother asked, pausing on the landing stage. 'Weren't you supposed to be sightseeing this morning?'

'Don't worry,' he told her. 'I've thought of something I should do first. We'll take the boat later.'

Turning back to the hotel as the launch disappeared in a cloud of spray, Flora took his hand. 'What have you thought of?'

'Nothing, but I needed space to breathe. We'll bag the boat when it returns.'

'If you really mean to speak to the priest today, the Scuola visit won't be possible. We'll have to postpone,' she said hopefully.

'Not so!' He shook his head in mock sadness, unable to suppress a smile. 'You don't escape that easily. The Scuola happens to be in San Polo and so does Santa Margherita. According to the count.'

'We can do both?'

'It seems we can, though what good it will do... but the Tintorettos, they'll be a treat to enjoy!'

5

The journey to San Tomà was uneventful and, as they stepped off the *vaporetto*, a sign high on the wall pointed them towards the Scuola Grande.

'See!' Jack said, taking her hand. 'Signs – just what we need.'

Walking through the streets of San Polo revealed a new Venice from the city Flora had so far seen. The old artisan quarter was a district of quiet lanes, narrow passageways and meandering canals, with some of the houses they passed being the oldest buildings in Venice: walls washed in red ochre, iron balconies gently rusting and terracotta roofs that dipped and swayed in dizzying fashion.

'It's quite different.' Flora stood and gazed up at the window boxes filled with flowers. 'So old and absolutely no souvenir sellers.'

'Not in this part of San Polo, but the Rialto market isn't far. I guess there'll be plenty of stalls there.'

'Near where we ate?'

He nodded. 'Pretty close. It's the liveliest area, I'd say. Plenty of tourists to keep it busy.'

'I like it *here*. It feels lived-in, as though there are still native Venetians in this part of the city, unconcerned with visitors and simply going about their daily routine.'

A large, dusty square had opened in front of them, the Campo San Rocco according to Jack's map and, at one end, an impressive white stone building – the Scuola Grande. Last night, before falling asleep, Flora had read a few pages of the one guidebook she'd brought, not wanting to feel completely ignorant. The Scuola, she'd read, had been established by a group of wealthy Venetian citizens in the fifteenth century, dedicated to San Rocco – popularly regarded as a protector against the plague – and concerning itself with a profusion of trades and crafts. Nearly a hundred years later, Tintoretto had provided it with paintings.

'Apart from housing your wonderful Tintorettos, any idea how the building is used? I can't imagine that local artists and craftspeople belong to the school these days.'

'I'm not sure, though I did see a poster yesterday advertising a classical concert here. If this is like other *scuole*, there'll be two halls, a lower and an upper, either of which would make a superb venue for music.'

A modest fee allowed them entrance to the *sala terrena*, or the lower hall, its four walls filled with paintings paying homage to the Virgin Mary in a depiction of her life. Unusually, Flora found herself agreeing with Sybil – religious art, it seemed, left her indifferent, too. Not so Jack. He spent so long gazing at *The Annunciation* that she had finally to grab him by the arm and drag him up the staircase to the *sala superiore*.

The upper hall was magnificent, from its brilliantly glossy floor to a ceiling filled with scenes from the Old Testament and walls that displayed a string of episodes from the New. A tour de force that together told the biblical story from the Fall to the Redemption.

'Quite a place,' Jack remarked, his neck cricked at a painful angle in an attempt to absorb the ceiling's full majesty.

It wasn't the paintings, however, that lit Flora's interest, but the carvings fringing the panelled walls, an array of figures brought to life in wood. In brilliant detail they celebrated all manner of skills and trades: carpenters, artists, musicians, writers, teachers, decorators.

There was one, she reckoned, that looked like the painter himself, holding a brush and palette, and she tugged at her husband's shirtsleeve to gain his attention. 'Look, Jack. I think this might be Tintoretto.'

'It is, signora.' A priest, who had been circling the perimeter of the hall a few steps behind them, smiled at her as she turned. 'You like the figures?'

'They are wonderful.'

'I agree. I come often to walk this upper hall, not for the paintings – I have art in my own church – but for the carvings.'

'Your church is nearby?' she asked.

The priest should know Santa Margherita. Jack might have his map but any help in finding their way through the maze of small alleys would be welcome.

'It is behind the Scuola, just streets away,' the man replied. 'Santa Margherita.'

Flora felt her mouth drop and closed it immediately. 'You aren't Father Renzi, by any chance?'

'But yes.' The priest looked baffled and slightly uneasy.

'My... um... stepfather has mentioned you.' Jack had joined them. Saying aloud the word 'stepfather' had cost him, Flora thought. 'Count Falconi,' he added.

The priest's face cleared. 'The count is a good friend. A very good friend. From my old district.'

'We were on our way to see you, in fact. Count Falconi asked us to visit.'

'He did? Why was that?' A pair of deep brown eyes registered puzzlement.

'We' – Jack half turned to her, seeming unsure how to continue – 'we look into things. Dig around. Ask questions.' It was difficult trying to explain exactly what they did do. 'We help sometimes, when the police have dismissed a problem.'

This last explanation appeared to work and the priest's expression was suddenly intent. 'Massimo thinks you can help me?'

'He does, although we aren't very sure ourselves. But if we could talk...'

'We talk outside,' the priest said decisively. Their conversation in the great hall had been carried on in little more than whispers. 'There is a café opposite the San Rocco church. I will show you.'

San Rocco was only steps away from the Scuola and they soon found a table in what little shade was left. Having ordered a round of *aranciatas*, Father Renzi returned once more to his friend.

'Massimo has told you of my problems?'

Flora leaned forward to say quietly, 'We understand that a valuable painting has gone missing from Santa Margherita and that your housekeeper has disappeared.'

'Both very bad things. The painting is part of my church's history, but Filomena – that is the most distressing. It is urgent I find her.' In some agitation, he pulled at the beard mushrooming from his chin.

'Can you tell us what you know? Anything that might help.' Jack didn't sound hopeful.

'There are things I should say, but I will have to go back in time.'

'As far as you need,' Jack said, as the *aranciatas* arrived at the table.

Flora sipped slowly, enjoying the trickle of cold liquid down her throat. She was eager to hear the priest's story.

'There is a family in the village where I served for many years,' Renzi began. 'A small town really. And they have a son, Luigi. A few years ago, he was caught thieving and was put into jail.'

'Is he still in prison?' Flora was quick to ask, suspecting that Luigi might have returned to his old habits.

The priest shook his head. 'The boy has served his sentence. He was released over a year ago.'

'A free man then, but is he still thieving? Could he have stolen the painting?' Jack brought her suspicions out into the open. It was the same question, Flora reflected, that she had asked the count.

'I cannot believe it,' the priest said. 'Why would he do such a thing? He stole before and looked what happened. To risk prison again for a painting he could not sell? The Rastello is famous and no dealer would touch it.'

'Unless the boy had contact with a professional gang, willing and able to move pictures around Europe. A lucrative smuggling racket exists between here and Albania, I know.'

'How *do* you know?' Flora was intrigued.

'From research I did for a book. I was sure it would come in useful! Under Enver Hoxha Albania is a closed country, but there are always openings for men who want money, and Albania has an interesting coastline: a wild landscape and a profusion of rocky coves where a boat can land unseen.'

Flora frowned. Albanian smugglers or not, she was still trying to fathom the priest's involvement. 'Father Renzi, what role did you play in the boy's story?'

The elderly man looked blankly across the square as though seeing a very different scene, and it was minutes before he spoke. 'Ah, there you have it,' he said at last. 'It was the role I played for which I have suffered.'

There was another long silence. 'It was an ambitious theft that landed the boy in trouble. Too ambitious. I think Luigi had been stealing for some time, small items from neighbours' houses and then he would sell them at a market somewhere. But he met a man new to the area one night in a bar – he was celebrating a birthday – and this man was more experienced at burglary. He had grander plans than stealing the neighbours' small possessions. Together, they broke into the palazzo of one of the richest men in our district. Nino Vitali is a businessman from Turin and uses his palazzo only for holidays, but he is a wealthy collector and the house contained many objects of value.'

'And these two stole from it?'

'They tried, but the palazzo had far more alarms than they expected, and they had to run, very quickly – it meant they could steal only a little. Also there were dogs.' The priest gave a small shudder at the thought. 'They fled, but Luigi Tasca was seen by one of the servants Vitali keeps at the house. A steward. He was certain that he saw two men running and one that he recognised – Tasca – but the light was not good and there was a small doubt.'

'And his accomplice – the experienced burglar?'

'The police went straight to him, of course. He was well-known to them, but they found nothing in his rooms and no evidence against him. He swore that he was at home that night and had no idea where Luigi was. It was only the steward's evidence that suggested the man was lying.'

'But how did this affect *you?*' She was struggling to form a clear picture.

'The police came calling on Tasca and he gave me as his alibi. He said he had been at my house at the time of the burglary. He had gone looking for his friend, Matteo – Matteo Pretelli is Filomena's nephew and the two boys were very good friends. They often used to meet at Filomena's apartment, the one she had in my house.'

'Matteo's aunt is Filomena?' Jack checked. A longer cast of characters than he'd expected was beginning to unfold.

'Exactly.' Father Renzi looked pleased at his understanding. 'Luigi Tasca said he intended that evening to go to Matteo's house to look for his friend, but then decided he was more likely to find him at his aunt's apartment. When he got to my house, however, Matteo wasn't there and Luigi did not see his friend. Instead, he told the police that he saw me. Or, at least, that I saw him. At precisely the time the robbery was committed.'

'Why didn't he keep to his original plan of going to his friend's house? He could have said that he met Matteo there at the time he was supposed to have broken into the palazzo and Pretelli would likely have lied for him. Much simpler.' Jack shielded his eyes from a sun that had emerged from behind the parasol.

'I have no idea but, if he had done so, it would not have been as simple as you say. His alibi would have been destroyed immediately – Matteo had travelled to Milan for the day and could not possibly have seen him.'

'But when he used *you* as his alibi?' Flora prompted.

'Ah, yes, I am coming to this. It is where the problem arrives. I denied that I had seen him and from that moment I became the enemy of the Tasca family. They blamed me for the disaster that overtook their son and took their revenge.'

'The count mentioned something of that. But what exactly happened?'

'It is painful to talk of.'

'If we're to be any help,' Flora said, 'we should know.'

The priest put down his glass, the drink untouched. 'I was caught in a trap. The Tasca family were my devoted parishioners and I liked them personally. They are a large family but always they come to mass and the children attend bible class every Sunday. If I denied that I had seen Luigi, the boy's alibi would fall to pieces and it would be the steward's word against his. Who would the jury believe?'

'His alibi collapsed and they believed the steward?' Jack hazarded.

'The jury did. And the family never forgave me for my refusal to help.'

'But you couldn't tell a deliberate lie. Not as a priest,' Flora protested.

Renzi shook his head, a sorrowful smile on his face. 'My dear, a priest in these small communities is more than a servant of God. He is a mainstay, a friend, a comforter, a father. The Tascas expected me to come to their son's rescue and I did not. That is when the problems began.'

'Which were?' Jack fidgeted in his seat, seeming wary of being drawn further into this maelstrom but feeling he must ask.

'Many difficulties. The family refused to attend my church and persuaded others to do the same. They ignored me in the street when I greeted them, tore up my garden and left rubbish instead of flowers. Worse' – the priest's face was filled with pain – 'they spread lies about me – that I drank heavily, took from the collection, made my altar boys uncomfortable. They posted anonymous messages around the village, although everyone knew who had written them. Unpleasant and untrue accusations that I could do nothing to stop.'

'And the church authorities moved you to Venice to get you away?' Flora asked, wondering why they had done little else to stop this assault on a loyal servant.

'I asked for a new post and they saw the wisdom of my request. It broke my heart to do this, but I had no choice. I have tried hard to make it work, but I miss my village, my town, and always will. Filomena, too.'

Jack leaned forward. 'Is this the first trouble you've encountered since you moved?'

The priest looked surprised. 'What kind of trouble are you thinking?'

'Has the family continued to bother you since you've been at Santa Margherita?'

'Not at all. I have heard nothing from them.'

'Has anything else been stolen from the church?' Jack pursued.

The priest hesitated. 'Nothing,' he said at last. 'There was a candelabra... a few months ago... I noticed it was missing, but Filomena told me she had taken it to the goldsmith for repair. She had dented it accidentally when cleaning. She is growing old, you see, and can be a little careless these days.'

'And that's all, just the candelabra?'

He seemed to hesitate again, but then gave a nod.

'And Filomena – you've no clue where the lady could be?'

'None. The painting disappeared into thin air and so has Filomena. I fear very much that harm has come to her.'

'Have you mentioned the problems you had with the Tasca family to the Venice police?'

'I would not wish to do so. It would be as though I was accusing them and I cannot truly believe they have any part in this. I have been three years in Venice and, as I told you, have heard nothing from them.'

'Could you talk to them perhaps?' Flora suggested. 'To be sure that they know nothing? Talk to Luigi Tasca himself, maybe.'

'It is not possible. None of the family will speak and it would stir more trouble – they would say that I was once again trying to blacken Luigi's name. And I must let the police carry on their investigation – they have made it plain I should not interfere. Their minds are made up. Filomena has chosen to go away, they say, no one has made her, and the artwork will be recovered all in good time. The art squad from Rome is excellent; they will trace what has happened to the painting.'

'Essentially, they've washed their hands of the business.'

'It would seem so.'

'Well, you may not be able to talk to the Tascas, but we can.' Flora was already thinking of what she would ask them.

The priest put out his hand as though to detain her. 'You will be careful. They are an angry family and I do not know what they might do.'

'We're very good at being careful,' she said cheerfully.

Are we? was Jack's less comfortable thought.

6

The priest got to his feet and solemnly shook hands with them both. 'You will excuse me now? I must return to my house in case there is a message from the police.'

It seemed unlikely, but Jack wasn't about to bring Father Renzi's spirits any lower than they already were.

'But, if you should ask any questions and you have any news, you will come to Santa Margherita?' The priest still lingered by the table.

'We will, I promise.' It was easy enough to promise, but difficult to see how they could unearth anything substantive, knowing no one in Venice and with little Italian.

'Father Renzi.' Flora jumped up, as though stricken by a sudden thought. 'Do you know a Franco Massi? He came from Asolo, too, I believe.'

'Franco? But, of course. The Massi family are well-known in that district. Franco has been in Venice for some years and I know that he has done very well. But also that he does not forget his beginnings. He has been a very good son – for the most part. I hear that he often returns to see his parents. They are growing older, of course.'

It was obvious to Jack that the priest had not heard of Massi's death. Perhaps he avoided newspapers or never listened to the local radio. He supposed they should break the bad news, but first...

'When you say Franco has been a good son "for the most part", is there some doubt?'

The priest waggled his head from side to side. 'A small doubt only. His parents were not happy that Franco broke his engagement. They liked very much the girl he had chosen and were hoping for a marriage. And, of course, for grandchildren! That is not likely with their younger son.'

'Do you know why he broke it?'

'Signora Massi told me when I was last in Asolo that Franco felt his parents would need more of his help as the years passed. He has a disabled brother, you see, and fears that caring for the younger boy will become harder. He thought, I imagine, that with a family of his own, it would not be possible to give his parents the support they will need.'

It seemed a poor excuse to Jack, and to Flora, too. 'Why then did he suggest marriage in the first place?' she asked. 'The family's situation can't have changed.'

Renzi spread his hands. 'Who would know? The heart, my dear, has its reasons.'

She looked unimpressed with the aphorism and was gazing pointedly at him, Jack realised. It was time to speak. 'Father Renzi.' He cleared his throat. 'I think you cannot have heard the news. Franco Massi is dead. Two nights ago he fell into the Grand Canal and drowned.'

The priest looked aghast. 'He is dead! This cannot be.'

'I'm afraid it is.'

'But this is terrible. How can he have fallen? How could he not swim to safety?'

'The police are saying it was an accident,' Jack said carefully. 'That he must have hit his head as he fell and been rendered unconscious.'

'This is terrible,' Renzi repeated. 'His parents will have hearts that are broken. Franco has always been their hope, their light. I must speak with them.' His tone had a new urgency. 'Telephone to Asolo immediately.'

'Before you go,' Flora said, as the priest made to walk away, 'do you know Bianca Benetti? She was Franco's fiancée.'

Hearing the name, Father Renzi retraced a few steps. 'I cannot say that I know the young woman well, but I have met her. Just once. They were here – Franco and Bianca – having coffee in the square and he rushed up to me. Come to meet a beautiful girl, Father, he said. And she was beautiful... but... the poor child, how she must be suffering.'

The priest stood motionless, staring blindly into space, until Flora's second question brought him back to the present. 'Would you know where she works?'

'Yes, I think so.' He sounded a little vague. 'Franco must have mentioned it. Yes.' He nodded to himself. 'It is a hotel on the Giudecca. Close to the Cipriani where Franco is... was... employed. That boy has done so well. Such a good future in front of him.' The priest shook his head, his beard quivering slightly.

'The name of the hotel?'

'Minerva, I think. Yes, Hotel Minerva.'

A final wave, and Renzi walked towards one of the small lanes that intersected with the square. Jack's eyes followed the disappearing figure of the priest, then felt another pair of eyes trained on him. Hazel eyes.

'Don't tell me,' he groaned. 'We're on our way to Hotel Minerva.'

It was only fair, Jack thought, as they walked back to the San Tomà stop. He'd been indulged with a visit to the Scuola Grande and, surprisingly, they'd been rewarded with more than the Tintorettos. If Flora was determined to help Father Renzi, and it seemed she was, discovering whether Franco Massi had any connection to the priest's difficulties would be a first step, and a visit to his fiancée at the Minerva might just help. Once back on the Giudecca, the hotel shouldn't be hard to find.

Their conversation with Bianca was likely to be brief, he reckoned, and should leave them time to enjoy an afternoon at the Cipriani. Particularly, an afternoon at the swimming pool: in his mind a stretch of deep blue water glinted in the sun, a cushioned lounger sat beneath a huge umbrella, and an ever-watchful pool attendant served fruit and sorbets and ice-cold drinks. It was a treat that had been in his thoughts ever since he'd spied the pool from an upstairs window. It was quite unusual for a Venetian hotel to boast such a luxury and this one, he judged, was near Olympic size.

'Lunch?' he asked, as they clambered aboard the *vaporetto* on their way back to the island.

She wrinkled her nose. 'I'm not sure I could eat anything. I'm still full from breakfast.'

'Me too. Shall we skip a meal? If we're desperate, we can always buy paninis on the way.' He was as eager now as Flora to find Bianca Benetti, although for somewhat different reasons.

Ferried back to the Giudecca by the Cipriani launch, and having shrugged off the need for a panini, they found Hotel Minerva with ease. A ten-minute walk by the side of the lagoon, through attractive gardens and past numerous small shops and several restaurants, brought them to the Calle San Giacomo. A sign at its entrance directed them to follow the passageway to the hotel at its end.

The Minerva was a good deal smaller than their own hotel and clearly less luxurious, but clean and comfortable with a pleasant receptionist behind the desk.

'Bianca Benetti?' she queried. 'Yes, she is here. Bianca is one of our housekeeping staff. I will ring to see if she is available to come.'

They were invited to take a seat in the lobby and, after a lengthy wait, were gratified to see the pretty girl that Flora had met in Abbeymead step out of the lift and look around. Flora stood up and waved to her.

Bianca nodded, a head of thick curls bouncing in acknowledgement. Even dressed in the hotel's uniform of brown-striped dress and cream pinafore, Bianca made an impression, her curvaceous figure brightening the somewhat drab attire.

'It is Flora, no?' she said, her English heavily accented.

'That's right. I remember meeting you at the Priory.'

'That was a good time,' the girl said a trifle sadly. 'I miss England. I miss Sussex.'

Flora knew the feeling although, strangely, she had felt little homesickness this time, and had to keep reminding herself to telephone Alice, as she'd promised, and reassure her that all was well and neither she nor Jack had so far fallen into a canal, though she wouldn't mention the man who had.

'Please, come and sit down.' Jack made space for the girl on the Venetian-red sofa and she sank down beside Flora.

'Sally asked me to call and say hello if we had time this week,' Flora began gently. 'I didn't think we would but... we heard the news... about your... about Franco... and thought that we really must come.'

Bianca stared at her feet, and for the first time Flora noticed how drawn she looked.

'We are so sorry, Bianca.' Better to pretend ignorance of a broken engagement. Father Renzi might not, in any case, be right.

'Accidents happen,' she said, her voice lacking any trace of emotion.

Flora was taken aback. Even if Franco *had* broken the engagement, he'd been this girl's fiancé.

'Franco—' she began delicately, only to be interrupted.

'How did you know of Franco?'

'He checked us into our hotel – we're staying at the Cipriani. After we heard what happened to him, and realised he was engaged to someone we actually knew, we felt we had to call.'

Bianca's smile was taut. 'Not any more engaged. We said goodbye last month. I am sorry to hear that anyone has come to harm in the canal, but Franco – he is nothing to me now.'

There was a long pause while Flora strove to think of something to say. She had expected a heartbroken fiancée, even a heartbroken ex-fiancée, but Bianca's cold indifference was discomfiting.

'I have spoken to Sally, you know,' the maid said. 'She told me you were coming here – on your honeymoon.'

The sudden change of conversation had Flora blink. It was evident they would not be speaking of Franco, as she'd hoped.

'Really?' she stuttered. 'I didn't know you and Sally spoke that often.'

'Sally is a good friend. She understands.'

What exactly Sally understood was difficult to fathom – it seemed unlikely that Bianca was about to clarify – and, really, it was Franco who interested them.

Flora decided to try again. 'Can I ask when it was that you last saw Franco?'

The girl looked surprised. It must seem a strange question, Flora acknowledged, but then Bianca shrugged at the oddity as though she couldn't remember or couldn't be bothered to.

'You don't remember him telling you any worries he had?'

The maid's expression was derisive. 'Franco? Worries? No chance. He was king of his own little castle.'

And what did that mean? But before Flora could ask for enlightenment, the receptionist had walked over to the small group and tapped Bianca on the shoulder.

'I am sorry to interrupt,' she said in English, 'but you are wanted, Bianca. Room 233 are unhappy with their pillows.'

The girl rose gracefully to her feet. 'I must go, but I hope I will see you again before you leave Venice. You should take a boat trip. Here.' She delved into her apron pocket and brought out a card. 'This is my father. He is a boatman and has a brand new vessel. He knows all of Venice very well and will take you wherever you want.'

They scrambled to say a hasty goodbye before the maid whisked herself away and into the lift on her mission to room 233.

'Well, that didn't work too well,' Jack said, getting to his feet. 'She evidently wants nothing to do with Franco, even a dead Franco. We seem to have wasted our time.' He'd been unable to stop thinking of the swimming pool.

'Maybe not entirely.' Flora tapped the card. 'We should take a boat trip.'

7

Walking into the Cipriani, Flora made straight for the reception desk, Bianca's card in her hand. The older of the two men on duty was head of the large reception team, she knew, and it was to him she showed the business card.

'We're thinking of hiring a boat for the day and I've had a recommendation,' she began. 'Would you know this gentleman?'

The man afforded the name a brief glance, then gave a slight cough. 'We do not usually give recommendations, signora.' He passed a hand over sleeked-down grey hair before returning the card and met Flora's enquiring face with a professional smile.

'I'm not actually asking for a recommendation,' she pointed out. 'Only if you know this name.'

'I do,' he admitted, 'and I would advise that if you wish to take a boat, you allow us to organise the hire for you.'

'There's a problem with...' she glanced down at the card, 'Piero Benetti?'

'Piero Benetti? *Assolutamente!*' The younger man on the desk, who had clearly been listening in, earned himself a severe look from his superior.

'You know him then?' Flora transferred her attention to the young receptionist.

He cast his colleague a nervous look. 'I would not say that I know him. *Non esattamente.* But I saw Benetti when he came here. To the hotel. And he caused much trouble.'

'Really, what trouble would that be?'

'The signora should not worry,' the older man said smoothly. 'We will find an excellent boat for you and your husband, and at a very good rate.'

'The trouble?' This was too interesting to ignore.

The senior receptionist took stock of Flora and must have decided that she wasn't a woman to give up. That she wasn't going away. With obvious reluctance, he said, 'Signor Benetti had a problem with a member of our staff and felt it right to express his anger.'

'Is that a complicated way of saying he lost his temper?'

'He did.'

'*E come!*' the younger man added, earning another severe look from his mentor. 'We must replace two large vases. The ones you see there. Smashed to pieces.'

'And the member of staff with whom Benetti had a problem? Would that be Franco Massi?'

'Yes, signora.' The grey-haired man gave a delicate sigh. 'Now, if there is anything further...'

'Nothing, thank you. You have been very helpful.'

Bemused, the two men looked at each other until the younger, recalling he was in some disgrace, grabbed hold of a ringing telephone.

Jack had gone ahead and, by the time Flora joined him in the bedroom, he was already in swimming costume and sandals. 'Come on, slow coach,' he urged. 'Let's make the most of what's left of the day.'

Flora shuffled through her suitcase in search of a bathing suit. 'Bianca's father had a problem with Franco,' she murmured. 'He came here to the Cipriani and made a massive scene.'

'His daughter had just been dumped by Massi. It's understandable.'

'But to barge into a hotel, a hotel like this, and create a huge argument – he actually broke several vases – he must have been pretty violent.'

'A testament to love for his daughter?'

Flora saw her husband's grin and gave up. 'OK, I may be exaggerating, but it's still something to remember. Look, you go ahead, Jack – find a shady spot for us both. Ah, here's my costume.' She held up a red ruched halter neck with a sweetheart neckline. 'Just a pair of sandals I need now. I'll be down as soon as I've found them.'

Ten minutes later, trailing her feet through deliciously cool water, she had to agree with Jack. This was the way to spend an afternoon in Venice. Not in walking the scorching lanes, or immured in art galleries, wonderful though they were, but sitting on the edge of this fabulous pool while Jack sliced his way up and down the long stretch of water.

After several lengths, he came to a halt and swam to the pool's edge. Looking up at her, his flop of hair plastered to his forehead, he gave her a gentle scold.

'You really should learn to swim, Flora. I could teach you.'

'I'm happy enough here,' she said.

'But it's fun. An important life skill, too.'

'I'm happy,' she repeated.

She was genuinely scared of deep water. A few years ago, she had come close to drowning and paddling her feet was now the nearest she intended to get. Jack was right, of course.

Learning to swim was something she should have done as a child – as an adult it was too steep a challenge – but Abbeymead was some miles from the sea which meant that journeys to the coast were infrequent and dependent on public transport and, though there was a swimming pool in the nearby town, for much of her childhood it had been closed on and off from the threat of polio.

She scrambled up and, hopping from one foot to another across paving that sizzled, made it to one of the sunloungers Jack had bagged earlier. Lazily, she lay back, contemplating a sky the colour of ultramarine, her gaze travelling downwards to the pink walls and terracotta roofs beyond the hotel's perimeter, to a glistening white dome, and in the near distance, to the red brick of a bell tower. What a setting for a swimming pool!

'Shall we get a drink?' she asked, as Jack arrived at her side, reaching across to throw him a towel. 'Here! You're dripping on me.'

'I need you wet! But a good idea. A *limonata*, maybe? The waiter's on his way over.' He nodded towards the approaching figure.

When Flora followed his gaze, however, it wasn't one of the pool staff she saw but the younger of the receptionists she'd spoken to less than an hour ago.

'Signor, signora, you have a telephone call,' he called, before he'd even reached them.

When they were slow to respond, he said more urgently, 'From England. It costs much.'

'Something's happened at home!' Flora jumped up, grabbing her sundress. 'Something bad. The All's Well? The cottage?'

'Who is it?' Jack asked the man calmly.

'It is a lady. A Signora Yenner?'

'Jenner. Alice! Oh, dear Lord, she's ill!' Frantically, Flora cast around for her sandals.

'If Alice were ill, she'd hardly be telephoning.' But Jack's reasoning went unheard.

'I should have phoned, I knew I should, but somehow the time never seemed right.'

'Well, it is now, so stop panicking and go and speak to her.'

'You'll come, too?'

'But why?'

'Because I need you with me, Jack.'

Obediently, he pulled on a pair of shorts and casual shirt. 'My clothes will be utterly soaked, you realise that.'

'They'll dry,' she said shortly.

'Flora, love, is that you?'

'Yes.' Flora gripped the receiver until her knuckles shone white. 'What's the matter, Alice? What's happened?'

'You didn't telephone.'

'I meant to, I really did. I'm so sorry,' she said lamely, and waited for the blow to fall. Alice must have terrible news. But her friend stayed silent.

A short pause. 'Is everything OK in the village?' she ventured, praying it would be.

'I reckon so.'

The creases on Flora's forehead deepened. 'And you're well?'

'More or less, my love. We've had good weather so the arthritis isn't playin' up like it can do.'

'The All's Well?' she asked, holding her breath.

'That Rose is doin' all right. I'm not happy with how she behaved with Hector and never will be – she hurt my Sally badly – but she's managin' the shop well enough, I must say.'

'And the cottage?'

'I passed by t'other day and your house looks fine.'

Jack had been listening in and out of the corner of her eye

she saw him gesticulating, mouthing an irritated 'What!' It seemed extraordinary to Flora, too, that Alice was paying for an expensive call to tell her precisely nothing.

'I went by Overlay House, too,' her old friend offered. 'And I've met the new chap, as it happens, the new man who's renting. Met him at the baker's – the day after you left, it was – and I arsked how he was gettin' on at the house. He pulled a bit of a face and said OK, he supposed, but it needed a fair bit of refurbishment. I bet it does, I thought! He seemed nice enough but it's a funny business. I dunno if I'd trust him far. He's moved here from Lewes, did you know? – says he wanted somewhere quieter. I wouldn't have thought Lewes was exactly noisy, so it's a bit strange. He doesn't appear to work, either. Mebbe he's got money. He was talkin' about doin' stuff for one of the bonfire societies, but that's not a job. They're all volunteers, the ones who make the costumes and the floats.'

At this point, she was forced to pause for breath and Jack took the opportunity to grab the phone from Flora's hand. 'Alice, what's happened?' he said quietly but firmly. 'Why are you really ringing?'

There was silence, the only sound faint echoes on the line. 'It's Sally,' she said at last, naming her niece and the owner of the Priory.

'Sally's unwell?' Flora said into the mouthpiece.

'Not ezactly. But she's been that worn down. I told her to go to Norfolk – there's one or two Jenners still in the county and I could get in touch. Some lovely beaches there, sand and all, but then that girl phoned and Sally decided she'd go to see her.'

'What girl and where?'

'The one Dominic Lister hired. That Italian lass.'

'Bianca Benetti?'

'Probably. Sounds like the name. She's been phoning Sally this last week. Real upset. Something about her dad and her boyfriend. She said she really wanted to see Sally, talk to her, face to face. Said she'd always been a good friend and, when Sal said that *she'd* been feelin' a bit off colour, the girl told her take the train to Venice and she'd find her a room.'

'Are you saying Sally is in Venice?' Flora was struggling to understand.

'She's on her way. I just told you.' Alice was sounding agitated, but added quickly, 'She won't bother you, honestly. She definitely won't come lookin' for you.'

'And that's the reason you've phoned?'

'Yes,' Alice mumbled. 'I'm sorry, my love. You and Jack deserve a good holiday together and Sally could have gone anywhere for hers, but there... I didn't like to tell you. I thought if you phoned, I could just kind of drop it in, but you didn't phone so I got a bit desperate. I thought you needed to know, just in case when she gets there you might meet her by accident.'

'Just in case,' Jack remarked drily, as they said goodbye to a clearly relieved Alice, unburdened now by the momentous news. 'I'd say it was a certainty.'

'It might not happen.' Flora tried to conjure a smile from him.

'She's staying with the Benetti girl, Flora, and you're intent on pursuing this Massi business. It has to be a certainty.'

Walking back to the pool, she put her arm around him and hugged him close. 'If we do meet Sally, what does it matter – really?'

'I suppose I'd hoped that for a few days we could leave Abbeymead behind, that I could spend them alone with you. Just you and me together. Was that too much to hope?'

Flora had no answer. It seemed it was.

8

'If Sally is staying with Bianca while she's in Venice, it could prove useful.' Flora was trying for optimism, but her words produced only a groan.

'That's exactly what I mean.' Jack paused on the stairs on their way back to the room, a challenge in his eyes. 'If it isn't Abbeymead taking our time, it's some mad investigation you're desperate to pursue.'

'You're just as desperate – normally. Don't pretend otherwise!'

'But not this time. Not on what should be a very special holiday.'

'We've promised Massimo *and* Father Renzi that we'd do what we could to discover what's been going on – maybe we shouldn't have promised, but we did.'

'OK,' he said, taking her hand, 'but what does Bianca have to do with any of it? Nothing, as far as I can see.'

'Asolo,' Flora said, with certainty. 'Asolo is where the priest's difficulties began and where there's still a family who hates him. It's too much of a coincidence that Father Renzi was driven from the town and now faces a dreadful situation in

Venice. This latest trouble has its roots in the past, I'm convinced.'

'But Bianca – I still don't see why it's important to talk to her. Apart from the fact that she's no wish to talk to us. She made that pretty clear.'

'She was at work. It was difficult. And we weren't given the time to speak to her properly. I think we should try again. Persuade her, if we can, to forget how angry she feels about Franco – for a short while at least – and cast her mind back to conversations she had with him. Conversations when he might have told her something – not daily worries, she was quite scathing about that – but suspicions he might have over what was happening in his home town. He would know Luigi Tasca. He would know Matteo Pretelli. And he returned home regularly. On one of those visits perhaps he discovered something about the priest or about the Tascas.'

'That isn't just a long shot, Flora, it's out of sight. When is Franco supposed to have passed on this vital information? The man dipped out of his engagement weeks ago and now he's dead.'

She gave a small hunch of her shoulders. 'I know it's unlikely that Bianca will be any help, but we have to follow the few leads we have. If they go nowhere, we can say honestly to the priest and your fath— and the count... that we tried but weren't successful.'

He unlocked their door and walked through into the bedroom, crossing to the long windows and flinging them wide. 'We could say that anyway and forget the whole business.'

'But that would be a lie.'

'It would, but would it matter?' He turned to her. 'What's most important – finding out who stole Father Renzi's painting, or our honeymoon?'

Flora plumped herself down on the bed. 'It's not just a painting, though, is it? There's the safety of an elderly woman at stake – and justice for a man who could have been killed for simply knowing too much.'

A deep ridge appeared between Jack's eyes. 'If it wasn't for the housekeeper, I'd give up the questioning right now.'

'But you won't?'

He gave a shake of his head. 'I won't, not until she turns up, hopefully unharmed. But Franco Massi's death is another matter. That could well have been an accident, and why should it have any connection to what happened at Santa Margarita? Apart from the fact that Franco and the priest come from the same town, there's no obvious connection.'

'I've a hunch.'

Jack joined her on the bed, smoothing the strands of copper hair from her face. 'Oh, one of those!'

Flora's hunches had become the stuff of teasing between them.

'Yes, one of those. I think we should eat at La Zucca again. Tomorrow, perhaps?'

There was bewilderment on his face. 'But why? Why go back there?'

'It's another avenue. Another path to explore. If Bianca knows nothing when we speak to her again, perhaps someone at the restaurant will. Franco was furious on the night he died and his quarrel was with the owner of La Zucca.'

'If Franco was concerned the restaurant owner was involved in something shady, which is what you're suggesting, why would he have recommended the place to us a few hours earlier?'

'Something happened in the hours between?'

'Like what?'

'Franco was very, very angry,' she said stubbornly. 'There has to have been a reason for that.'

'No doubt, but it could be something totally unconnected to Asolo, to the Tascas, to the priest. In fact, it's almost impossible to think it would be connected. Perhaps the restaurant gave a Cipriani guest a poor meal and Franco came to protest.'

'It was more than a protest, but you're right,' she said calmly. 'There could have been any number of reasons for the quarrel. But if it was personal... if the restaurant owner has links to Asolo...'

'And how do we find that out?'

'We ask him.'

It sounded simple. It always did with Flora, and usually turned out to be anything but, while the question of their honeymoon and how they should spend it remained unresolved. For months, they'd been planning their trip to Venice: reading books, deciding where they'd visit, anticipating everything about this glorious holiday – the flights, the hotel, the city. It mattered hugely and yet, since arriving, they'd been faced with a possible murder, a stolen painting, a missing woman and now, apparently, the imminent arrival of a friend from home. Every day should have been one of pure enjoyment, so how had they landed themselves in this mess?

It wasn't all Flora's fault. She hadn't asked Count Falconi to call on them. Hadn't asked for his mother's visit either, Jack thought darkly, and she hadn't encouraged Sally to make the trip. All she'd really done was raise the suspicion that Franco Massi had been deliberately killed and linked it, as only she could, with the troubles suffered by Father Renzi. It had been sufficient, though, to plunge them into a new adventure which, knowing Flora, wouldn't end until she got to the truth.

He had no wish to make a second visit to La Zucca. As far as he could see, it would help little and could stir up even more trouble. Yet there was no obvious objection he could raise to eating there again. Their previous meal had been well-cooked, delicious even, and tomorrow should be an evening to look forward to. Except for the fact that his wife intended to interrogate its owner, and the owner was unlikely to respond happily.

If Jack refused point-blank to go there, he knew Flora well enough to realise she would find a way to go by herself. And that was something he most definitely didn't want.

A faint hope during the night that La Zucca might be closed on a Monday, since many of the restaurants in Venice took a break that day, had disappeared by morning when one of the receptionists on duty assured him that, on the contrary, La Zucca was so popular that it now opened six days a week.

It seemed that Jack must think again. He needed a plan, he told himself. Any plan. Perhaps if he kept Flora busy today, exceptionally busy, she might be too tired by the evening to travel back to the city and would be willing to settle for a meal on the island. It was even possible that by then she might have had second thoughts over confronting the restaurant owner in his den. Or she'd thought of other avenues to explore – with Flora, you never knew.

With this idea in mind, sketchy as it was, he suggested that after breakfast they take the hotel boat to St Mark's and saunter first along the Riva degli Schiavoni and from there into Castello, a quarter of Venice they hadn't yet explored.

'We could make for the Arsenale first, but call at the Giardini on the way. We never did get to the café.' He hoped he sounded suitably casual.

The happy smile she gave in response made him feel a tad guilty, but Jack was on a mission – to deflect her. It was for her own good, he argued silently, and that's what was most important.

'I'd love to do the walk,' she said, her enthusiasm increasing his guilt. 'Let's go early. Venice in the cool of the morning will be bliss and, once it's too hot, there are masses of cafés or bars we can shelter in.'

· · ·

Within an hour of their breakfast coffee, they were turning in through the iron gates of the Giardini and following the gravel pathway to where Jack was sure they would find the café.

Flora stopped to survey the gardens on either side. 'The grass is already quite burnt. Almost brown. Not at all like Sussex.'

'And getting more unlike by the day. It will be a whole lot browner by the end of the summer. Literally, dying for rain. I guess that's when the floods arrive, the dreaded *acqua alta*.'

'High water?' she ventured. 'See, I shall soon be fluent!'

'High water,' he agreed, laughing. 'When the tide rises and the lagoon sweeps in. But not until autumn – so we should be safe!'

They had turned a corner in the path and come to a small, red-roofed building standing to one side, its shutters down and surrounded by a general air of desertion.

'The café is closed. How disappointing.'

'We'll eat there one day,' she promised. 'And, in any case, it's far too early for lunch. Even for you.'

At least it meant they would keep walking, Jack thought. Out on to the Riva again, the sun now higher in the sky as they strolled towards the Arsenale, crossing over the bridge into its main square. Despite the increasing warmth, Flora's energy, he noted gloomily, seemed undiminished.

He glanced around the open square. 'This place looks as though it's crumbling. How sad. Years of disuse and neglect, I guess. It deserves better.'

'Was it once an army barracks, do you know?'

'Something close, but it was the Venice navy who were here – their shipyards and armouries. This was their base when the Republic controlled a huge part of the Mediterranean.'

'There's not much sign of that now.' Flora turned in a circle. 'Except for those lions. The lions are pretty impressive.' The two marble beasts, one lying, one sitting, flanked an enormous arch, its iron gate firmly closed against them.

'Not much to see, though. Come on, let's move. The sea air is giving me an appetite. Shall we go back over the bridge and look for a café?'

'I'd like to walk on, if that's OK with you. For a while, at least. I'm enjoying exploring.' Jack's spirits sank lower. The trip to La Zucca hadn't gone away.

'What's that island?' she asked sometime later, stopping to point across the lagoon.

They had passed the Giovanni and Paolo hospital and Flora was looking across at an expanse of green.

'It's San Michele, the cemetery. Nicely situated directly opposite the hospital,' he said wryly.

She lifted a hand to shield her eyes. 'I think I can make out a mausoleum and some small domes and maybe a few avenging angels. It looks an interesting place. I'd love to take a boat trip there.'

'This afternoon?' he asked eagerly.

'Maybe another day. Today, I think, we should keep walking – it's hot but nowhere near as hot as it has been.'

Jack stifled a sigh. It had been a ropey plan to start with and now was clearly not working at all. At this rate, he'd be the one too tired to take the boat back to St Mark's this evening. Perhaps he could plead that as an excuse – extreme fatigue or maybe a bad back, or a blister on his foot. Anything to keep them away from that restaurant. He couldn't lose the very bad feeling he had about La Zucca, though why he had it, he wasn't sure – other than a natural dislike of what would almost certainly be a confrontation.

Another mile or two further, or so it seemed, his spirits lifted slightly when, by chance, he spotted a small trattoria situated on one of the shaded alleyways running down to the lagoon, its tables spilling across the pavement. Brightly checked tablecloths flapped in a breeze that had recently begun to blow, and the café's window of salami and round cheeses looked inviting.

He snatched a surreptitious look at his watch. 'Twelve o'clock already,' he said brightly. 'Why don't we eat here? We can make it a snack and there's an empty table waiting for us.'

It proved a good choice. The light lunch, when it came, was exactly right: a bowl of minestrone, a caprese salad, followed by a plate of grilled calamari. Despite her supposed lack of appetite, Flora ate her way through the several dishes, talking animatedly of the gardens, the Arsenale, the view from where they sat. Everything, Jack thought, except this evening's crucial visit.

Was it worth carrying on with his flawed plan? But he could think of nothing else, so after paying the bill, he turned to ask, 'More walking?' Over his shoulder, he looked longingly at a water taxi that was powering by.

'Why not? We have to reach home somehow,' she said.

And reach home they did, walking through what seemed to Jack most of Castello, the northernmost *sestiere* of Venice and one of its largest. One that few tourists bothered to visit, making a stroll through its streets an attractive prospect – if only his feet would stop hurting. He was sure now that he really did have a blister.

By the time they reached the Cipriani kiosk to phone for a ferry back to the Giudecca, Jack had consigned his plan to the devil.

9

It had been an interesting day, Flora decided, and a clever idea of Jack's to use the slightly cooler weather to see something of a Venice they hadn't yet explored. She was certainly tired, but tired or not, was looking forward to the evening and a visit to a restaurant that she reckoned was behind most, if not all, of the trouble they'd uncovered. An hour or so lazing and she'd be ready to go.

Jack yawned, joining her on the bed and wrapping his arms around her. 'I don't know if I can eat much tonight,' he murmured.

'Really? That doesn't sound like you. We could always forget the main course, I suppose. I don't think they'd object. Have just a starter and a pudding – their desserts looked lovely.'

'We're definitely going out to eat?' he asked innocently.

She turned her head to look at him, her expression puzzled. 'Why wouldn't we? We're going to La Zucca. You do remember?'

. . .

How could he forget the restaurant or the repercussions he feared from Flora's meeting with an owner who, inevitably, would be less than pleased? And so it turned out. They had eaten their main course of chicken *cacciatore* – neither, in fact, had fancied a starter – and by luck, or ill luck, Jack grumbled to himself, it was the owner rather than their waiter who walked out to their table on the terrace and presented them with the dessert menu.

Flora smiled brightly up at him, a sure sign she was in questioning mode. 'You have a beautiful restaurant here,' she said.

'Thank you, signora.'

'Beautiful surroundings, too. So close to the Grand Canal. You must be very busy.'

'*Il ristorante è popolare.* It goes well,' he acknowledged.

'We're just finding our way around Venice,' she confided. 'It can be confusing.'

He nodded pleasantly and handed them both a new menu, intending to leave them to make their choice.

'We've been talking of travelling more widely, though,' she said before he could walk away. 'Exploring the Veneto.'

'*Il Veneto* – is very beautiful, too.'

'Can you recommend anywhere we should visit in particular?'

Here it comes, Jack realised.

The owner spread his hands in a gesture of resignation. 'There are so many places. *Tutto é bellissimo.*'

'Do you come from Venice yourself?'

'No, signora.' He tried to walk away.

'Perhaps we could visit your home town.' Flora's smile became brighter. 'Where would that be?' And when he appeared not to understand, she asked again. 'Where do you come from? *Da dove viene?*'

'Asolo.' He answered abruptly.

'Asolo is in the Veneto?' she asked, adopting a useful ignorance.

'It is, signora, and very beautiful.'

'Thank you. We might visit. And I'll have the *amaretto gelato*, please. How about you, Jack?'

As soon as the owner had strode back into the restaurant, Flora turned to him as he knew she would.

'You see? There *is* a connection.'

'And what are we to do about it? He didn't appear exactly helpful, did he?'

'No, he didn't,' she said thoughtfully. 'I may go for a little walk after the ice cream. To find the toilet.'

'Flora...' he warned.

'I'm allowed to go to the Ladies. And if I should lose my way...'

Jack leaned across the table, his voice low. 'What, exactly?'

'I could explore. There must be a lot more to the restaurant than this terrace and the tables inside. A cellar maybe.'

'And if you find a cellar, what then?'

'I've no idea, but it's surely worth a little scrummaging. A man is dead, a painting stolen and an elderly lady who should be safe at home is still missing.'

The gelato, brought this time by their waiter – Flora remarked on the change – was mouthwatering. The owner, she checked again the name over the door, Silvio Fabbri, had disappeared into the dim interior of the restaurant. There were a few lamplit tables inside but the warmth of the summer evening had the majority of customers choose seats on the long terrace.

Crunching her napkin into a ball, she got to her feet and gathered up her handbag. 'I won't be long,' she said.

'Don't be – and never mind the cellar. Stick to the bathroom,' Jack advised.

'But of course!'

A waitress was serving the several indoor tables and pointed Flora in the right direction. A flight of stairs towards the back of the restaurant led to a half landing and the women's washroom, but then continued on, leading down to... she would find out.

Checking over her shoulder that she was unwatched, Flora sped down the staircase to discover that the restaurant boasted an enormous basement which must, she calculated, stretch beneath the businesses on either side of La Zucca. It was far larger than she'd expected. And far more interesting. From the furthest end came the clank of pots, the smack of china, the shouts of people under pressure – that would be the kitchen. But the sounds were at a distance and, turning in the opposite direction, she began to explore what else this cavernous space contained. Doors were her first thought. At least six, side by side, all shut and all probably locked.

But maybe not. Flora walked up to the first and was about to try the handle when a slight noise caught her ear. No more than a faint scuffle. She turned quickly but before she could face whatever had made the noise, a hand gripped her shoulder, hard and painful. She caught her breath and waited.

'Signora, you are lost?'

She twisted round and his clasp lessened slightly. A young man, tall and muscular, with dark curly hair. His smile seemed to mock, a smile that Flora didn't like.

'The bathroom,' she said, hoping he'd swallow the excuse. 'I'm looking for the bathroom.'

'But you have come too far, signora,' he said in English. '*Troppo lontano.* Please, I show you.' The clasp on her shoulder intensified once more and Flora felt herself propelled towards the staircase she had recently descended.

'Up,' he said. And it was a command rather than a request.

'*Matteo, sei tu qui sotto?*' The voice from above was harsh and impatient.

'Si, sto arrivando. I am coming.' The man named Matteo gave her a little push and she was forced to climb the stairs, coming face to face with a second young man, this one wearing an angry expression and a none too clean shirt.

He ignored her and spoke in rapid Italian while Matteo, it seemed, attempted to soothe him. To reassure him? she wondered. Dialogue crackled back and forth until her guide seemed suddenly to realise that Flora stood close by and was listening.

'This is where you want, signora.' He waved a hand towards the cubicles she'd seen earlier.

Flora thanked him and smiled at his companion. In return, she received a scowl.

'What happened?' Jack asked, fearing the worst, as he'd done all day. 'You look tense. Are you?'

'Only a little. The restaurant has a huge basement, Jack, and doors everywhere. I'm certain there's something down there they want to hide. I was stopped by a young man – the owner's son, maybe? – who made sure I went no further. His name was Matteo...' She trailed off. 'Wasn't there a Matteo in the priest's story? Matteo... Pretelli.'

'There must be thousands of Matteos in Italy.'

'So, another coincidence?'

Jack ignored the challenge. 'You went looking and Matteo—'

'Suddenly, he was there. I hadn't heard a sound and then a hand was on my shoulder. And not a gentle hand either. He more or less forced me to walk back up the stairs.'

'You were trespassing. They don't want customers wandering where they shouldn't.'

'Maybe, but it *is* an enormous basement. The cooks take up a fair space, I imagine, but apart from the kitchen, there are half a dozen rooms. I wanted to know what was behind those doors. I still do.'

Jack grimaced. 'We're not going to find out. At least, not tonight – if ever. I think we should pay and disappear. You've done enough exploring for one evening.'

He was right, Flora knew, and hoped that she hadn't spoiled for him what had been a thoroughly enjoyable day. But for the episode in the basement – and for a moment she'd felt real fear – it had been a wonderful evening. Eating together, talking together. Really, this is what they should be doing, she told herself, as they began their walk back to St Mark's and the Cipriani berth: days spent sightseeing or lazing by the pool, evenings eating by the lagoon or beside one of the small canals that made Venice the city it was.

But she couldn't relax, not entirely. If it had only been a matter of a missing painting, she might have shrugged it off, left it to the squad from Rome to solve the mystery, but knowing that a woman, an elderly woman at that, was involved – a woman the priest feared had come to harm – made it impossible to forget. Impossible to do anything but try to discover what had happened to her. And Father Renzi, too. Flora had liked him a lot, had felt desperately sorry for his predicament and wanted very much to see him regain a life that was peaceful and untroubled.

Despite her qualms, there was no doubt in her mind that she had to continue to dig. There would be the chance of a second honeymoon, she comforted herself, sometime in the future, and hoped that Jack would see it that way, too.

'I think it would be wise to give La Zucca a miss for a while,' Jack said, as they wandered through the streets to St Mark's piazza.

The evening had been difficult, he thought. That was the

word. Difficult but not disastrous, certainly not as bad as he'd
feared. Maybe Flora would be content now with what she'd
discovered and they could forget any future visits. Disappointment, however, lay ahead.

'I'm glad you said for a while.' Flora tucked her arm in his.
'We'll have to search that cellar – or the police will. I mean, six
doors to six rooms and all of them closed!'

'And all of them stuffed to the ceiling with goods for the
restaurant.'

'You don't know that, and how would that even be possible?
But I agree – we won't go back just yet.'

A breathing space, at least, he thought.

They had walked halfway back to the square and were
sauntering through a narrow, ill-lit passageway, an archway of
brightness ahead, when a figure came rushing past them,
cannoning into Jack and sending him crashing against the stone
wall of the building that towered above them.

A young woman who had been walking a few paces behind
tutted loudly and, with Flora, helped Jack to his feet.

'*Ruffiano*,' she said. Then in English, 'Ruffian. You OK?'

'Yes, thank you. *Grazie mille.*'

She smiled at them both and walked on.

'He *was* a ruffian,' Flora began to say when she realised that
Jack was clutching his arm in a worrying fashion. 'You're not
OK, are you?'

She came close and through the gloom peered at his shirtsleeve. A bloom of red had spread across the white cotton.

'You've been stabbed!' she said. 'Oh, dear Lord, you've been
stabbed!'

'I felt something,' he admitted. 'But it won't be serious, not where it is, just messy. Have you a handkerchief? Better still, use mine.'

Flora fumbled in his pocket for the square of linen, her hand shaking slightly. Then, in the dim light, folding his sleeve back, she could just make out a slash mark, no more than two inches wide, but pouring blood.

Jack craned his neck to squint. 'It's a superficial cut, by the look of it. If you can bind it...'

Flora wrapped the handkerchief around the wound, tugging the ends into as tight a knot as she could manage, then holding him by the other arm, walked them as quickly as possible to the waterside. To the Cipriani phone and safety.

By the time they stepped off the launch at the hotel's landing stage, the bleeding had stopped and Jack was adamant that he had no need of a doctor. Unsure of her powers as a nurse, Flora was worried, but had to trust to his judgement. He'd been a soldier for six years, after all; he must know more about wounds than she ever would.

Once in their room, she undid his shirt buttons and very gingerly peeled off the bloodied cotton, dropping it into the bath along with the bloodstained handkerchief. Time enough to launder them later. For now, it was important to wash, dry and protect what was an unpleasant gash.

It was fortunate that, despite Jack's mockery, she'd brought a veritable medicine chest with them and now it came into its own. Soap and water and a dusting of boracic powder should keep the wound healthy, but when she tried to unroll a bandage she'd packed, he held up his hand in protest.

'It will be fine as it is. But thank you.' He dropped a kiss on the top of her head. 'Right now, I think a brandy might be just the thing, don't you?'

She shook her head. 'No, I don't. I read somewhere that alcohol can inflame a wound.'

'And I read somewhere,' Jack countered, picking up the phone to call reception, 'that alcohol could be just the thing to dull the pain!'

A few minutes later, two balloons of golden liquid arrived at their door. 'We should take them onto the balcony,' he suggested. 'It's still warm enough.'

She followed him outside and, for a while, they sat in silence looking over the lagoon and the illuminated mass of San Giorgio Maggiore. A spectacle to enjoy.

Flora had hardly spoken since they returned and he could see she was troubled. 'A penny for them?'

'It might cost more than a penny.'

Her expression in the half-light was difficult to read and he saved his response until she pointed to his arm, now encased in a fresh shirt. 'Did that happen because of me?'

He frowned. 'Because of you? How?'

'I was poking around, as Alice always says. And I was caught. I don't think Matteo believed I was looking for the bathroom.'

Jack struggled to make the connection. 'You think... you think my attacker was from the restaurant? But why? He was some random no-good, probably high on alcohol or worse.'

'But was he? Was he simply a thug? He didn't hold us up at knifepoint and demand money, which is what I'd expect. He ran at you quite deliberately, slashed, and then ran away.'

'That's what I mean. A random drunk.' Jack raised his glass. 'Try the brandy and you'll feel better.'

But, after taking a sip, it seemed that Flora didn't. Her forehead was furrowed deeply and her gaze had fixed on some indeterminate point in the distance. 'The man who rushed past us in that alleyway,' she said slowly, 'the man who stabbed you... I think he was the person I saw at La Zucca. The one who called down to Matteo.'

'You couldn't have recognised him,' Jack protested. 'It was nearly dark in that alley.'

She took another small sip and said even more slowly, 'He was short and stocky. A quite different figure from his friend.'

'Short and stocky could apply to a great many Italian men.'

'I'm sure it was him,' she said doggedly.

'Another hunch?'

'More than that, Jack. It was his clothes, too. They seemed familiar. The shirt he wore was the same blue – I saw it even though the light was dim – and it smelt the same.'

'Let's accept for one moment that it *was* the man you saw at the restaurant. What possible purpose could there be in following their customers and injuring them?'

'A warning?'

'In that case, why slash at me? All I did was sit at a table and eat my dinner. You were the one doing the poking around.'

'I'm a woman – maybe he baulked at stabbing me.'

'So, he hurts me instead.' Jack swirled the brandy around his glass. 'How does that work?'

'If he hurts you, he hurts me, too,' she said simply. 'That restaurant has something to hide, I'm certain, and the knife was a warning for us to keep away. I want to know who that man is. And who Matteo is. If those men have any connection to Asolo, the priest will know them. He might even have photographs of his time there, photographs of his congregation.'

'You're going to ask me to go back to San Polo, aren't you?'

She beamed. 'I am, but only when your arm has stopped hurting.'

10

When, the next morning, Jack took himself to the pool for an early swim, Flora was relieved. The injury couldn't be as serious as she'd feared and, as long as they took the day quietly, all should be well. Did talking to Father Renzi qualify as a quiet day? she wondered. If so, she might persuade Jack to return to Santa Margherita before they continued their sightseeing.

'The arm's still working,' he said cheerfully, clumping through the bedroom door. 'A little stiff, and I had to swim side-stroke. But fifteen lengths! And why are you still in bed? That's definitely not allowed!'

He strode across the room, pulling back the top sheet and tugging at her legs, causing Flora to yell a protest. 'Stop it! And you're dripping on me again.' Tangled in the sheet, she landed with a bump on the floor.

'You're being exhausting, Jack. Go away! Or rather go and stand under the shower and then I can bag the bathroom for myself.'

By the time Flora emerged, washed and dressed, it was touch and go whether they would make breakfast; somehow, though, they arrived on the terrace in time to grab a seat by the lagoon. Her mood was brighter and made a good deal sunnier by the primrose yellow sundress she'd decided to wear. It had been a last-minute purchase, one of several for sale in the Steyning dress shop she sometimes visited. Against the faint tan she'd acquired, it looked better in Venice than it ever had in Sussex.

'Love the dress.' Jack's grey eyes were gleaming silver this morning, she noticed. No doubt puffed by his success at pulling her from the bed – for which she hadn't yet forgiven him.

'If that's by way of an apology...'

He shook his head. 'The real apology will be our visit to San Polo, to the manse – is a priest's house called a manse? Those peaches look good, don't they? After that swim, I could eat a bowlful.'

'We're going to see Father Renzi?'

'It's what you suggested, isn't it? And maybe it's not a bad idea,' he conceded, helping himself to two of the largest peaches.

Whatever the priest's house was called, they arrived outside it before the Santa Margherita clock had struck eleven.

'Before we knock at his door, I'd like to take a wander around the church,' Flora said. 'Do you mind?'

'Fine, though there was nothing much about it in my guide-book. I had a read last night, once you started snoring.'

She gave him a poke in the ribs which had him cling to his left side. 'My arm, my arm,' he moaned theatrically.

'You're clutching the wrong one,' she said over her shoulder, making for the church entrance.

The interior of Santa Margherita was surprisingly light, belying its dour outer appearance. White marble pillars, a white and ochre marble floor, and a row of plain glass windows down one entire side of the church, lifted any gloom that the grey-washed ceiling might have engendered. A huge illuminated cross hung from the ceiling and at a prie-dieu beneath it, Father Renzi was kneeling.

Jack looked at her, his eyebrows raised. What to do? They could hardly interrupt the man's prayers but how long did a priest pray? They could be waiting for the rest of the morning.

They were lucky, however. As they stood silently in the aisle, unsure what best to do, Renzi rose to his feet, his knees cracking loudly in the still atmosphere. Smoothing out his cassock, he genuflected before the altar, then backed away and almost collided with them.

A broad smile filled his face when he saw who his visitors were. 'You have come to my church?'

A little embarrassed that the church had been an afterthought, Flora was quick to say, 'To Santa Margherita and you, Father Renzi.'

'Then you must have *merenda* with me. Come, my house is a few steps away.'

'*Merenda?*' she whispered.

'A mid-morning snack,' Jack whispered back.

The priest's abode was a stone's throw from the church he served and, guiding them through the back door of what looked to be a sprawling building, he took them directly into the kitchen, unabashed, it seemed, by the disorder: a sink full of crockery, a cooking pan apparently mislaid on the window sill, a large basket of groceries left unpacked and the cloth that covered the table crumpled and stained.

'Coffee,' the priest muttered. 'We must have coffee. And *pane zucchero*.'

It took time for him to remember where the coffee was stored, then to find the percolator and finally to heat the water. As the minutes ticked by, Flora was itching to help but felt it too awkward to offer. The coffee, when it finally appeared on a battered tray, proved incredibly weak. And there was no sign of the *pane zucchero*.

'We will go to the sitting room,' he announced, gesturing to them to follow him into what proved an equally disordered room. Newspapers and magazines – parish magazines, Flora guessed – were piled high on a spindly-legged table, cushions had found spaces on the floor rather than the chairs, and the curtains at the room's one window had only been half pulled, as though midway through the operation someone had thought of something else to do.

Father Renzi glanced abstractedly around, seeming dazed and hardly knowing the place. Turning to them, he apologised. 'I am sorry,' he said sadly. 'Things are not running well. Without Filomena, I am a little lost.'

Flora waited until they had swallowed half a cup of the weak coffee before she posed the question they'd come to ask.

'We've been talking over your story, Father,' she began. 'The burglary in Asolo and the prison sentence Luigi Tasca was given, and we were wondering if you might have photographs of him when he was younger. Photographs of Luigi *and* his friend. I imagine both boys would have come to any social events the church ran, and someone might have taken a picture or two.'

The priest thought for a moment. 'I have no photograph albums. It is not something a priest would keep. But there is an old parish scrapbook somewhere – I'm sure I brought it with me, or Filomena did. And you are right, Signora Carrington, the church in Asolo hosted some wonderful events: a summer fair each year, a Christmas meal, an outing in the New Year for the older people. If you have a few minutes, I can look for it.'

They would have more than a few minutes, Flora thought, if the scrapbook could take them closer to what might be going on at La Zucca.

On the mantelpiece, the wood-framed clock loudly ticked the time away, and it was a good quarter of an hour later that the priest returned. His cheeks were flushed and his beard sported tangled strands of what looked like cotton wool.

Flora had to restrain herself from picking them off, one by one.

'I have it,' he said, buoyantly. 'It was in the attic! Sometimes Filomena is too tidy.'

The same could certainly not be said of Father Renzi, and his housekeeper, Flora imagined, must have a full-time job keeping at least the semblance of order in this ramshackle house.

He opened the scrapbook and immediately a shower of paper poured forth, covering the faded rug: photographs, concert programmes, leaflets with details of church services, the summer fair, the cake competition.

'I meant to finish the scrapbook when we moved here. Glue all of it into place and in the right order, but there never seems to have been the time.'

'It doesn't matter.' Flora took up a handful of paper.

And it didn't. On the rug was spread an entire record of the priest's time in Asolo. Unerringly, she picked out a small, square photograph from the pile on her lap, the faces very slightly familiar.

'Who are these two? Would you know them?'

The priest leaned forward and nodded, pointing at the curly-headed boy on the left of the picture.

'That is Matteo Pretelli. He always helped me put up stalls for the fair.'

Flora felt a tremor of excitement. She'd been right. The man who had frogmarched her out of the basement had indeed been Pretelli. And his companion? she wondered.

'The other boy?' she asked, hopefully. It was a face she knew but not quite.

'That is Franco. Franco Massi. Poor lad.' It was a while before the priest spoke again. 'The boys must have been more or less the same age there, around eleven years old. Franco always helped, too.'

So that was why the face had again seemed slightly familiar. Flora felt a little disappointed but also very sad. Looking at the young boy, his whole life yet to be lived, and unknowing how soon it would end.

'And this is Matteo Pretelli with his aunt.' Father Renzi passed another small photograph to her.

Filomena looked exactly as Flora had imagined. A little dowdy, wearing a dull grey frock almost to her ankles and carrying a faded leather handbag. But the face above the dress's simple Peter Pan collar was one that shone. Beautiful skin, she thought, and shining brown curls. Was that where Matteo got his?

'And Luigi Tasca? Is there a photograph of him?' Jack had been silently studying the pictures she'd passed to him.

'I don't think so,' the priest said. 'I remember... the boy didn't much like photographs. Let me see.'

For some time, Renzi burrowed through the mound of loose paper and Flora was about to suggest that they forget the search and leave the priest in peace, when he pounced on a badly creased sheet of newsprint.

'Here.' He waved his trophy at them. 'It's from a local paper. I thought I'd cut the item out. It was when Luigi went to trial. I read all the accounts and wanted to keep some kind of record.'

He handed the article to Flora while Jack jumped up to look over her shoulder. A blurred image of a young man took pride of place, climbing out of a police van with the entrance to the law court clearly visible in the background. Even blurred, she knew immediately that the man was the same as the scowling individual she'd met the previous evening. It was Luigi Tasca who had been at La Zucca last night and Luigi Tasca, Flora would swear, who had followed them down that alleyway with a knife in his hand.

The priest gathered together the heap of paper and tucked it back into the scrapbook where Flora was sure it would stay for the next fifty years and maybe the fifty after that.

'Was there a reason you wished to know about these boys?' he asked.

'We're just asking questions at the moment,' Flora said vaguely.

'There is nothing wrong, I hope. You have met no problems?'

'None at all.' Jack's denial was perhaps a little too hearty.

'I remember saying to you that you must be careful. You *will* be careful?'

'We will,' he assured the man, this time sounding a little more convincing.

'I have been worried since you were last here,' Father Renzi confessed. 'I should never have gone to the count. And he should never have asked you for help. It is not fair on a young couple celebrating their marriage.'

Neither of them made a response but when they'd left the house and were walking towards the San Tomà *vaporetto* stop, Jack said, 'No, it isn't fair. But we're well and truly in the middle of it now.'

'And we go on?' she asked, tucking her hand into the crook of his good arm.

'And we go on.'

11

She thought over Jack's comment as she waited with him at St Mark's for the Cipriani launch to appear at the quayside. He was right, of course, they were right in the middle of something, but what, exactly, remained a mystery. The story had begun with a man falling to his death in the canal – no, it had really begun with that quarrel they'd witnessed at La Zucca – then close on the heels of Franco's death, they'd learned a valuable painting was missing from a local church and a priest's housekeeper had vanished into thin air. Finally, Bianca had appeared on the scene, a girl Flora had barely known in Abbeymead, now in Venice and coping with a failed engagement and a father furious with what had happened. How did these disparate events, these different people, connect? It was fine to be in the middle of something but only if you had the faintest clue as to what. Were they looking at a robbery? A kidnap? A murder? Or could all these events be explained in other ways?

They had clambered aboard the hotel launch and were halfway across the Giudecca Canal when she felt a certainty as to what they should do. Touching Jack's arm to gain his attention, she said, 'We should take a boat ride with Piero Benetti.'

'Because?'

'He must have known Franco Massi fairly well – his daughter was engaged to the man and there must have been times when Benetti talked to him. Shared meals with him, perhaps. If Franco ever spoke of Asolo, Benetti might remember and be able to tell us more than his daughter is willing to say.'

'According to the hotel reception, Franco, before he died, wasn't exactly flavour of the month with the man once destined to be his father-in-law. So, is Benetti likely to say anything useful? And then there's the restaurant and its lethal inhabitants. Don't we have enough on our hands with them?'

They were sailing past the pink walls of the Cipriani to stop at its landing stage before Flora spoke again. 'I think we should go back to the beginning.' She sounded certain. 'To Franco. He was the man who died. We should start with him and with the people who knew him, and hope the pieces will fall into place. And the boat trip wouldn't be wasted – we could ask Benetti to take us to one of the islands. I've seen pictures of a place I'd love to visit. It has streets of beautifully coloured houses.'

'That will be Burano.'

'Then let's go there. Make it part of our sightseeing. I can ask the Cipriani to ring Benetti and book the trip for us.'

'They'll warn you off again,' he said, glumly. 'And probably with good reason.'

But when they strolled into the hotel, it was the younger receptionist who was behind the desk, his senior colleague evidently off duty today.

'Piero Benetti?' His lips pursed a little. 'Ah, yes, signora, you showed Signor Trentino his business card.'

Signor Trentino was evidently the head receptionist.

'I know he wasn't too happy with the idea but we'd like to go ahead,' Flora said, adopting a confident air.

'If you are sure, signora.' He looked questioningly at Jack, standing to one side. Her husband gave a resigned nod. 'Benetti has a reputation for being a man of short temper,' the receptionist counselled. 'He can be violent at times, I've seen it myself. And certainly he threatened Franco Massi.'

'I hardly think he'll turn violent on a trip to Burano, do you?' Jack spoke in an amused voice. 'A sightseeing trip,' he explained, 'Benetti's bread and butter, I would have thought.'

'Of course. Of course. I will telephone. For tomorrow?'

It had needed Jack's acquiescence, Flora fumed, to get things moving. Would there ever be a time when a woman was considered sensible enough to make her own decisions?

Inwardly ruffled Flora may have been, but she was glad they were to meet the hot-tempered Benetti. The idea that Franco's murder might have nothing to do with Asolo was one she couldn't lose entirely. And talking to Benetti could be a step in that direction. If, by chance, Franco had confided any trouble he was facing – asked Benetti for advice, maybe – Asolo might have featured in their conversation, but equally it might not. Franco could have feared something else, feared someone else.

Jack appeared less confident of the trip's success. 'I shouldn't put too much hope in discovering anything monumental,' he cautioned, as they brushed their teeth side by side that night. 'Separate basins, Jack,' Flora had exclaimed when they'd walked into the bathroom for the first time, a space almost as large as her cottage sitting room.

'Maybe and maybe not.' She shook the toothbrush free of water. 'But we'll still have a splendid day out.'

Piero Benetti was at the Cipriani landing stage at ten the next morning. Flora could immediately see the resemblance to his daughter and wondered if she should mention they had met Bianca.

'You have a beautiful boat,' Jack said, helping her to a seat at the stern. 'A beautiful name, too, the *Mirabelle*. Is it new?'

Flora was no judge of boats but, even to her untutored eye, the vessel was special: its polished mahogany deep and rich, its brass fittings gleaming, and a new and unblemished flag flying at the prow. The outside seats they chose were comfortably upholstered, their figured cotton perfect, she decided, for a fancy pair of curtains.

'Old taxi finished,' Benetti said, his voice colourless. 'Big crash.'

That wasn't good to hear. Flora had managed to conquer her fear of water sufficiently to travel on boats – ever since coming to Venice she'd been forced to jump on and off them – but a dangerous collision was something else.

'Stupid tourist,' Piero announced.

Despite stupid tourists, business must be very good, she assumed, to afford to replace an old water taxi with a boat such as this.

'Was Bianca with you when the accident happened?' she asked, hoping to begin the conversation she was after.

'Bianca, no. She work all day. You know my daughter?'

'We met her a few days ago.' Perhaps best not to mention Sussex just now. 'She was the one who gave us your card. We thought of you as soon as we decided to take a trip to Burano.'

'She is good girl. Sometimes.'

'Only sometimes? Does she give you trouble?'

He gave a long sigh. '*Bambini!*' Then abruptly turned his back on them to rev the boat's engine and send the *Mirabelle* racing into the wide-open expanse of the lagoon.

End of conversation, she thought wryly, closing her eyes and lying back in her seat for the sun to smother her in its warmth.

'Sleepy?' Jack leaned across and stroked her cheek with a finger.

'A bit,' she admitted. Their time in Venice was proving just a little too exciting and, for the last two nights, she hadn't slept well. 'But I'll try to keep awake!'

'There'll be time enough for you to doze. We won't be at the island for at least another half an hour.'

She snuggled into his body, reassuringly solid, feeling the breeze on her face and in her hair, and hearing the swish of the waters as they cut a passage towards Burano. No sleep, but gradually a dreamlike state, in which, joyously, her mind was emptied of every concern that had intruded into their holiday.

It was Jack putting his hand on her knee that brought her out of the dream. 'We've arrived,' he said in her ear.

Flora opened her eyes, surprised that somehow the lagoon had disappeared and in its place was a narrow canal where they were berthed alongside a line of small boats.

'Let's take a look.'

He pulled her to her feet and together they walked to the boat's rail, gazing across at the houses clustered around the harbour. Flora's first impression was of colour. Bright, dazzling colour – pink, orange, turquoise, yellow, white – an extraordinary rainbow that stretched as far as her eye could see.

'Is it what you expected?'

'I've seen a picture of the island, but the reality is absolutely stunning.' She continued to stare at the scene in front of her. 'It's a Fauvist painting brought to life! Is there a reason for the colours, do you know?'

'My guidebook mentions a legend that the fishermen of Burano painted their homes the same colour as their boats, so that if they faced disaster at sea the boat's colour would tell people at which door to knock and relay the sad news. I've no idea how true that is. It could be one of those tales. But time to explore the painting?'

Leaving Flora to collect her sunhat and handbag, Jack arranged with Piero the time they would return. While she had dozed, he'd watched a silent Benetti at work. A good sailor, he reckoned, but one with a short fuse. If the wheel failed to respond quickly enough to his touch, he jerked at it. If an instrument didn't register what he expected, it was banged with a closed knuckle. And when another one of the many boats on the lagoon came too close, there were subdued curses. Not a man to cross, Jack decided.

Reaching for Flora's hand, he started down the gangway and together they began a stroll up the main street, both of them taking delight in the brightly hued houses. Soon they were competing with each other to find as many different colours as they could. The balconies, they noticed, were almost as brilliant as the buildings themselves, filled with flowers and attached to nearly every house they passed.

'I can see why artists might come here,' Flora said. 'The island must be an inspiration – it's a fantasy of colour.'

'It became really popular after the First War, but I read somewhere that Leonardo da Vinci discovered Burano centuries before, though I'm not sure I believe it.'

'The island is quite isolated,' she said thoughtfully. I can't imagine what it would be like to live here in winter.'

'Tough, I think, and likely to get tougher if the waters continue to rise. This place and the other islands, and Venice itself, could be under threat and not that far into the future.'

'Will the tourists still come? I guess it's tourism that earns the island its money.'

'They'll come as long as they can, I imagine, but it's prob-ably fishing that brings in more. At breakfast the other day – when you'd gone on your mission to find a handkerchief! – the waiter was telling me the seafood here is magnificent and a frac-tion of the price you pay in Venice. We'll make sure we have a decent lunch, so look out for a likely restaurant.'

They had come on this trip specifically for the chance to talk to Piero Benetti but, as the hours slipped by and they explored further into the island, their mission was almost forgot-ten: a coffee in the colourful square of Piazza Baldassare Galuppi, a visit to the church with its beautiful old statues and mosaics, and several astonished minutes gazing at the bell tower which leant at such a crazy angle it should rightly have fallen down years ago. It seemed that the simple enjoyment of sauntering, hand in hand, through eye-catching streets had pushed them to relax in a way they hadn't since they'd first come to Italy.

'I'd like to buy a few souvenirs before we leave,' Flora said, as they began to retrace their steps along the main road. 'I thought maybe some lace – as we've walked, I've been noticing the window displays. I'd love to take something back for Alice. Perhaps for Kate as well, if it's not too old-fashioned.'

When Jack's eye was caught by a beautifully dressed shop window they were passing, he pulled her over to take a look. 'What about this place? Do you see anything you like?'

Flora stared through the glass. 'Plenty,' she said, fixing her gaze on a trio of lace sunshades sitting proudly on a pedestal. 'Those are beautiful! Are they handmade, do you think?'

'Almost certainly. Burano exports lace all over the world.'

She pressed her face to the window, taking in every curve and stitch of the three sunshades. 'They really are exquisite.'

'Let's go in. I can't imagine Alice using a sunshade, but you might see something else you like.'

'All too possible, I'm afraid, and all of it expensive.'

Nevertheless, she followed him inside, wandering slowly past shelves filled to the brim with bales of differently patterned lace. Flora admired everything she saw: intricately worked tablecloths, runners and napkins to match, fans and collars, and fabulously worked blouses.

The shopkeeper came forward, a hopeful expression on his face. 'You would like to try?' He unhooked one of the blouses from its rack.

'No, no,' she said hurriedly, fearful of the cost.

'It is handmade. Needle lace,' the man explained. 'Very

difficult work – each woman makes only one stitch that is her own, so the garment must be passed from one to the other.'

'It's quite beautiful, I can see, but... this is what I'd like.'

Jack saw her point to a case of lace bookmarks, small and delicate. One of them depicted the Madonna and child and she swooped on it. 'This is lovely. And so unusual. And these – the one of the lagoon and there's one of the Doge's palace. They will be perfect for my friends. Thank you.'

Once the shopkeeper had wrapped the small presents in coloured tissue and tied them with a satin ribbon, he presented the parcel to her with a solemn handshake. 'If you are interested in Burano lace, signora, there is a school of lace not far from here. You may visit and watch the women at work.'

'I'd love that!' She turned to Jack, her face bright with antici-pation. 'Can we go?'

He looked at his watch. 'If we do, we'll run out of time. Or we'd have to miss lunch.'

'And that would be a tragedy,' she said teasingly.

As it happened, Flora was delighted they hadn't missed lunch. By dint of turning off the main street and into a small *calle*, they found a restaurant patronised by local people and with meals at what appeared a bargain price. Their surroundings might have been basic but the food they ate was anything but. A first dish, a risotto with fish and asparagus, proved one of the tastiest Flora had so far eaten, followed by a *secondo* of *branzino al forno* with a fresh salad dressed in oil, honey and oregano. A jug of the local white wine appeared and soon disappeared. When it came to dessert, though, she knew her limits.

'Pudding?' Jack asked, after the waiter had cleared their plates.

'Not in a million years.' She was very glad she had worn a dress with a forgiving waistline.

'The *cannoli* look pretty good,' he tempted.

'I'll be leaving you to find out!'

He looked again at his watch. 'Maybe not. Our captain doesn't appear the most patient of men. We'd better not be late for him.'

'Although...' he said, as they walked back into the street, 'there's just enough time for *my* shopping.'

Surprised, Flora watched him race across the nearby bridge to the walkway on the other side of the small canal, then race back, a posy of white freesias in his hand.

'For you, signora.' A solemn bow accompanied the flowers. 'To celebrate a wonderful day!'

Flora threw her arms around him, dangerously close to crushing the flowers, and, to the delight of an elderly passer-by, kissed him thoroughly.

'Now we must run,' he warned, disentangling himself. 'Or we'll be in trouble.'

Piero Benetti was waiting for them on the quayside and, though he wasn't exactly scowling, neither was he full of joy. Sensing that she couldn't make him more despondent than he was already, Flora decided to have the conversation she'd been wanting since they'd first boarded the *Mirabelle*.

Laying the posy carefully to one side, she walked unsteadily over to the man at the wheel.

'Will you be seeing Bianca this evening?' she began.

'No,' he said shortly. 'Why you want to know?'

'Only to pass on our good wishes. She seemed a little upset when we met her the other day. She told me there had been a problem – with her fiancé.'

'That man.' He muttered something inaudible and probably highly offensive.

'You didn't like Franco Massi?' It was a fairly good guess.

'Like him? *Una merda!*'

Jack's eyebrows rose. It *was* offensive.

'He is all smart, the big man one day. He make promise, he take money, but then... pah!' He threw his hands in the air.

Money? What money? Flora was desperate to ask but knew that, if she did, Benetti would stop talking. Instead, she said, 'Do you know why Franco changed his mind?'

'Why he left my *bella* Bianca? For his family, he say. For his mother, his father, his brother. *Spazzatura!*' There was a pause while he glared ahead, silently shaking his head from side to side. 'A bad day she go to England.'

'She met Franco in England?'

'No, no. She met here. Venezia. He goes to the Minerva, this is hotel where she work.'

'And he met Bianca there?'

There was another inaudible mutter.

'I'm not surprised they became friends,' Flora said, but garnered no response. 'They'd have so much to talk about,' she persevered. 'Both of them having worked in England.'

'Bianca, it is bad she go there. England very bad. It mean trouble.'

'Really? But it must have been exciting for her to work abroad for the first time. And it was in *Venice* that she met Franco.'

'It give her bad idea,' he growled, and without another word thrust the tiller roughly forward, sending the *Mirabelle* shooting across the lagoon.

12

'That is one angry man,' Jack observed as they walked up the path to the hotel foyer.

'Angry enough to push Massi to his death?'

'I don't see why not. He was angry enough to come here and harangue the reception staff – risking any business the hotel might give him in the future. And it seems he had more than one reason to be furious.'

'The money, you mean. That surprised me.'

They were walking up the marble staircase to their first-floor room and Jack put a finger to his lips. It was better to keep the discussion for the bedroom and she agreed.

As they walked into the apartment, Flora caught sight of her face in the crystal-framed Murano mirror. More freckles, she mourned, but at least her arms and legs had turned a satisfying colour and she felt extraordinarily alive.

'You look quite beautiful, you know.' Jack wrapped both arms around her and bounced her on to the sofa that faced the long windows leading to their balcony.

Laughing, she landed half on and half off the seat. 'You've obviously enjoyed today!'

'I have, and do we have to talk about Benetti right now?' He said it with feeling.

'We do – for a while.'

'And then?'

She reached across to give him a gentle kiss. 'Benetti,' she said, her tone businesslike. 'What *was* the money he referred to, do you think?'

'All I could imagine was that Massi must have borrowed from him or Benetti gave the pair a gift of cash when they became engaged.'

'And now he sees it as money wasted.'

'Well it was. A painful waste, particularly after he'd suffered a collision that wrecked his taxi. He would have had to find a very large sum for that splendid new boat.'

'I wonder how he did find the money? Perhaps he's had to go into debt. If so, it's no wonder he's unhappy with Bianca. But whatever her shortcomings, it's evident he's very proud of her.'

Flora reached up to rearrange the ponytail she'd worn on and off since arriving in Venice – a way to stay cool, she'd discovered – smoothing back the otherwise recalcitrant waves to fasten them neatly with a tortoiseshell buckle clip.

'Yes, he is proud,' Jack agreed. 'In a strange way. And angry *for* her as well as *with* her. Bianca shrugged it off when we spoke to her, but it *was* a rejection that she suffered and she's bound to feel humiliated.'

'And if she really loved him, desperately upset. No wonder Benetti took up the cudgels on her behalf. It was inevitable he'd tackle Franco face-to-face. When he came here to the Cipriani it was to have it out with the man, but they sent him packing before he could. So instead – why not waylay Franco on his way back from La Zucca that evening?'

'It's possible, but how we find out...'

The open windows were an invitation to a breeze that had begun to blow across the lagoon and, refreshed, Jack got to his feet and walked out onto the balcony. For a while, he stood looking out on the busy scene below, watching the stream of boats that plied to and from the city and the islands.

'The mention of money was interesting,' he said, walking back into the room, 'but did you catch what he said about troubles? That stayed in my mind. Were they troubles Bianca encountered when she was in England? He had nothing good to say about her stay there.'

Flora swung her legs onto the sofa and stretched out against the pile of cushions. 'The remark struck me as odd, too. I wondered if anything happened in Abbeymead or Brighton that we don't know about. Sally never mentioned any problem. In fact, once Bianca left the village to work at the Old Ship, I don't think she saw much of the girl – even though they appear to have kept in touch.'

'If the troubles *were* connected to England, whatever they were, they couldn't have had anything to do with her meeting Franco. Benetti was quite clear the two of them didn't meet until she'd returned to Venice.'

'So... another kind of trouble? I suppose if something serious did occur in England it could have added to the upset Benetti felt over the broken engagement. More fuel for the fire. One thing after another.' She sat up, tucking her legs beneath her. 'Jack—'

'Don't ask!'

'Alan Ridley *might* know something. Bianca must have lived and worked in Sussex for around two years.'

'Even if we unearthed a problem in England, would it have any bearing on what's happened since?'

'You can never tell. How many times do we know when the past has come back to bite people when they least expected it?'

Jack walked back to the sofa and she shuffled along to make room for him. 'OK.' He sounded resigned. 'I'll ring Brighton police in the morning, after breakfast, and hope to find the inspector in. He won't be too happy, though – he's bound to think it trivial.'

'He could check on them both,' Flora said, impervious to the warning. 'Franco as well as Bianca. He worked in London for several years and it would be good to have more information, particularly as no one here is likely to know anything about his life abroad.'

Each morning, breakfast seemed to take a little longer. The temptation to linger was strong: a flower-strewn terrace, a parasol-shaded table, and boats to watch. So many boats, a fascinating parade constantly in motion. And always an attentive waiter ready to serve them platters of fruit and pastries, jugs of coffee and, for Jack, smoked salmon or a dish of eggs Benedict.

This morning was no different and it was well after ten o'clock before they left the terrace and wandered into the lobby. They'd gone only a few steps before they were hailed by Signor Trentino who, today, was the sole member of staff at the reception desk.

'You have a message, *signore, signora*.' The receptionist held a slip of white paper, fluttering it in the air.

'The signora did not wish to disturb you at breakfast,' he said, as they approached, 'but ask that I give you this.'

Jack took the note from him. 'It's from Sally,' he said briefly, turning to Flora. 'I guess we were expecting it.'

'And?'

'She'd love to meet for a chat, but only if we'd like to. How can we say no?'

'We can't. We'll have to say hello.'

'Say hello and perhaps get her to explain why, of all places, she decided to come to Venice.' He hadn't meant to sound flinty, but felt a nagging irritation that not even here, a thousand miles away, could they be free of village life. 'She's suggesting this evening – a drink at the Minerva bar. What do you think?'

'Why not? It's inevitable we would meet at some point. And the Minerva...'

'We'll be meeting Sally, not sleuthing,' he warned, then caught Signor Trentino's eye and said hastily, 'Could you ring this number please and say we'll be at the hotel at seven this evening?'

'Of course, *signore*,' the man said smoothly. 'Is there anything else I can help with?'

'Actually, there is, thank you. I need to make a telephone call – to England – and I'm not sure how best to do it.'

'The hotel switchboard will be happy to help. If you would be so kind as to give me the number you require, I will ask the *telefonista* to make contact and pass the call through to the telephone alcove. You will find it on the right, as you step into the garden.'

'Excellent. We'll wait there?'

'It will take a little time, and if it is not possible to connect, I will send a man to tell you.'

But it was possible and quicker than Jack expected. They'd waited only a few minutes beside the alcove when the phone rang and Alan Ridley's voice sounded down the line.

'Jack Carrington! Aren't you on your honeymoon, old chap?'

'We are, Alan, but—'

'There's always a "but" with you two. Don't tell me that young woman you've married—'

'Flora,' he interrupted brusquely, feeling the familiar annoyance that Ridley seemed unable or unwilling to use Flora's name.

—'Flora,' the inspector continued stiffly. 'Don't tell me she's got you investigating. Not on your honeymoon. Not in Venice!'

'It's a small thing only.'

'It always is.' Ridley was sounding unusually cheerful, Jack realised. Success in solving a difficult case, perhaps?

'I wouldn't bother you, only something's come up.' Don't say it always does, he muttered inwardly. 'A link between Venice and Sussex – in particular, a link with Abbeymead and Brighton. One of Sally Jenner's friends – you'll remember Sally, I'm sure, she runs the Priory hotel – one of her friends has returned home to Venice but worked for some time in Sussex. We wondered if perhaps the girl was mentioned in any police file.'

'Why—' the inspector began to ask.

'Her name is Bianca Benetti,' Jack said quickly, unable to explain why they were interested in Bianca's stay in England. It was too complicated.

'Benetti,' Alan Ridley mused. 'The name is ringing some kind of bell, though I've no idea why.'

'If you could spare the time, can you check for me? It's a minor thing, as I said, but it would help the holiday go smoothly.'

There was a pause, the inspector evidently thinking hard. 'If I were you, Jack,' he said at last, 'I wouldn't fret. Honeymoons rarely go smoothly, it's a well-known fact.'

'Really? Not that—' Jack began, but instantly gave up any attempt to disabuse Ridley that the holiday was a disaster. Time was just too short. 'There is another name you could look out for at the same time,' he said hopefully.

'You don't want much, do you?'

'The chap is called Franco Massi.'

'How do you spell that?'

As he spelt out the name, he could hear the inspector scribbling.

'OK, I'll have a quick gander, but I'm not spending too much time on it. I'm off on a break myself in a couple of weeks. Broadstairs – d'you know it?'

Jack denied any knowledge of the town.

'Nice little place. Great beaches – miles of sand, not the pebble we've got here – and the best bed and breakfast in the country. Can't wait to get away!'

Deciding to forgo the Cipriani ferry to St Mark's on a new sightseeing trip, they walked to the nearest *vaporetto* stop, passing the Redentore on the way. Jack was keen to take a wander through the huge Palladian church, a sixteenth-century thanksgiving for Venice's deliverance from the plague.

Flora, though, had no great interest. 'I don't think I want to,' she said. 'It's big and cold and very white.'

'And that's a problem?' Jack was laughing.

Looking up at the vast cupola, she was conscious of a movement at the edge of her vision. A figure, there and then not there. It had disappeared through a side entrance to the church. Why the side entrance? Why not up the front flight of steps and through the magnificent Doric pillars? She gave a swift glance around. They were alone, no passers-by, no tourists – they would flock here next month for the *festa* which, with fireworks, celebrated the end of a terrible plague. Maybe the figure had come to pray quietly – that was always possible. It had been the flash of bright blue that triggered memory. That, and a certain shambling stride. A lot of men wear blue shirts, she scolded herself, a lot might walk in that creeping fashion, not just Luigi Tasca. But the fear remained.

'Well?' he asked her, still smiling.

Flora made a decision. She was being foolish. She would say nothing. 'The church feels unfriendly,' she tried to explain. 'It's giving me goose pimples just looking at it.' Was that the church's doing or that flash of blue shirt?

'Can churches be unfriendly?' he asked, while they waited for the next *vaporetto*. 'That seems a contradiction.'

'I think they can. But perhaps it's just that I've seen too many. There are over two hundred in Venice alone – which is a terrifying figure.'

'We're going to the Vivaldi concert tomorrow,' Jack reminded her, 'and it's to be performed in a church.'

'That's different,' she insisted. 'Vivaldi's church is much smaller and it's where he worked for most of his life. *And* it will be filled with wonderful music. Oh, the boat's here already.'

She nodded towards the little ship wallowing towards them, spray surging around its deck as it plunged through the lagoon on what was an unusually windy morning.

The journey across the Giudecca Canal took no more than ten minutes and, arriving at the Zattere, a wide and wonderful promenade stretched ahead of them. Built as a landing dock hundreds of years previously, the quay was as exposed as it was wide and, despite the wind that still blew strongly, it wasn't long before they began to feel uncomfortably sticky, the sun beating down from a near cloudless sky. A fifteen-minute saunter from the *vaporetto* brought them to a corner café that fronted a narrow canal, its blinds offering a welcome stretch of shade. Stopping to cool down, they gazed across the water and realised they were looking at something very special.

Jack consulted the guidebook he'd decided to bring with him today. 'According to this,' he said, 'we're standing opposite the oldest shipyard in Venice.'

The scene could have been one from two hundred years ago: gondolas being repaired, gondolas being constructed.

'A hundred different pieces and seven types of wood for each gondola,' Jack read. 'It's a craft handed down from one generation to another.'

'And such skill,' Flora murmured, watching as a craftsman slowly sanded one of the many sections of wood that, once shaped, would eventually make a finished boat.

'For how much longer, though? Will future generations be

willing to learn?' Then, in a change of mood, he gave her arm a squeeze. 'Could you eat an ice cream?'

'When can't I?'

Slowly demolishing their ice creams, strawberry for Flora and *malaga*, a kind of rum and raisin, for Jack, they strolled back to the Zattere and along towards the harbour of San Basilio where they found a bench in the shade.

'You might want to know you've a dribble of strawberry on your chin,' Jack said.

'And you've rum and raisin on your nose. More usefully, do you have a handkerchief handy? I can't get to mine.'

With some difficulty, he fumbled in his pocket and brought out a large square of linen. 'You first.' Grinning, he handed her the handkerchief. 'Looking like this, we wouldn't be too welcome on any of those.' He pointed to the line of expensive yachts berthed in the harbour. 'Ragamuffins, they'd say. Not a lira to their name!'

'No money maybe, but far better taste.'

'What do you mean, no money? We'll order the yacht tomorrow! In the meantime, lunch calls.'

'After ice cream?'

'A miserable gelato isn't going to feed a man and breakfast disappeared an age ago. There are dozens of bars and restaurants along the quayside and I have my eye on one in particular.'

Their walk back from the Zattere, through Dorsoduro and over the Accademia bridge to St Mark's, was a fair distance and made beneath the broiling sun of early afternoon. An uncomfortable walk, especially when you were feeling very full, Flora admitted to herself: she'd soon forgotten the ice cream amid a welter of bruschetta and grilled mullet. A splendid lunch.

It was a hot and weary twosome, though, who telephoned the Cipriani for a ride back to the hotel.

'I don't know if I can bear to walk to the Minerva this evening.' Flora yawned, her head slumped on his shoulder. 'Or even open my mouth to talk.'

'Sally will be disappointed if you don't go.' He fell silent, thinking how best to say what he wanted. 'Flora,' he began, when they were midway across the lagoon, 'I think maybe you should meet Sally alone.'

Flora straightened in her seat, suddenly energised. 'You want me to go on my own? But why?'

'I think it would be easier, less awkward if I wasn't there. She wouldn't feel so bad about interrupting our honeymoon.'

'Maybe she *should* feel bad.'

'You know you don't mean that. And if you intend to talk to her about Bianca, I reckon you'll get far more from her if there's just the two of you and a glass of wine.'

'There *will* be plenty to talk about,' Flora said hesitantly. 'And Sally is bound to know more than we do.'

But on the verge of agreeing, she was hit by a sudden frisson of fear. Above the surface of the waves an image glimmered – the figure at the Redentore. The Minerva hotel wasn't far from the church, she imagined, and what if the blue-shirted man was lurking close? She needed her husband beside her.

'On the other hand,' she countered, 'Sally could find it odd if you weren't with me. It could make her feel even worse about the "gatecrashing". I think you need to come, Jack. And she could have useful information. It was Bianca who asked her to visit and, by now, the girl must have spilt whatever beans there were to spill. Why Franco really pulled out of the engagement, for instance.'

Jack could hazard a fairly accurate guess. Cold feet. He'd had plenty of them himself, but he kept a diplomatic silence.

13

The Hotel Minerva boasted only one bar but it was already crowded when Flora and Jack arrived a few minutes after seven. It was a cosy space with a terrace overlooking the Giudecca Canal and was already filled with chattering customers.

Sally, dressed in a glamorous black sheath, was at the bar and, hearing her name called, swivelled round on her stool to greet them.

She jumped up to hug first Flora and then Jack. 'It's so good to see you both – and isn't Venice heavenly?'

They could only nod in agreement, both of them slightly stunned by Sally's transformation. A black sheath? A bright red chunky necklace with lipstick to match? And shoes with three-inch heels! Flora was admiring of this new Sally, envious even, but she did wonder what Alice would have to say. If Sally wanted a quiet life, and she probably did, she would lose the lipstick and the heels before she reappeared in Abbeymead.

'I'm not sure we'll manage to find seats,' she was saying, 'but we could go somewhere else—'

'No need.' Jack had spotted a table that had just become free. 'If we're nifty, we can grab the one on the terrace.'

Flora was the niftiest and took possession before another group of friends could stake a claim.

'Italian wine is delicious, don't you think?' Slipping into a seat, Sally held up her half-filled glass.

'Three glasses then?' Jack turned back to the bar to join a queue that had grown since they'd arrived.

'Jack's a sweetie,' Sally said, 'but I'm glad to have the chance to speak to you alone, Flora. I wanted to say I'm really sorry about what seems like my intruding. I would never have come to Venice only... Bianca phoned, asking me for help, and she sounded terrible. I really did wonder what I was coming to, but actually I think all she really wanted was to talk – she doesn't seem to have many friends. And to be honest, I was desperate for a break, and the thought of a week in Venice was so tempting. But I knew you and Jack were here and on your honeymoon. And it was... awkward.'

Flora reached out to clasp her hand. 'It doesn't have to be and you have a perfect right to visit. We're doing our own thing and I'm sure you are, too. There's masses to see and we're unlikely to be bumping into each other every five minutes. But—'

She broke off. The picture of Bianca that Sally had just painted hardly matched the girl Flora had met a few days ago at this very hotel. It could be that Bianca had been determined not to show her feelings, despite being deeply troubled over the loss of her fiancé, but on the other hand... sounding terrible on a telephone call to a friend she hardly ever spoke to? Begging that friend to come to Venice immediately? Something didn't chime right.

Sally's gaze had become fixed on her, her friend's eyes full of worry. 'I really am sorry, Flora,' she stammered out another apology. 'About my being here.'

'No, no,' she hastened to say, realising how Sally must be interpreting her silence. She should stop thinking and start talking. 'It's not a problem, Sally. Honestly. And it's nice to catch up with what's been happening in Abbeymead. Not that I've missed the village, which is strange. It must be the first time ever.'

'Not strange to me. This city is magical – how could you want to be anywhere else? And the brilliant thing is that I've still a few more days to enjoy it.'

'So... Bianca telephoned you, you say?' It somehow mattered for Flora to be sure of the girl's true feelings.

'Out of the blue. We've sent the occasional card since she moved back to Italy: birthdays and Christmas and a postcard when I went to the Lake District with Dominic. And we've spoken from time to time on the phone, but getting her call was a huge surprise.'

'What did she say, exactly?'

'That her father had been very unwell. She was desperately upset about him, worried that he'd fall sick again even though the doctors seemed happy. I tried to reassure her, say all the right things, but then suddenly she announced that her engagement had fallen through. She actually began crying down the phone. It seemed to me that she didn't have anyone here she could talk to, but I was dumbfounded when she asked me to come.'

'When you say her father had been unwell, how unwell?' Flora swooped on the information she hadn't known before. Piero Benetti had appeared perfectly fit on their trip to Burano.

'He'd had a heart attack. He's OK now, back to work, I believe, but it was uncertain for a while and hugely worrying for her. She's his only child.'

'No other family?'

'His wife was too sickly to have more children and died when Bianca was a small girl. She seems very close to her father though they don't always get on. Bianca has her own ideas and they're not always his. He planned for her to work in an office when she left school – actually found her a job in a local boat-builder's, she told me. But she hated it from the first day and begged him to let her leave and travel. What she most wanted was to improve her English. She reckoned that would mean she could move to a better job. In the end, after a lot of nagging, it seems he agreed she could go for a short holiday as long as she lived with people he knew. She stayed in Worthing – his late wife had distant relatives there.'

Sally took a long drink of her remaining wine. 'Her father was delighted when she came back to Venice, she said, but now this fiancé business seems to have really stirred him up. From what I can gather, he was impressed by Franco Massi, at least to begin with. Probably believed the chap genuinely loved Bianca, but then Franco walked out on her. Dumped her just like that. No real reason. I can see why her father is so angry – and anger's not good for a heart.'

A final sip and Sally had emptied her glass. 'Oh, Jack's been successful!' She smiled broadly. 'Reinforcements, Flora!'

Flora looked across the crowded terrace. Somehow her husband was finding a way through the scatter of tables and drinkers, balancing three full wine glasses between his hands.

'So how was Abbeymead when you left?' he asked, handing the women their drinks and purloining a spare seat from a neighbouring table.

'Much the same.' Sally gave a smile that could only be called weary. 'Kate and Tony are battling to manage the café while looking after a baby who has colic, poor darling. Auntie seems happier, now that I've managed to recruit more staff for the kitchen. Oh, and Hector and Rose have named the day.'

This last snippet of information was given as airily as Sally could manage, but neither Jack nor Flora were deceived. Hector Lansdale was always going to be a prickly subject. For a time, the Priory's sous chef had been Sally's conquest until he set eyes on Rose, Flora's assistant at the bookshop, and set the

Abbeymead tongues wagging. Rose Lawson was a woman who had already had one husband, and that for the village was deemed quite sufficient.

'I'm glad the Priory is doing so well,' Flora said, trying to bridge the uneasy silence that had fallen. 'And glad that Alice is feeling more cheerful.' As head chef, Sally's aunt was a kingpin of the hotel.

'She's amazingly cheerful, in fact.' Sally leaned across the table. 'She suspects a plot!' This was said in a stage whisper. 'You'd better get back to the village quickly with your sleuthing hats on or she'll steal your thunder!'

'The new tenant?' Flora hazarded a guess.

'The very same.' Sally burst out laughing. 'Auntie thinks he may be some kind of spy. Why, she asked me, has he moved to Abbeymead? Why doesn't he work? He's no more than fifty, apparently. And if he's got money, why choose to rent Overlay of all places? I know you loved it, Jack, but these days the house has become quite run-down.'

'Do you think there's anything *to* suspect?' Flora was inclined to take Alice's qualms more seriously.

'No, of course not, but I'm not saying so. If it keeps Auntie happy, it's worth having fun with. It's quite comical after all the times she's scolded the pair of you for poking around, and here she is setting up as her own detective.'

'Let's hope not,' Jack said lazily. 'We don't want any competition!'

'About Bianca...' Flora was eager to return to the subject. 'What reason did Franco give for ending the engagement?'

'Like I said, no real reason. A pathetic excuse at best. Bianca certainly thought so and so did her father. Franco said his parents were elderly and increasingly needed his help, particularly now that his younger brother's disability had become worse. If he was married with his own family, he said, he couldn't give his parents the time or the care they should have.

And living in Mestre – he and Bianca were buying a flat there –
while he still worked on the Giudecca meant long days and
even less spare time. It *is* pathetic, don't you think?'

Flora nodded. 'His parents haven't suddenly grown old. He
must have considered the problems he'd face before he asked
Bianca to marry him.'

'It's more likely that Mestre put him off.'

They stared at Jack. 'It's not exactly a smart place,' he said,
'but presumably it was what they could afford.'

'Why would that put him off?' Flora was puzzled.

'Think about it. The man worked in a luxury hotel, the best
in Venice. The disjunction between that and living in a semi-
industrial area would be jarring.'

'But he would never expect to live in Cipriani-style,' Flora
objected.

'No,' Sally said thoughtfully, 'but he probably wanted better
than Mestre. Bianca took me there yesterday and showed me
the flat they were going to buy. It looked OK, reasonable, I
suppose, but from what she said of Franco, I really couldn't see
him living there.'

'What did she say of Franco?'

'That he was extremely smart. It was the first thing she
noticed about him. How well-groomed he was, how his clothes
fitted perfectly, what beautiful manners he had.'

Remembering Franco's suave greeting when they'd arrived
at the Cipriani and what she'd seen of his room there, Flora
inwardly agreed.

'How did they meet?' she asked.

'He'd come to the Minerva to deliver a personal letter,' Sally
said, 'to the hotel manager from the manager of the Cipriani,
and he bumped into Bianca – literally – in the foyer. She was
carrying a pile of linen at the time, she said, and tea towels and
pillowcases flew all over the place. When Franco helped pick
them up and apologised, she answered him in English—'

'Really?'

'Perhaps trying to impress,' Jack put in.

'Perhaps,' Sally agreed. 'But it led them to realise they'd both been in England and they talked about it a little. He asked her out for a drink when she came off duty that day – and the rest followed. Bianca's a pretty girl and there seems to have been plenty of men interested, but Franco was the one who impressed her. And I guess *he* was flattered by her attention.'

'I can see she'd be impressed,' Flora mused. 'He was a good deal older than her and like you say, good-looking and confident.'

Sally rubbed her chin. 'She did confess to me that she'd thought him a boyfriend to make other girls jealous. And I've a feeling she was thinking of her future, too. After all, Franco worked in the most expensive hotel in Venice and Bianca might have hoped he would help her up the ladder. She has her eye on becoming a receptionist herself – she doesn't want to clean toilets for the rest of her life. But, having said that, I'm quite sure she was genuinely heartbroken when he walked out on her.'

Jack lifted his glass. 'Great wine, Sally. Great choice. I suppose it might have worked between them,' he said quietly. 'Franco was a man on the up and she was evidently keen to join him.'

'Not in Mestre, from what I've seen of it,' Sally said. 'Living there wouldn't have helped them move up.'

There was a moment's silence, before Jack said, 'Even Mestre prices are relatively high, I believe. How were they going to afford the flat you saw?'

The money that Benetti mentioned, was Flora's immediate thought. Had that been for a flat for his daughter?

'Her father lent it to them,' Sally said, confirming the hunch. 'That's what Bianca told me. It was money Signor Benetti had saved for years and earmarked for the new boat he'd ordered. Quite a sacrifice.'

'We met Piero Benetti yesterday,' Flora confessed. 'Bianca gave us his card and we asked him to take us to Burano. He has the new boat – we travelled in it and it's beautiful – so he must have had his money returned. We thought it a wonderful trip, although Benetti didn't appear too happy. He seems to blame Bianca's time in England for most of her troubles.'

'It's because when she went to England, she wasn't supposed to stay. Her father expected her back in Venice and was very upset when she told him she'd found a job in Sussex. Even more upset when he learned she was working as a chambermaid. He wanted more for her, I think, but he loves her hugely and eventually went along with it.'

'How did she fetch up at the Priory?' Jack asked.

'She saw one of my advertisements in the *Worthing Echo*. The usual thing, I needed more staff, and on the spur of the moment Bianca decided to apply. Of course it was Dominic who interviewed her and gave her the job, even though she had no experience. But that was Dominic.'

There was a pause while they all silently agreed that that was indeed Dominic.

'She lasted six months in Abbeymead but found the village too isolated, too lonely, particularly in winter, even though by then the pair of us had become friends. But I was always busy and couldn't see a lot of her, and I wasn't surprised when she decamped to Brighton, which is a great deal livelier.'

'Do you know why she left Brighton to go back to Italy?'

'Not really. She called one morning to say she was going – it seemed very sudden – but she left me her Venice address and telephone number. We've kept in touch on and off, but I've never asked her why she decided to go home. I've always assumed that maybe she was homesick.'

Sally took a last sip of the second glass. 'Another round?' she asked gaily. 'I'll do the honours this time.'

When their friend was out of earshot, Flora said very quietly, 'It might be that Inspector Ridley will know.'

'Know why Bianca left suddenly? No complications, Flora – it will be homesickness, as Sally said.'

But Flora wasn't satisfied. There was something more to it, she was certain – something that had caused Bianca to up sticks and whisk herself back to her homeland. And she had every intention of discovering what that might be.

14

Jack might not want complications but he wasn't entirely convinced either by the notion of homesickness. It seemed a little too pat. Bianca had left Brighton abruptly and, if she was as happy to confide in Sally as she appeared to be, why hadn't she talked of her feelings? The longing for home was understandable, an emotion familiar to anyone living abroad, but she'd said nothing of her reasons for leaving and it was Sally's assumption only that homesickness had sent the girl back to Venice. Though Jack didn't want to, he had to admit that Flora was right in questioning the girl's sudden departure. Hopefully, Alan Ridley's call might throw some light on the matter.

'While you're sunbathing in the garden, I'll read on the balcony,' he told Flora the next day, as she was busy gathering her belongings together for the lazy morning they'd planned. 'Alan's call might come through and I don't want to miss it.'

'No complications, Jack, remember!'

'It's as well to dot the i's,' he said defensively. 'Or I'll never hear the last of it.'

She gave him a kiss on the cheek. 'Let me know what happens. I'll be by the duck pond.'

He didn't have long to wait, having barely managed one page of his holiday read before the shrill of the telephone had him hurry from the balcony. Lifting the receiver, it was to hear the banging of doors and the sounds of a scuffle thrumming down the line.

'Jack, old fellow? Sorry about the commotion. Another drunk for our cells, and at this time in the morning.' Jack looked across the room at the Murano glass clock. Almost ten, nine o'clock in Brighton.

'I got on with the search you wanted,' the inspector continued. 'In my spare time.' This was said with heavy irony. 'Actually, it didn't take long. Franco Massi proved a complete blank. Nothing whatsoever on him in our records. But Bianca Benetti – I wondered why the name sounded familiar and now I know.'

'And?' It had been worth asking, he thought. Trust Flora!

'She worked at the Old Ship, as you said, but left after a fracas at the hotel. A major confrontation in the foyer that involved her and a hotel guest. Apparently, the man concerned owned a chain of hotels in the West Country and was in Brighton to scout for properties along the south coast – with an eye to developing his business, I imagine. But he fell out with Bianca or Bianca fell out with him—'

'But she was a chambermaid,' Jack objected. How did you fall out with a chambermaid so badly the police had to be called?

'I'll come to that in a minute. Until I read the whole report, all I could remember was that whatever the dispute, it turned into a full-scale riot and the hotel manager was forced to call the police to restore order.'

'You remember his call coming through?'

'I didn't take it, old chap, my deputy did – but, as it happened, I was there, at the hotel. Which is why I remembered the girl's name. I had a cousin staying at the Ship that week and he'd invited me for lunch. I'd walked through the

entrance just as one of my constables was laying down the
law.'

'Did you find out what had gone on exactly?'

'I didn't at the time – lunch called – but now I've looked up
the report, I have. The guest, a Mr Holland, complained to the
hotel manager that Bianca had been harassing him ever since
he'd checked in, asking to be taken on in one of his hotels as a
trainee receptionist and, to get rid of her, he'd agreed. But it
wasn't an arrangement he wanted to keep, and was leaving the
hotel without confirming a job offer or leaving the girl his
details. She must have been watching out for him and when she
realised he was hopping it, breaking his promise and, worse,
laughing at her, she lost her temper and threw a bowl of fruit at
him. The reception always kept a bowl of fruit on the desk, I
understand. Perhaps not now, though.'

'Not exactly a full-scale riot, I'd say.'

'Hold your horses. You've not heard it all. A waiter who was
walking through the foyer at the time – I reckon he was keen on
Bianca – thought she was being attacked and powered in on her
side. He punched the guest in the face, grabbed him in a bear
grip and refused to let go – until one of my chaps produced a
pair of handcuffs. By then, the foyer was looking less than
pristine.'

'Bianca was dismissed immediately, I imagine.'

'You're right, along with the waiter. The hotel manager
somehow persuaded the guest not to bring charges – some kind
of sweetener was offered, I imagine – and the girl, according to
the ferry records at Dover, sailed to Calais two days later.'

'And from there on to Venice,' Jack commented.

'If that's where the lass is. She'd have left without a reference, that's for sure.'

'Yet she found a job here in another hotel.' It must have
been Sally, he thought wryly, who'd been happy to supply a
reference.

'That's not the last of it either.' There was the hint of a sigh down the telephone. 'When I asked for the file on the rumpus at the Old Ship, Norris reminded me that he'd spoken to the Venice police a month or so ago.'

Jack frowned. 'About Bianca?'

'About Bianca,' the inspector confirmed. 'Holland, the man she had the barney with, has developed a serious health problem – blinding headaches, lack of balance, which he blames on the fight he had at the hotel. He's gone to his solicitors intending to sue Bianca, the waiter and the Old Ship and, in turn, his solicitors have gone to the police in Venice. Not certain how it works in Italy, but the chap is adamant he wants to sue them all. The *commissario* who spoke to Norris asked if we had any details of the incident on file. Mr Holland's legal team has asked the Venice police to question the girl and at the moment they're not sure what they're dealing with.'

'Thanks, Alan.' Jack stared at the wall, trying to absorb what had been a torrent of information. 'That's helpful... I think.'

'Always one to help, old fellow, but you really need to get on with that honeymoon. Leave Signorina Benetti to us.'

Replacing the receiver, Jack continued to stare fixedly at the wall, the sound of the bedroom door finally rousing him from his thoughts.

'I forgot my suntan cream,' Flora began, making for the dressing table. Then, noticing the expression on Jack's face, she asked, 'Ridley telephoned? Does he have anything on Franco?'

'Not Franco.' Jack dragged himself from his reverie. 'Bianca. Guilty of affray, I think they call it. A brawl at the Brighton hotel where she worked between Bianca and a guest who didn't keep his promise.'

'Which was?'

'That he'd employ her as a receptionist in one of *his* hotels.'

Flora's hand hovered over the drawer and stopped. 'Really? That *is* interesting... remember what Sally told us? That Bianca is very keen to leave her job as a chambermaid, that she wants very much to become a receptionist. A ladder perhaps to hotel management. So, her dream hasn't died, and even Sally, who's been a good friend to her, thinks that Franco's position at the Cipriani was part of his attraction.'

She paused, the tube of suntan cream in her hand. 'I wonder... I wonder if that might be one of the reasons she contacted Sally, begging her to come here. I mean, apart from having few friends and needing a shoulder to cry on. If Bianca no longer sees a future for herself in Venice, is she hoping to return to England? To train as a receptionist at the Priory?'

'You're making her sound weaselly.'

'She's desperate, Jack. From what Alan's just told you, she was so frantic for promotion that she was willing to start a physical fight. Is she still using violence, do you think, to gain her ends?'

Jack frowned. 'What you're suggesting is that she could have killed Franco. It's not likely, though, is it? She'd be killing her golden egg. Franco was her future.'

'Except that the girl evidently has a temper. She lost it at the Old Ship. Perhaps she lost it again when she saw her future slipping away.'

'Her father has a temper, too,' Jack reminded her. 'And he has a far stronger motive for murder than a lost job. He's furious that his daughter has been rejected by a man he trusted and furious that, in the process, he's lost a great deal of money.'

'Has he lost it? Somehow, he found the funds to buy a beautiful new boat – whatever deposit the couple paid on the Mestre flat must have been returned when they cancelled the purchase.'

'He can still be angry – it's been a messy business – and we shouldn't write him out of the plot just yet. And what about all our other characters? Have you forgotten the dubious restaurant and its dirty deeds?'

Flora walked over to the squashy sofa and flopped, stretching herself full-length on the pile of soft cushions. 'I haven't forgotten the restaurant. I wish I could,' she said, yawning. The sun streaming through the balcony windows knitted her in a blanket of warmth. 'But I think I may forget the garden this morning.' She yawned again. 'I'm so comfortable here, it's making me dozy.'

Too dozy to set her brain in motion when she needed to think. Lodged deep inside her was a conviction – one Flora couldn't satisfactorily explain – that Asolo was still the key that would unlock the mystery: to the theft, to the kidnapping, even to the murder. Yet neither Bianca nor her father appeared to have any kind of connection to the place. There must be one, she thought drowsily, her eyelids closing against her will. Maybe this evening...

The Santa Maria della Pietà or Vivaldi church was situated on the Riva degli Schiavoni, a short walk from the quayside where the hotel launch had its berth and an even shorter walk from the Doge's Palace. On the Bridge of Sighs, from where prisoners once took their last glimpse of Venice before incarceration in the doge's prison cells, they stood for a while, watching a succession of gondoliers as they passed below. The rowers' toes, Flora noticed, faced outwards ballet style as, with skill, they directed their lopsided craft beneath the bridge and into the network of small canals that furnished the route for each new band of tourists.

From here, they could see the white-pillared church they were making for and already a smattering of people were being greeted by the priest standing at its door. The concert, with its regular performance of *The Four Seasons* violin concertos, was one of the most popular the church hosted, and Jack had been lucky to obtain tickets for them at fairly short notice.

He reached out for her hand, giving it a small tug. 'This is a wonderful view but we'd better make tracks. The church is already filling up.'

It was another beautiful summer evening, the air soft and warm and, as Flora stepped through the front entrance into the lobby, she was surprised to find the church almost as mellow – she'd expected the temperature to plunge in the usual ecclesiastical chill, and had brought with her the thickest cardigan she could find. Without fans and in the heat of very high summer, this interior could be stifling, she imagined.

Once in the church proper, Flora paused to look around. An abundance of paintings was her first impression, every wall filled, while above them the ceiling flamed with a tumultuous vision of storm clouds, trumpeting angels and tumbling *putti* singing for all their worth.

Jack, tickets in hand, beckoned her towards a pew three or four rows back from the low stage and, once seated, she could see better how cleverly the church had been built. The oratorio was oval-shaped and the atrium surrounding it had clearly been designed to dispel noise from the quays and the harbour outside. The church was like a white egg, she thought, smiling at the simile. A fresh, white egg, with flashes of red from curtains and kneelers providing a contrast.

But it was the balconies and choir stalls, elegant in wrought iron, that took most of her attention. It was from the choir stalls, she'd read, that the young girls living in the orphanage supported by the Pietà had given regular performances of sacred and secular music.

'Do you see?' Jack nudged her to look upwards, his eyes bright with pleasure. 'Tiepolo's great fresco.'

'I do, but did you know,' she asked, a sly grin emerging, 'that Vivaldi's father was a barber who played in the orchestra at San Marco?'

Jack might know about frescoes but it was good occasionally

to know something he didn't! The church, she'd learned, built by Massari in classical style, had once been the chapel of a foundling hospital, one of several in the city playing a central role in the Venetian Republic's musical life. Antonio Vivaldi, having been ordained a priest, had himself taught at the Pietà orphanage on and off throughout his life.

'I suppose it was inevitable the barber's son became a musician,' she added.

'But not inevitable he became a virtuoso violinist.'

She dredged her mind for a moment before whispering, 'I bet you didn't know that Vivaldi was called the "red priest" for the colour of his hair.'

Laughing, Jack pulled a face. 'OK, you win. For now. But please stop reading that guidebook!'

The book was soon forgotten, however, along with the hard, wooden pews, once the four violinists began to play.

From the first movement, Flora was swept away by the sheer beauty of the music, the wonderful acoustics of the church playing their part. Her body was left behind as mind and heart followed the sweep of the seasons: in autumn, the harvest with song and dance and drink, in winter the melancholy of wind and ice before the joy of spring and new life – birds singing, fountains flowing – and finally, the buzzing of insects and the blazing sun of summertime.

Only then did Flora become aware of the pew where she sat, of the church and the people and Jack at her side. He leaned towards her, a question in his eyes.

'You enjoyed it?'

'Enjoyed? I must have. It's just I... no words,' she said simply.

'No words needed,' he agreed.

Glancing over her shoulder, she took in the audience for the first time, now picking up handbags, adjusting jackets, making ready to leave, as the last ripple of applause echoed around the old, white walls. Many, like them, were clearly visitors to the city, but a substantial number of the concertgoers seemed likely to be local. Three rows behind them she noticed the black clothing of a priest, his back half-turned, as he edged his way out of the pew and into the aisle.

Father Renzi, she was sure! She was too far away to call out to him, but as he joined the line of people waiting to leave the church, he turned his head and glanced over his shoulder, looking Jack and Flora fully in the face. It *was* Stephano Renzi and she gave him a friendly wave.

There was no answering wave. No smile. No effort to respond at all, his expression empty and unknowing. She gave another wave, smaller this time and less confident, but that too went unacknowledged. As she watched, the priest turned back towards the entrance and shuffled forward with the rest of the audience.

'That was Father Renzi,' she said, urgently pulling at Jack's sleeve. 'Did you see him? It's plain he saw us, but then turned away.'

Jack *had* seen the priest. 'He may be in a hurry,' he excused, 'and doesn't have the time to talk.'

'Jack,' she protested, 'this is the man who's begged us to help him find his housekeeper, if not his painting, and he doesn't have time to say good evening! Doesn't have time even to wave hello? Why did he walk away like that? Why ignore us so blatantly?'

'I've no idea.' Jack gathered up his jacket. 'But I don't think it's something that should worry us.'

Flora was conflicted but said nothing until they were outside the church and once more walking back along the Riva to where the Cipriani launch waited for them.

'I don't agree,' she said, breaking the silence. 'I think we should be concerned. Something's happened to Father Renzi since we last saw him. It must have, to make him act so oddly. But what?'

Jack came to a halt. 'I really think you should forget the incident, Flora. If something has gone even more amiss, we'll learn about it soon enough.' He took her hand and kissed it. 'We've had a wonderful evening and it's not over yet. There are still a few more hours – let's enjoy them.'

It *was* an evening to enjoy, she had to accept: music still played in her ears, moonlight spread its silver across the lagoon, and the warm sweet air hugged them close. These were hours to remember for the rest of her life.

But still, that moment in the church – the priest's refusal to acknowledge them – that had been deeply uncomfortable and she couldn't forget.

15

___

At breakfast the next morning, Flora was unusually quiet, nodding her thanks to the waitress who brought them coffee and munching her way silently through successive pastries. Last night's events were still vivid in her mind. Despite Jack's conviction that whatever new trouble the priest might be in would soon become clear, she felt agitated. Too agitated to wait. But, sensibly, what could she do…?

Jack interrupted her thoughts. 'Did you make that hairdresser's appointment?' he asked, as he finished a last cup of coffee. It had been something she'd mentioned casually when they'd been dressing for the concert last night.

'Not yet. Why?'

'I thought you might like to go this morning.' He fidgeted with a spoon. 'While I'm at the university? I'd really like to visit their library – just an hour or so,' he added quickly.

That was a surprise. 'Are you going for research?'

'That's it,' he said, seeming grateful she hadn't dismissed the trip out of hand. 'Arthur's idea. He's been keen for some time on a mystery with Italian politics as a setting – the last time we spoke, he suggested it could be the next novel. What he'd like, I think, is a book that plays with connections, if there are any, between the establishment in Rome and the Sicilian mafia, though I've always been nervous of tackling the subject.'

'Because you could be sued?'

'Something like that, or worse,' he joked. 'But Arthur thinks it would make a great thriller, fictionalised hugely, of course, and I have to agree.'

'Have you said yes?'

'Not yet. I thought I'd take the chance while I'm here to read some of the papers that Ca' Foscari holds in its library – memories of post-Second World War Italy and possible links between the mafia and Roman politics. Stuff on the role the mafia played in the war, perhaps. Would you mind my disappearing for an hour or so?'

'Leaving me alone?' She shook her head. 'It will be a chance to have my hair done. A special treat – I can't remember the last time I had someone fuss over me.'

'Any idea where you'll go?'

'Not at the moment. Maybe I'll take the boat across to St Mark's and just walk. I'm bound to find a salon I like.'

Flora returned to her pastry, thinking hard. An appointment with the hairdresser was a nice idea but, in the circumstances, it could wait. Uppermost in her mind was the priest's unexplained behaviour. If Jack wasn't interested in finding out the cause – he'd made no mention of Father Renzi this morning – she would go exploring by herself. To the priest's house. To his church, if he wasn't at home.

She tried to picture the map she'd seen of the various *vaporetto* lines and had a hazy memory that the San Tomà landing was not that far distant from the university. Maybe two or three stops further on from where Jack planned to alight. After speaking to the priest, she could retrace her journey and catch a *vaporetto* down the Grand Canal to meet Jack at Ca' Foscari.

'I could meet you,' she offered.

He looked surprised but agreed with only a small show of reluctance – he was the one asking a favour, after all – but it was clear that he had doubts Flora would ever find her way to the university.

'Shall we say one o'clock? In time for lunch.'

She grinned. 'Naturally, reading is bound to give you an appetite!'

Jack glanced quickly down at his watch. 'If I'm going to make lunch, I'd better leave now. But have you finished?'

'Not quite,' she said breezily. 'I think I could manage another croissant and I've plenty of time. Go and enjoy your research and then come out to play. The sun should still be shining.'

Flora allowed another hour to elapse, taking her time over the rest of her breakfast, before collecting her handbag from the bedroom and wandering through the garden to the landing steps to await the return of the Cipriani boat. Despite Jack's unspoken doubts, she was feeling confident about managing this trip. She knew now how to buy a ticket for the *vaporetto*, which line she should take, and in which direction.

At St Mark's, the line one *vaporetto* she needed appeared almost immediately and she found a seat on the open deck. She hoped she'd find the priest at home but, in any case, she could walk across to the church – he was bound to be in one place or the other. Would he speak to her, though? After last night's incident, she had to admit there was a strong likelihood that he'd refuse.

But, as so often, Flora refused to be daunted. She would approach him carefully, that was the key. Maybe mention casually that she happened to be in the locality and was meeting Jack for lunch, but thought she'd take another look at his beautiful church. She could go on to say how much she'd enjoyed the concert last night, and had he, too? Though, of course, he must have been to the Pietà many times previously. Once they'd been talking for a while, it should only be a small step to broaching the subject of his odd conduct.

They had pulled in at the San Tomà stop and, when Flora stepped out onto dry land, she was feeling positive. She'd been this way before and knew exactly where she was going. Winding a path through the alleys she and Jack had traversed earlier, she was struck at how few people were around. But then there wouldn't be crowds – this was very much a working district. Even so, she couldn't quite lose the feeling that she might be walking into a lion's den.

Was that because of Renzi? A fear that he wasn't the man they'd first thought him, and here she was, alone, and meeting him in what was likely to be an empty house. But he was a priest, a gentleman, and a gentle man. Why on earth would she feel threatened by him? It was her wretched imagination again, working overtime.

Knocking at the door of the presbytery, she waited to hear footsteps approaching. But it was silence that greeted her. She knocked again. Was the priest at home but refusing to come to the door? If so, there was little she could do. A final knock and she decided to cut her losses and walk to the church instead. It was here that they'd found Father Renzi on their first visit, kneeling before the altar.

Passing from bright sunshine into the dark interior of the church, it took Flora a few seconds before her eyes focused. This time, though, there was no figure at prayer. In fact, no figure at all. She walked up the main aisle towards the half circle of the altar. Fresh flowers – tall vases of calla lilies and feathery green stood on either side – testifying, no doubt, to the devotion of Renzi's female parishioners. Drops of water on the stone steps suggested the flower arrangers had called only recently.

And perhaps were still here – she had caught a slight sound coming from the sacristy.

'Hello,' she called out.

When there was no reply, she walked around the altar to the small room at the rear of the church. The door was ajar and, tentatively, she pushed it fully open. The sacristy was empty, but another sound had reached Flora's ears, this time from the body of the church. It must be one of the flower ladies but how had she missed the woman? Walking quickly back to the main aisle, she was met by emptiness. Once more, there was no one. Were her ears playing tricks on her? Or was it simply that she was desperate to see someone? Anyone.

She was halfway along the aisle on her way back to the main entrance when it seemed to Flora that she saw a shadow move. Shadows in a church should sleep undisturbed, so was it her eyes playing tricks on her now? For a moment, she stood perfectly still. Then, walking quickly up the aisle, she rushed through the open doorway and out of the church.

Once more in the fresh air, Flora breathed deeply, but it was a momentary relaxation only. Footsteps! She was sure there were footsteps, somewhere behind her but close. She swung round, ready to face whoever, whatever, it was, but to no avail. The piazza was empty. Oddly empty and, beneath a grey covering of cloud that had emerged from nowhere, it felt threatening.

Desperate to find her way back to the *vaporetto* stop and to what felt like safety, she dashed without thinking down the alleyway she was certain would lead her to the Grand Canal. As the twinge of panic faded, however, a horrible realisation dawned. She had chosen the wrong *calle* – they all looked so much alike – and was passing shops, a square, another church, that she had never seen before. Were the footsteps she'd heard still there? Flora couldn't be sure. And could no longer be sure of the way. Nervously, she peeled off into a passageway that had opened up to her right, thinking it looked more familiar.

But fifty yards down this new *calle*, she was met by a dead end. A palazzo's locked wooden gates barred her way. Now frantic, Flora wheeled around and, seeing another turning to her left, began to rush down it at full speed. This time she found a small canal at its end, and no bridge to take her over. It brought her to an abrupt halt and, for a moment, forced her to stand still and take stock. She had allowed panic to make her foolish.

Had she really been pursued? Was she still being pursued? She couldn't be certain. Trying to orientate herself, she forced her mind to be calm. The *vaporetto* stop was lost to her but, if she walked due south from here, as long as she could judge correctly, she should reach the university. Reach Jack and a pair of safe arms. She had been naive in thinking she could manage this trip alone, and without a map. Even from her scant experience of Venice, she'd realised that alleyways were unpredictable, and could sometimes end suddenly in dark, deep canals, or plunge into hidden arcades, or even emerge, without warning, into a breathtaking view.

Retracing her steps a short way, she noticed a *calle* she hadn't seen when rushing at full tilt. It was narrower and darker than the others, but it seemed to be going in the right direction – south towards Ca' Foscari – and as far as she could make out, stretched into the distance, houses on either side, without a dead end or a canal in sight.

Feeling more cheerful, she picked up her pace, putting to one side the fear that had taken hold. It had been her too-vivid imagination – again. The noise in the church, followed by footsteps? A workman, possibly, who'd then happened to be going her way. Shadows that moved? A trick of the light. There had been a small dread that she'd carried with her ever since the knife attack on Jack that they were being watched and conspired against – the figure at the Redentore, the blue shirt, a shambling man who, to her mind, had looked very much like Luigi Tasca – but for the moment the fear was dismissed.

Halfway along the *calle*, she had to stop. A tiny stone from the lane – its surface had been roughly finished – had become wedged in her shoe, and she had to bend to shake it free. As she did so, she heard those footsteps again, and this time they stopped abruptly. Stopped when she'd stopped.

Flora remained motionless, listening. The rattle of a shutter further down the alleyway sounded loudly in the silence. Venice was a closeted city and the houses on either side were shuttered tight. She looked behind her, but the *calle* was empty. Ahead, an archway spanned the lane. In a sudden burst of light, the sun broke through the lowering cloud, and the shadow cast by the arch's corbelling looked for all the world like three figures lying in wait. She could feel her heart once more racing, but told herself not to be stupid. Walking on, though, her ears were sharp and attuned.

A few seconds later, the echo of a heavy tread on the rough ground came clearly. Flora quickened her pace, but the echo quickened, too. She was desperate to get to the end of this interminable *calle*, looking either side of her for possible escape: a door ajar, a window open, someone, anyone, she could ask for help. But the street remained shuttered and silent.

By now, she was almost running and whoever was behind her was running, too. She would turn and confront her pursuer, she thought. Then realised how ridiculous that would be. Luigi Tasca, if this *were* him, had thought nothing of wounding Jack; worse, he could well be a killer. Flora's breath was coming fast and she had no idea how long she could sustain this pace. Her legs were beginning to tremble and, frenziedly, she broke into a full run, her breath now coming in sobs. She had to find her husband, had to get to Jack.

'Signorina?'

She had run smack into the solid figure of a man. Instinctively, she raised her fists, ready to fight.

'Signorina, you are OK?' the voice asked gently.

Flora's fists lowered. What was she doing? This was not her pursuer.

'The university,' she managed to gulp out.

'*Ma sì. È qui.*' He waved a hand to his left, to yet another small passage. '*Due minuti,*' he promised.

Should she take the *calle*? There was little choice and, thankfully, within the promised two minutes what looked very much like a university building came into sight. Stumbling through the open gates, Flora was half crying, half laughing. The porter on duty studied her uncertainly, and no wonder.

'Sorry,' she said, her breath coming in spurts. '*Mi dispiace.*'

He pointed to a wooden bench. 'You have a seat, signorina.'

'Thank you. It's signora, by the way – my husband will be here very soon.'

And he was. Of all the times in her life that she had been glad to see Jack, this was probably the most precious.

At the sight of her, his eyebrows rose, but a broad smile filled his face. 'This *is* a surprise! You found your way here!'

'I did,' she said, trying to look unconcerned. She needed time to think, unsure whether she should speak of this morning's terror, but sensing quite strongly that it might be best to remain silent on her abortive visit to the priest. 'Did you have a good morning?'

He nodded. 'Actually, quite brilliant. Arthur is a star suggesting the idea. I reckon I've enough—' He broke off. 'Your hair?'

'Don't worry. I didn't go. I couldn't find a salon I liked.'

'Thank goodness for that. I thought I should be noticing something different.'

'No difference. The same old Flora. Shall we go?'

'Anywhere in particular?'

'To lunch first, if you're hungry, then back to the hotel and the swimming pool? The cloud is clearing again.' She looked up at the rapidly expanding patches of blue. 'How about an afternoon on a sunlounger?'

It would be a chance to catch her breath.

16

The following morning, a slight mist covered the lagoon leading Jack to suggest it was a day to visit a gallery. Apart from the Scuola Grande and the paintings hanging in Vivaldi's church, they had seen little of Italy's glorious art and he was keen that Flora managed a glimpse, at least, of the Accademia.

He was about to mention a trip across the lagoon to St Mark's and a gentle walk from there to the gallery when, after cutting a peach into precise quarters, Flora said, 'I think we should go to Asolo.'

Jack was temporarily confounded. 'Not the priest again.'

'The priest again,' she affirmed.

Flora had kept her silence on yesterday's adventure, but it had done nothing to set her mind at rest. On the contrary, it had made her surer than ever that a connection existed between what was happening to Father Renzi and the small town where he'd once been priest. Someone must have been watching his house in San Polo, watching Santa Margherita and, when she'd walked there yesterday, seen her knock on the priest's door and followed her into the church. For some reason, she had posed a threat. Her pursuer – and there was no doubt they'd been the footsteps of a man – had clearly meant her harm or why not call out for her to stop, shout an explanation of why he was following? He'd not done so and his pursuit had been dogged. It was only when she'd outrun him and reached safe harbour that he'd given up.

'Something has happened since we last spoke to Father Renzi,' she said with conviction. 'At the concert, he was a changed character. Not the courteous man we'd met before, the friendly man who was very, very keen that we help him find Signora Pretelli. Quite suddenly, he didn't want to speak to us. And since that incident at the Pietà, he's made no attempt to get in touch.'

The grey of Jack's eyes had darkened. 'It's a strange development, I agree, but if we think something has changed, something new has happened to the man, we should be going to San Polo and speaking to Renzi himself, rather than travelling miles to a town neither of us know.'

'We should,' she admitted, 'except I think it would be a wasted journey.' She'd had time now to reflect on yesterday's events. 'I'm fairly sure Renzi will refuse to say what's occurred to change his attitude. At best, we'll be met with a blank face and told everything is fine. And it isn't. I know it.'

Meditatively, Jack stirred his coffee. 'I'd love to see Asolo,' he admitted. 'If only for itself. The town is reputed to be very beautiful. But in order to help Father Renzi? How will a trip there tell us anything?'

'It's the place it all started. It's where Franco comes from, where Filomena and her nephew come from, and the horrible Tascas, and where Renzi was the priest for years.'

Jack continued stirring his coffee. 'All true, and you may be right.' He gave a sudden smile. 'You very often are, though I'm not convinced that Asolo is the key to the mystery. Still... it *is* a very lovely town.'

'You're willing to be persuaded?'

He nodded. 'I guess so. Even if we discover nothing, it will be a great day out,' but then added, more in hope than expectation, 'you wouldn't rather take a trot around the Accademia?'

'We'll go to the gallery before we leave the city, I promise. Tomorrow. But today, let's take a train to Asolo. I imagine you *can* take a train there.'

The hotel reception confirmed that you could indeed take the railway to Asolo, but it would mean a change of trains, a change of station, then a bus, and then a smaller bus. They would advise hiring a car, with or without a driver, which they could book in a matter of minutes.

In for a penny, Jack decided. 'A car is certainly a better choice, and could you book a driver as well?' He saw Flora's look of surprise and no wonder. It was by far the most expensive option.

'But, of course.' The receptionist beamed. 'I will book it immediately. Guido will take you to the Piazzale Roma and you will find the car waiting for you.'

Guido, they presumed was the Cipriani boatman.

'Can we afford it?' Flora asked, anxiously, as they climbed the stairs to their room to gather essentials for the day ahead.

'We can't afford not to. Do you want to spend most of the day on a broiling bus or an endless succession of trains? This way, we'll have time to interrogate the whole town!'

Passing through the lobby on their way to the hotel boat, they were stopped before they reached the door. The receptionist had darted from behind her desk to wave at them.

'You have a telephone call, Signora Carrington.'

'Me?' Flora looked confused.

'But yes.' The girl awarded her a professional smile. 'It is a friend, I believe. You may take it in the kiosk. It is more private there.'

Still clutching Jack's hand, Flora crossed the foyer with him to the alcove that contained the public telephone. She held the receiver so that he could be sure to hear before pressing the button that would transfer the call. It was Sally's voice that came down the line.

'Sorry to encroach on your holiday again, Flora, but I had to phone. I need to go home – to sort out the Priory. There's trouble there, though I can't imagine what's been going on. Anyway, I'm leaving this evening on the eight o'clock train from Santa Lucia and I won't have time to say goodbye in person. I felt I had to spend my last day in Venice with Bianca. She's so very upset.'

'Something has happened to her?' Flora half turned to her husband, pulling a small face.

'Not Bianca, her father. He's not at all well. He's had trouble with his heart before and now he's feeling quite ill again. It's the debt, I think.'

'The debt?'

'For the new boat. He had to borrow to pay for it, apparently, and there's some problem about repaying the money. I'm not sure exactly what and I don't like to ask.'

'Perhaps you'll find out today,' Flora suggested.

'Perhaps. I just want to buy her lunch and hopefully boost her spirits a little. But I'll see you both when you're back in Abbeymead. When do you leave?'

In answer to Flora's raised eyebrows, Jack held up three fingers.

'We've three more days here,' Flora said. 'Not long. But have a safe journey, Sally, and we'll see you very soon. Oh, and give our love to Alice.'

'Well, what do you make of that?' she asked, replacing the receiver.

'Not much, except that Sally is playing the good Samaritan before going home to knock a few heads together. Meanwhile, my lovely wife, we have a beautiful town to explore!'

. . .

Piazzale Roma was busy. As the entrance to the city and the only place in central Venice accessible to motor vehicles – the square acted as the main bus station – it teemed with cars, coaches, motorbikes. And lorries carrying every kind of goods.

Maggiore, the hire car business, had its offices next to a ramshackle garage and as soon as Jack stepped off the Cipriani boat, he could smell the diesel permeating the air. Taking Flora's hand, he made for the office door. There were papers to sign and a driver to meet, a grey-haired stalwart, a Signor Gallo he noticed from the badge, who pointed them to an open-top Alfa Romeo, at least ten years old but classically elegant in deep blue with a red leather interior.

'Asolo?' Jack said, unsure if their destination had appeared anywhere in the reams of paperwork he'd signed.

'*Si, Si,*' the man said, solemnly opening the wide single door and gesturing them to take the rear seat. In a minute, he'd pressed the starter, the engine had burst into life and they were on their way.

'We take road to Treviso,' their driver said over his shoulder.

'Treviso?' Flora queried in a low voice.

'Asolo is north of Treviso,' Jack reassured her, 'but I imagine we'll bypass the town. This is Liberty Bridge, by the way. It's the only road access into Venice from the mainland.'

'Liberty Bridge? The war again?'

He nodded. 'Built by Mussolini in the thirties, but after the war renamed for the end of the Fascist regime. It runs into the Via Della Libertà.'

'Of course it does!'

Expertly, Signor Gallo swung the car into the line of traffic making its way out of the city and onto a causeway that ran parallel to the railway bridge. In a short while, they were out on the road and the city had been left behind.

Through the window, clouds of filthy air began to drift towards them.

'Porto Marghera?' she asked and Jack nodded.

'If Mestre is anything like it, no wonder Franco decided he couldn't live there. Not after the Cipriani!'

Turning off the road that bypassed both Mestre and Marghera, Flora settled down to watch the passing landscape. The road, snaking its way towards Treviso, travelled between wooded hills, their lower slopes terraced for vines, and through numerous small villages, each with their square-topped church and war memorial. In the far distance, the sight of the snow-capped Dolomites caught her eye. The mountains were rarely visible from Venice, beleaguered as it was by waves of humidity rising from the lagoon.

As Jack had prophesied, they changed route on the outskirts of Treviso and after paying at a toll booth, Signor Gallo pulled into a rest area.

'You want drink?' he enquired from the front seat.

'Good idea.' Jack was enthusiastic. 'We can stretch our legs at the same time.' He helped his wife from the car. 'I reckon we'll be driving for another hour, at least.'

Flora didn't mind – another hour, another two hours, or longer. Getting to Asolo was what mattered. The town, she was hopeful, would unlock the puzzle they'd been set.

17

Jack had been pessimistic, Flora decided, when some forty minutes later, the driver pulled into a parking area outside Asolo and consulted his watch.

'You come back?' he asked, tapping the dial of his timepiece.

'Six o'clock,' Jack suggested. Then to Flora, 'That should give us time for lunch, as well as finding people willing to talk to us.'

'Always food,' she sighed.

'We're in Italy! Of course it's always food.'

Looking around her as they walked the short distance into the town, Flora could see why such lavish praise had been heaped on this small settlement, nestled so neatly into the wooded hillside. Ahead of them lay a jumble of terracotta rooftops amid a cluster of cypress, with here and there the turrets of what looked to be old villas peeping between the trees. It was a town of cobbled lanes and small squares, of rose-filled gardens and frescoed walls and, towering over all, the Renaissance fortress – basking today in the golden light of a full sun.

Passing through an archway, they began a walk along one of

the many arcaded streets, this one leading to the Piazza Garibaldi, the main square which, when they reached it, appeared remarkably quiet.

'It's so peaceful here and so beautiful. The pace of life must be very slow,' she observed, as they took a seat at the square's café.

'Lemonade?' he asked, as the waiter hovered at his shoulder.

'Please.'

'The town is certainly beautiful, but it was never going to be enough for Franco Massi, was it?' Jack leant back in his chair, enjoying the view.

'I can see why he might want a different life,' Flora agreed. 'Bright, ambitious, good with people – he was hardly a man to till the land.'

'So, now we're here, what do we do?' He picked up the glass of cold lemonade the waiter had brought. 'Have you made a plan? Of course, if you've changed your mind, we could simply picnic beneath the castle and drive back to Venice.'

'We won't be doing that and you know it! I do have a plan of sorts. I thought we'd find Franco's parents first.'

'And?'

'And talk to them.'

'They *have* just lost their son,' he reminded her.

'I know that, Jack, and if they don't want to talk, that will be it. But it's possible they might actually want to. They could be eager to speak of him.'

'I have my doubts, but it's worth an attempt, I suppose.'

When they asked their waiter for directions to the Massi house, they were told it was not, in fact, a house they needed but a smallholding on the outskirts of town. There was no taxi to take them, the man said apologetically, but it was a twenty-minute walk at most.

'We can walk,' Jack assured him. 'Does Signor Massi have a large business?'

The waiter cocked his head. 'He grows vegetables. Many fields – for the market. Fruit, too. And eggs. Chickens,' he explained, in case they hadn't made the connection.

By midday, they were standing at the end of a long, winding drive and despite the refreshing breeze, feeling exceptionally hot. The sound of a horn slicing through the silence made them jump. A tractor was pulling into the side of the lane behind them.

In his best Italian – which was poor, Jack had to admit – he managed to indicate they were bound for the house they could glimpse at the end of the drive, whereupon the driver gestured to them to squash into the buddy seat beside him. The ten minutes that followed were uncomfortable but vastly preferable to a trudge in the scorching sun.

It was Signora Massi who opened the door, a kindly-looking woman with hair scraped into a collapsing bun and wearing a much-washed apron. Behind her, a slight figure hovered in the hallway beyond.

When Jack again tried his Italian, hoping to tell her how they'd met Franco at the Cipriani and to express their sadness over her son's death, the shadow behind the signora suddenly became a person. A young boy, awkwardly dragging one leg, but with eyes the colour of chestnuts, spoke directly to them.

'Can I help?' he asked in English, with a smile that lit his face.

'I'm sorry,' Jack apologised. 'Sorry that my Italian is so poor.'

'You try,' the boy said. 'And that is good. My name is Daniele. I learn English from my brother. We speak English now and I translate for Mama.'

'My name is Jack Carrington and this is my wife, Flora,' he said gratefully. 'We're on holiday in Venice and met your brother' – it seemed a reasonable guess – 'at the Cipriani.'

'You stay at the hotel?'

'We're on our honeymoon. It's a very special holiday.'

How special it would turn out to be Jack didn't like to think.

Daniele gave them another blinding smile. 'Franco loved the hotel. He loved very much his work there.'

'That was obvious when he checked us in on our first evening.'

'*Venire!*' the signora suddenly commanded, breaking into a conversation it was doubtful she could follow, and hustling them into the flagged hallway and along a narrow passage to the rear of the house. Through an open door, Flora glimpsed a small room as they passed, set up as a workshop. A businesslike sewing machine sat atop a large table, and the shelves that filled one entire wall were packed with bales of material: cottons, crepes, and a small number of silks. Signora Massi was a seamstress.

The woman led them into a large airy room that ran across the entire rear of the house, a ceiling fan lazily stirring the warm air but offering some small relief from a heat that was becoming more intense.

'*Sedersi!*' she commanded again, and they did, finding the basketweave chairs cool and comfortable.

Their hostess hurried from the room, but in a few minutes had returned with glasses of cold juice, a mixture of cherry and lemon. Delicious, Flora thought, trying not to drink too greedily.

'Your son's?' Jack enquired, pointing to several framed certificates on the mantelpiece.

'Franco,' their hostess confirmed with pride.

'He was the clever one,' Daniele said, without a trace of resentment. 'Franco passed every examination, but there was nothing for him here.' The smile had faded and the note of sadness was evident. 'He wanted always to live in the city, in a beautiful apartment. In London, in Venezia. And he made big success. He was very good in his job. Very good with important people, people who had money.'

'He'd have to be,' Jack remarked drily. 'The Cipriani isn't exactly cheap. But you, you never wanted to follow him?'

The boy gestured to his leg. 'This does not work so well. I am tired many times and it is better I stay here. I can help my father.'

Again, it was said without resentment.

Signora Massi had sat silent as they talked. '*Tornava spesso*,' she offered.

'Even though my brother loved cities, he came back to Asolo,' Daniele translated, 'often.'

'Because your parents needed him?'

The boy looked uncertain. 'Maybe he needed Asolo,' he said diffidently.

Franco's story had been that his parents were ageing and it was his duty to help them and his disabled brother. But one look at her hostess had convinced Flora – and she was sure Jack, too – that it *was* simply a story. Signora Massi was sprightly and energetic, still working as a dressmaker if the sewing machine didn't lie, while Franco's father worked in his fields daily. As for Daniele, the brother who in future would need greater care, he moved slowly, it was true, perhaps painfully, but he was a cheerful lad and, it seemed, quite capable. Hadn't he just said that he helped his father in the fields? Bianca had been right to reject Franco's excuse – it was patently false.

If Franco had ever suffered worries for his family, they had to have been minimal, yet apparently the man had returned to his home town often and Flora wondered why. Was it that he wasn't particularly happy with his lot? That Venice hadn't turned out to be the nirvana he'd expected? That some feeling deep inside remained unsatisfied and, as his brother said, he'd begun to need his family more than they needed him?

Jack had been silent for some time, and she wondered if he

had been contemplating the same conundrum. When he spoke, though, he surprised her.

'We met a Father Renzi in Venice. I believe he was once the priest in Asolo.'

Well done, Jack, she thought. Neat and direct. Now, we might get closer to what we've come for.

The signora nodded. 'A good man. *Avrebbe dovuto restare.*'

'He should have stayed,' Danielle translated. 'We think he should never have gone to Venice. Bad things have happened there. When my mother telephoned Franco, he was not happy. He told her that the priest had troubles. Again.'

'Troubles,' their hostess agreed.

'Did he say what they were?' Flora asked.

'There were things that had been taken – stolen, Franco thought – from Santa Margherita. That is the priest's church,' the boy explained.

Things, Flora's inner voice queried. No mention of the painting, so what things were these? No mention of the missing woman either, and she wondered whether, in fact, the news had percolated this far. It seemed not.

But hadn't Father Renzi said clearly that he knew nothing of any other thefts? That earlier there had been no trouble? Yet, apparently, Franco had known for some time of problems at Father Renzi's church. Had he also known of the missing painting and the missing housekeeper – before he met his death? Is that why he'd gone to La Zucca that evening, suspecting the owner of being involved? Gone to intercede with Silvio Fabbri or to threaten him?

'We heard there had been trouble here in Asolo, too,' Jack said, while Flora held her breath, waiting to see whether or not their hosts would refuse to talk of it.

There was a long silence before Daniele said solemnly, 'The priest is a man of God. He must speak honestly, but in Asolo you do not always tell the truth.'

Flora shifted in her chair. 'You're thinking of what happened to the priest after Luigi Tasca went to prison?' she said quietly.

'You know of the matter?' Daniele looked startled.

'Father Renzi spoke of it to us,' Jack said. 'He was very frank. You see, he knows my... my stepfather.' It was said with difficulty, his distaste for the word clear. 'Father Renzi was keen to share his problems with the count.'

'Your father?' Signora Massi had caught the word.

'*Step*father,' he said deliberately. 'Count Falconi.'

'The count? *Oh! Un bell'uomo!*' she said, sighing a little.

'My mother is half in love with the count,' Daniele joked. 'And today you have come to Asolo to see him?'

'No.' Jack sounded flustered. 'Not today. We came to see your beautiful town and to say how sorry we were to learn of Franco's death.'

As soon as Daniele had translated for his mother, Flora tried a new approach. 'We met Bianca Benetti in Venice as well,' she said conversationally. 'She is a beautiful girl.'

The signora nodded. 'Bianca a good girl. And Franco good.'

Flora exchanged a look with her husband, neither of them sure what this somewhat cryptic comment implied. Perhaps it wasn't cryptic after all.

'You liked Bianca?' Flora asked the signora.

'A good girl,' she repeated.

It was fair to assume then that Franco's mother and, no doubt his father, had been happy with their son's engagement. Bianca's arrival had caused no conflict in the family.

Finishing her lemonade, Flora found her handbag and got to her feet, Jack taking his cue and following suit. 'Thank you so much for the drink,' she said. 'It's lovely to have met you, but you must be very busy and we've taken up too much of your time already.'

'You will explore Asolo?' Daniele suggested.

What Flora wanted most was to visit the Tascas' farm, to meet Luigi again and possibly his father, but there was no obvious excuse she could offer.

'We'll look around the town,' she said a little vaguely. 'Have lunch and then meet up with our driver.'

'I will walk to the gates with you,' Daniele said.

'No, really,' she began, fearful it would be a trial for him, but then stopped. He had a fixed look on his face which told her there was more he wanted to say, but not here in the house.

They had said their goodbyes and walked for some minutes, almost to the farm gates, when the boy came to a halt. 'Bianca was having a baby,' he said abruptly.

Flora locked eyes with Jack, both of them stunned.

'Not now,' Daniele said hastily. 'But it is why Franco asked her to marry.'

'What happened to the baby?'

The boy gave a small shrug of the shoulders. 'There was no baby. I don't know why.'

A miscarriage, she thought, but Bianca had said nothing of the tragedy and neither had Sally. Had Sally known what had befallen her friend? Was it possible – Flora paused at the thought – that there hadn't been a pregnancy?

'Did your mother know there was to be a baby?' she asked.

'Yes, she knew. Bianca told her. But they said nothing to my father.'

That went some way to explaining Signora Massi's strange remark that Bianca was good and Franco was good. In her eyes, they had done the honourable thing in deciding to marry.

'How did Franco feel,' she asked quietly, 'after Bianca lost the baby?'

It seemed that Daniele was reluctant to answer and they had walked another few yards before he said, 'Sad, I suppose.' Then burst out, 'But angry, too.'

'He was disappointed?'

Daniele shook his head. 'He thought it was a trick. That he had been tricked into the marriage.'

'And he wanted to forget the engagement?'

'He told me that he could not sign the lease of the Mestre flat. It was not what he wanted. So, he told Bianca that they should wait a while, that there was no need now for them to marry so quickly.'

'Did he mean to marry her eventually?'

'I don't know. He never said. I thought that maybe he would wait for a year or two.'

That wouldn't have pleased Bianca, Flora thought. She would suspect that Franco didn't want to marry at all.

'And Bianca?' she asked. 'How did she feel?'

'She was not happy. She came here to see my parents – maybe she hoped they would make Franco keep his word. They were shocked that he had broken his promise and sad for her. They expected the wedding. Her father, too, I think. Bianca is a good girl, they said, she deserves better. She will be our daughter and look after us.'

Bianca would have seen for herself that neither Franco's parents nor Daniele were in immediate need of help. He had lied to her and her visit here would have rammed home the truth. She would have felt the family's kindness towards her, their willingness to treat her as a daughter. Would have seen their shock at Franco's behaviour. What effect had all this had on Bianca? Had she returned to Venice and confronted him directly with his lies?

'My mother told Franco that he should honour his promise,' Daniele went on, 'and Bianca said this, too. She insisted that they marry.'

'Is that when Franco walked away?'

'It was. I leave you here,' he said, opening the gates for them to pass through. 'This road will take you to the town. I hope that you enjoy your day – and your lunch at the café. You must try the truffle omelette!'

18

The café when they walked through the door was almost empty, but the array of salad dishes on offer was tempting, though truffle omelette appeared missing from today's menu. Quickly, they made their selection and found seats at an outside table.

'What do you make of what we've learned?' Flora asked, snaffling a chunk of Taleggio cheese.

'That the Massis were happy with their son's choice of bride and unhappy that he let her down.'

'But the business of Franco feeling tricked.'

'It suggests, doesn't it, that he never truly wanted to marry? He was doing the decent thing and when it was no longer necessary, he wanted out. Married life in a small Mestre apartment wasn't for him.'

'I'm thinking it must have made Bianca very angry.' She cut a slice from a large tomato and matched it with a second bite of Taleggio.

'For sure. But does that get us anywhere?'

'I'm trying to understand what was going on in the girl's mind, Jack. As far as I can see, she hasn't spoken of this baby to anyone. How must she have felt when she was abandoned by

MERRYN ALLINGHAM

her fiancé because she was no longer pregnant? She'd fallen in love with the man – OK it was an expedient kind of love – but she obviously cared for him, and everything was looking fine. They were planning a wedding, her father had loaned the money for a deposit on a just-built flat, and the new baby would make them a family. Then, *pouf*, it's all gone.'

'All true what you say, but it doesn't mean she went looking for Franco to kill him. There were other people angry with him, too – don't forget, we still don't know what was behind that massive quarrel he had with Silvio Fabbri.'

Flora had silently to agree and turned back to her salad. There was so much that remained hidden. But when the waiter arrived to clear their plates and bring them the dessert menu, she ignored the treats on offer to ask, 'Do you know the Tasca family, by any chance?'

'Of course.' The young man brushed back his hair. 'Everyone know the Tascas. They are here a hundred years.' He gave a grimace. 'And for another hundred.'

'And Luigi Tasca? Does he live here still?'

Another grimace. 'Sometimes yes, signora. Sometimes, no. He is here and there.'

'I thought he might work on his father's farm.'

'*Forse*, perhaps, but not always. One day he paint the house, then he build fence, then he clean windows.'

'A drifter,' Jack muttered.

The waiter seemed to understand, nodding in agreement. 'He was soldier but then he has to go.'

'Dismissed?'

'Drink,' the waiter said succinctly.

'Do you know if he visits Venice often?'

The young man looked confused and Flora wasn't surprised – it had been an awkward turn of conversation. Hard enough to dig for the truth among strangers, she thought, but forced to ask questions in a foreign language, it was near impossible.

The waiter surprised her, however, when he nodded and said, 'Tasca has the motorbike. He goes to Venice with Matteo.'

'Matteo Pretelli? It's his aunt that lives in Venice, isn't it?'

'Signora Pretelli is very good cook.' A woman, the owner, they presumed, had come out of the café to join them. 'The boys, they visit for cake, I think! But you want Matteo?'

Why not? Flora thought. 'He works in Asolo?' she asked, her expression innocent.

'At the Tasca farm. You want to go there?'

'We were thinking of it,' she said casually. 'We understand that Signor Tasca runs an excellent business. We are farmers, too,' she lied blatantly. 'A man we met in a restaurant – in Venice – was a good friend of the signore. He suggested we paid a visit.'

The woman's forehead puckered, as she tried to follow Flora's words. 'Silvio Fabbri?' she asked at length.

'Yes! Do you know him?'

'Everyone know him. Everyone know everyone,' she said simply. 'Signor Fabbri in Venice many years, but he come to Asolo. He come to buy.'

When Flora looked questioningly at her, she said, 'Enrico Tasca, he sell vegetables and he sell fruit, all to Fabbri – for the restaurant. They are friends from little boys.'

'Really? We've just come from a visit to Signora Massi. Her husband grows fruit and vegetables, too, but he doesn't sell to La Zucca?'

The woman smiled complacently. This was easier for her to understand. 'One time he sell, but now restaurant is too big.' She spread her arms wide. 'Too much vegetable. Too much fruit. Massi has small farm.'

More interesting snippets, Flora decided, as Jack retrieved his wallet to settle the bill. Franco had quarrelled badly with Silvio Fabbri and Fabbri was in business with Luigi Tasca's father – another connection – but what, if anything, did either of them have to do with the theft of the painting or a missing woman?

Maybe Franco's anger that night had nothing to do with what had happened at Santa Margherita. It was what Jack had argued at the time, that Massi's fury could have been provoked by something completely different. Had that something different affected his family here? An injury to his mother or father, perhaps a business arrangement gone wrong? Tasca and Fabbri were closely intertwined, it seemed, and perhaps Franco had suspected questionable dealings between them, dealings that had prejudiced his own family's livelihood.

Or perhaps it was simply that he'd found Fabbri out in something underhand – after all, how had a man like Silvio Fabbri, coming from very humble beginnings, managed to buy an expensive restaurant? If Franco had discovered that Fabbri was guilty of dishonesty, when all the time he'd been recommending the Cipriani's guests to eat at La Zucca, he would have been very angry. He could have seen it as endangering the career of which he was so proud.

From this distance, it was unlikely they would ever discover what had sent Franco Massi into a towering rage that fateful evening, but the incident could still be the key to unravelling the reason for his death. And the key to finding his killer.

Perhaps a visit to the Tasca farm would give them the answers they needed. In her heart, though, Flora was doubtful.

The owner of the café had been clear in her directions: they were to take the first turning on the right from where they were sitting and follow the long lane until they came to the point that it snaked into a horseshoe. It was there they would find Enrico Tasca's farm.

Jack had been prepared for a sticky and uncomfortable walk

– the sun was now at its zenith – but the reality proved worse. By the time they had reached the horseshoe both of them were steaming and Flora's usually bright copper waves had become a mass of damp frizz.

But, at least, they had arrived and, even better, despite it being Sunday, there was a man working in the field nearest the lane – a young man. Was he, Jack wondered, one of their 'persons of interest', as the inspector was fond of saying? Might he even be Matteo himself? They'd learned this morning that the boy worked on this farm.

Flora, it seemed, had no doubts, marching up to the gate and calling to the toiling figure. 'Matteo Pretelli?'

Would he recognise her? he wondered. He crossed his fingers – they had met for only seconds in the basement of La Zucca where the lighting was extremely dim.

The young man, his oversized shirt clinging damply to limbs made powerful from years of labour, looked up from his planting. From where Jack was standing, there seemed no sign of recognition on his face.

'Sì?' He sounded uncertain, wiping the sweat from his forehead with a none too clean handkerchief.

'Could we have a word?' Flora asked. 'We've come from Venice and we'd love to speak to you.'

To Jack, that seemed a pretty inadequate explanation. Pretelli would have no clue as to who they were – at least he hoped not – or what their connection might be to any drama of which he'd been part. Nevertheless, the young man ambled towards them, perhaps not understanding Flora's English, and propped himself against the gate.

'We met Father Stephano Renzi in Venice,' she began, 'and he told us about you.'

'Sì?' Suspicion had crept into his voice at the mention of the priest's name.

'He said how you often came to visit your aunt, even when she had moved to Venice, and what a good cook she was.'

Matteo smiled slowly. 'A good cook,' he repeated, holding on to words he'd evidently recognised. 'She is good cook.'

The present tense, Jack noted, though that might simply be the young man's English. Unless... he believed his aunt was still alive, either because he hadn't been told of her kidnapping or because he knew where she was.

'Your aunt is missing. *Sua zia è scomparsa,*' he said, plunging head first into difficult territory, and hoping he hadn't mangled the Italian too badly. 'Did you know?'

He nodded. 'It is not good,' he said in English.

'You have no idea where she is?' Flora asked.

'*Dove?* No.'

'And your friend, Luigi, would he know perhaps? He visits your aunt with you, we've heard.'

'You know Luigi?' He hadn't answered Flora's question, Jack saw.

'We understand the two of you have been friends since you were children.'

Matteo's smile was genuine. 'Luigi my best friend,' he stated proudly.

'Even though he went to prison.' Flora was stepping on dangerous ground.

'You know this? How you know this? *È stato un errore.* A mistake. Luigi is good person. I see him in prison, and now he makes no more mistake.'

'He doesn't work here with you?'

'One day, two days.'

'And the rest of the time?' Flora was thinking, Jack knew, of how easy it would be for Luigi to spend time in Venice, time plotting the theft of a valuable painting.

Matteo shrugged, a gesture that suggested Luigi did little

work or, when he did, it was on a casual basis. Plenty of time then to get into mischief.

A splutter of an engine behind them had Jack turn to see a large man in overalls jump from a muddy and much dented Land Rover.

'*Qual è il problema?*' he asked Matteo.

'No problem.'

'*Poi torna al lavoro.*'

Matteo scowled. It seemed he was being ordered to get back to work. The red-faced man turned to them. '*Siete interessati nella mia fattoria?*'

'We like your farm,' Jack confirmed in English. 'We are visiting Asolo from Venice.'

'*Conoscono Don Stephano,*' Matteo added, pausing in his work.

The mention of Stephano Renzi had the man's shoulders stiffen, but he held out his hand to them and introduced himself. 'Enrico Tasca.'

Flora gave him her most dazzling smile. 'It's so good to meet you, Signor Tasca. We were hoping that we might. Hoping that perhaps you could help us.'

'Help? What do you mean?'

'Filomena Pretelli, Matteo's aunt, is missing and Don Stephano is very worried. We wondered if she was here. She lived in Asolo for many years, we believe.'

'She not here,' he said curtly.

'Don Stephano thinks that maybe she has had a breakdown,' Flora pursued.

'*Un crollo,*' Jack added quickly, trying to follow Flora's lead. 'Items have been stolen from Santa Margherita and the signora has become very upset. Did you know this?'

The man jiggled the Land Rover's keys in his hands, passing them from one to the other. At length, he said, 'Silvio tell me when I go to Venice. From church! It is bad.'

He seemed shocked, Jack thought. Sincerely. If it had been his own son stealing from Santa Margherita, Enrico Tasca appeared ignorant of it.

'Silvio?' Flora queried. 'Signor Fabbri? We went to his restaurant, La Zucca. The food is very good.'

The man nodded. 'We grow.' He pointed to the spread of fields in front of them. 'Good vegetables. Good fruit.'

'I'm sure. But Signor Fabbri – he has no farm of his own?'

A slight smile passed across the weather-beaten face as he pocketed the keys and held out a pair of grimy hands, a testament to years of rural labour.

'Not for Silvio,' he said, shaking his head.

That seemed to signal the end of the conversation. There was little more they could ask and prolonging the encounter would seem to solve nothing – they would be met by blank faces and a shrug of the shoulders. If either Matteo or Enrico Tasca were aware of Filomena's whereabouts, neither of them were saying.

But neither of them, Jack realised suddenly, appeared unduly worried. Yet this was a woman that both Matteo and Enrico's son had been close to, in this town and later in Venice.

Flimsy grounds for suspicion, he had to admit, but the connection between the Tasca farm and the Venice restaurant was more than simply a commercial arrangement, he was sure, yet no matter how many questions they'd asked, it had remained murky. Deliberately so?

19

They found their driver at the café when, after a weary walk from the farm, they arrived back at the main square. In their absence, Signor Gallo had made himself comfortable, the littered table evidence of a succession of coffees and sweet treats. But whenever they gave him the signal, he said, he was ready to leave.

The drive back to Venice was uneventful, though made longer by several hold-ups in the traffic and it was sunset before they arrived at the Piazzale Roma. With Flora huddled against him, Jack had been guilty of dozing intermittently for most of the journey, and it was only the driver swinging open the passenger door that woke him fully.

Waving farewell to Signor Gallo, he gave himself a mental shake. The day had had its bright spots the beauty of the town, in particular – and, in terms of their investigation, it hadn't disappointed entirely. But neither had it proved to be the key Flora had hoped. Their holiday was coming to a close, they had only a few more days in Venice and, rather than chasing shadows, they should be making the very best of the time they had left. He tried to focus.

'A *vaporetto* ride along the Grand Canal?' he suggested, as they walked out of the Piazzale. 'It's likely to be spectacular at this time of day.'

'It's our only option, isn't it?' Flora asked, her voice flat. She sounded very tired and unusually dispirited.

It *was* the only choice, Jack admitted, there being no easy way of telephoning the Cipriani but, with luck, it would prove a cheering end to a day in which their fortunes had been mixed.

As they neared the *vaporetto* stop, a vessel had already arrived, and a stream of passengers were cramming aboard. Holding hands, they ran for it, Jack making sure they took the two open seats left vacant at the rear of the craft. The view would be everything. Lights were already blazing along the canal as they made a slow progress towards St Mark's: elegant *palazzi* lit from top to toe, their reflections glittering across the canal, bringing its waters alive; brightly welcoming restaurants, their terraces decked in a profusion of fairy lights; and the boats, even the boats, plying their evening trade, had become vessels of gold. It was as breathtaking as he'd hoped.

Flora was now wide awake, her eyes everywhere. She's forgotten her tiredness, he thought, forgotten her disappointment at how little progress they seemed to have made; both of them rendered silent by the sheer beauty of an extraordinary city.

Once at St Mark's, they made the short walk to the familiar telephone box, still feeling no need to talk but in perfect amity. A call to the hotel had them swept across the lagoon and, in a short time, anchoring at the landing steps of the Cipriani.

In the foyer, a surprise awaited them.

'Sally! You *have* found time to say goodbye!' Flora exclaimed. 'How nice. But won't you miss your train?'

'I've had to change my ticket. I'm staying the night and leaving first thing in the morning. It's Bianca. Something awful.'

Jack's heart sank. More complications, he foresaw, as Flora

guided her friend to one of the foyer's sizeable chairs. She reached out and gently touched Sally's arm.

'Tell me what's happened.'

'It's Bianca's father.' Sally's eyes filled with tears and she fumbled for a handkerchief. 'The poor girl. She's distraught.'

'Piero Benetti?' Flora asked, sounding uncertain.

Sally nodded. 'He's dead, Flora. He just collapsed and died – right there in their kitchen.'

It was Jack who spoke. 'Was it another heart attack?'

'I imagine so. There'll be a post-mortem, of course. Bianca was with him – she said... she said that one minute he was talking to her and the next he'd clutched at his chest and fell to the floor. He was dead by the time she got to him.'

'How dreadful!' Flora had found her voice.

'It was. It has been. I've been at her house all day, trying to help. Trying to get her to eat something, anything. Lunch went out of the window, of course. But... the thing is, Flora, I simply have to leave tomorrow. I've already delayed too long and I can't take more time out. I didn't say before but Alice telephoned me a few days ago. I knew there was a problem as soon as I heard her voice, otherwise she would never have called. There's real trouble at the hotel – some kind of feud between two of the staff that's upsetting everyone else. I've put off going back as long as I could but I need to be there to knock a few heads together.'

It was an uncanny echo of Jack's words.

'And your train...'

'That's sorted, at least the ticket is. The new schedule means I'll be waiting around in Milan for a fair time, but I should be home the day after tomorrow. I hate leaving Bianca alone, though.'

'Hasn't she relatives who could stay with her?'

'It doesn't seem so. She has one or two good neighbours and I think they'll call and do what they can. But I was wondering... I understand you hardly know her, but could you and Jack call, possibly? Just once would help. I can give you her address. I know she'd be happy to have your company for a while.'

Jack could see that the request had put Flora in a quandary. Had put him in one, too. They had only a few days left in Venice and playing nurse to Bianca wasn't how either of them would have wished to spend them. But the girl had lost a father she loved dearly and it seemed she'd been left to cope alone; they should do whatever they could to comfort her, he supposed, although he doubted Bianca would see their presence as exactly comforting. But Flora would want to help, for Sally's sake – she was clearly very upset – if not for Bianca herself.

'We'll do what we can,' Flora promised, as he knew she would, 'but we're not here for much longer ourselves.'

'Thank you. Thank you, both – for whatever you can do. You'll let me know how things are with her, once you get back to Abbeymead?'

'Her address?' Jack prompted.

'Oh, here... here it is.' She passed Flora a crumpled scrap of paper. 'And thank you again. You're such a good friend. And you, too, Jack.'

Brushing aside the thanks, Flora walked her friend down to the Cipriani landing stage and asked Guido if, as a favour, he could take Sally back to the Minerva, no more than a five-minute boat trip. Trying to suppress his impatience, Jack waited for her return. How much of what was left of their honeymoon, he wondered, would be spent tending a heartbroken girl?

He was still waiting when the young man working behind the reception desk looked up and saw him, prompting a walk across the foyer to hand Jack a slip of paper.

'Sorry, Signor Carrington. I did not see you at first. There has been a telephone call for you this afternoon.'

'Thank you,' he said a trifle dazedly.

There seemed, all of a sudden, to be too much happening. Too many phone calls. Too many visitors. He'd not yet made complete sense of Sally's news. Dying instantly from a heart attack, particularly after prior warning, wasn't that uncommon, he supposed. And Piero Benetti had a temper – they'd experienced that for themselves – which couldn't be good for a faulty heart. Nevertheless, it seemed very sudden. And suspicious? One thing *was* certain, with Benetti dead, one of Flora's chosen suspects for Franco's murder had dropped out of the picture.

'Is it important?' Emerging from his reverie, he saw that Flora had returned and was staring at the note.

Opening it, he read the few lines it contained. 'Important? I don't know. You judge.'

She took the slip of paper from him, her eyes widening as she read. 'We have an invitation to Casa Elena?'

'A command, I'd say, not an invitation.'

'Maybe, but it is nicely phrased,' she said consolingly.

'Really? I get the feeling we're expected to jump to it immediately. Sybil Carrington has spoken and we must be there for lunch tomorrow.'

Flora subdued a sigh. The fraught relationship between mother and son could be difficult to navigate and spending the whole of tomorrow on tenterhooks, dancing around the two of them, was not what she'd envisaged for one of their last days in Venice. Nor, in fact, was holding Bianca's hand for hours.

'I suppose we'll have to go,' Jack muttered. 'The note sounds slightly desperate as well as peremptory.'

'And Bianca Benetti?'

'I'm afraid Bianca will have to wait. We can't do it all! For the Lord's sake we're on holiday and being summoned to go here, there, everywhere. It's ridiculous!'

It was unusual for Jack to lose his calm so completely, but a honeymoon in Venice had been a dream in the making – until real life had intruded too sharply.

'Bianca lives on the Lido,' she said soothingly. 'Sally told me. Is there any way we can combine the two visits? One to Casa Elena and one to Bianca, and save the last day for ourselves?'

'Not a chance. They're miles apart. If we have to go to my mother tomorrow, our last day will be spent providing a supply of handkerchiefs and a shoulder to cry on.'

'We don't need to be with Bianca all day. While we're at the Lido, we could go for a paddle. And you could go for a swim,' she said hopefully.

It took a while for Jack's frown to disappear. Then his face brightened. 'Yes, we could. And... we could have lunch at the Hotel La Perla. It's old-school posh. All Edwardian glamour and art deco. Right on the beach, too. You'd love it.'

'Decision made then. We go to the count's tomorrow and see Bianca the following day.'

'Then we go home,' he said, gloom descending once more.

'We have to go home but we can come back. Maybe not at the Cipriani next time – the Minerva perhaps?'

'You're right! We can and we will!'

Swooping down on her, he lifted her off her feet, swinging her in a circle, and making the young receptionist watching from behind his desk burst into laughter.

'No more!' Flora protested. 'Put me down. You have a journey to organise – to the count's magnificent estate.'

20

Once again, they found themselves at the Maggiore office in the Piazzale Roma, Flora hoping that this might be their last visit to the business, but the familiar figure of Signor Gallo emerging from the doorway had her smile.

'Signor Carrington and Signora Carrington. More adventures,' he said, tugging his newly pressed suit jacket into place.

'More adventures,' Jack agreed, though he sounded flat. 'But not so far afield today.'

Casa Elena was some twenty-five miles from Venice, Jack had calculated and, determined to enjoy the journey, Flora settled herself in the rear seat of the Alfa Romeo. It was a route that took them through a diverse landscape, fields of cultivation alternating with hillsides covered in vines, and occasionally a small castle perched on high, its ancient walls clear against the skyline. The glimpse of a wide river on Flora's side of the car had her ask the driver its name.

'Po,' he told her.

'Po?' She looked at Jack for enlightenment.

'One of the largest rivers in Italy. It flows into the Adriatic near Venice so it could be the Po. But he might be guessing,' he said quietly, nodding at Signor Gallo's back. 'There's a vast network of rivers – the Piave, Brenta, Adige, they're just a few – it could be one of those.'

For some fifteen minutes, they had been steadily climbing from the valley floor, pillows of cloud drifting into an otherwise unmarked sky. The air, too, had grown noticeably cooler. They were leaving behind fields fertile with produce and, in their place, climbing amongst hills, every inch of which was covered in vines. Only clusters of cypress trees, stark against the horizon, provided a contrast.

The driver was swinging the car wide around yet another bend, but then pulled up sharply to stop outside a pair of elegant gates that had come suddenly into view.

'Look at that crest,' Flora said softly, leaning forward and pointing to an elaborately worked shield above the entrance. 'Such beautiful colours.'

'Flashy.' Jack awarded the crest only a passing glance.

Signor Gallo had climbed from the car and was now tugging at a large bronze circle, highly decorated and attached to one of the stone pillars. Somewhere in the *Casa* ahead, a bell must be clanging and, sure enough, the gates slowly opened.

'They're electronic,' Flora commented, 'so why not a button, I wonder? But the bronze pull is stunning.'

'Like I said, flashy.' Jack was plainly in one of his dismissive moods and they were always best to ignore.

On either side of the drive, a long drive – Flora estimated it to be at least half a mile – a hedge of cotoneaster had been neatly clipped and, beyond the hedge, row after row of vines crowded together, their wooden supports standing straight as soldiers. A battalion guarding its treasure.

At the end of the drive, Signor Gallo brought the car to a halt outside the porticoed entrance of a large white building and, within seconds of their arrival, a uniformed maid had opened the massive front door and was waiting for them at the top of a flight of stone steps.

'We're here for lunch,' Jack told their driver, 'but we shouldn't be more than a few hours.'

Signor Gallo was about to resume his seat in the car when the count himself appeared from around the corner of the house. Mansion, Flora corrected herself.

'You are here!' he said. 'Wonderful!'

The count, wearing newly pressed slacks and a smart shirt of pale green seersucker, was looking his elegant best and seemed a good deal more lively than when they'd last encountered him at the hotel. A closer glance, though, and Flora noticed that sadness still lurked in his eyes. With one daughter dead and the other caged in a nunnery, it would be many years, if ever, before he recovered fully from the drama that had been played out in Provence.

Falconi bent to speak to the driver and, after a burst of rapid Italian, the car disappeared around the opposite corner.

'I have sent him to my cook,' the count told them. 'He will eat in the kitchen.'

The servants' quarters then.

'Please, come. Sybil is waiting. We have also a guest who will eat with us.'

Flora caught sight of Jack's expression – he was finding it hard to conceal a scowl. He hadn't wanted to make this visit, had been annoyed by his mother's abrupt summons but felt obliged to obey. Now, he was being told they were to share their lunch with a person unknown, suggesting that Sybil's demand could not have been as urgent as she'd made out.

Following the count into a vast drawing room, it was not, however, an unknown person who greeted them.

'You've met Father Renzi, I believe.' Sybil glided forward, air-kissing Flora and giving Jack a casual pat on the arm.

As always, she was dressed in the very highest of fashion.

Flora had neither the money nor the inclination to follow the designers of the day, but she did read the occasional fashion magazine and the figured cream linen dress, full-skirted and neatly belted with a slashed neckline, had to be by Givenchy, or someone remarkably like him. To complete her ensemble, Sybil had chosen a pair of cream leather stilettos – the count must love her dearly, was Flora's first thought on glimpsing them. Those shoes must wreak havoc with the parquet flooring.

But Sybil was at one with the house in which she now lived. The drawing room was painted a regal blue – duck egg, Flora divined – and a bank of long windows, with bounteous drapes in a toning colour, filled one entire wall. The sofas and armchairs were similarly upholstered, and so deep you could lose yourself in them and never be found. A scattering of Louis Seize marquetry tables completed the picture. A highly expensive picture.

Stephano Renzi had risen from his seat and hesitantly offered his hand to each of them in turn. He should be hesitant, Flora thought militantly. At the Vivaldi concert, he had deliberately snubbed them.

'We will go into lunch in a short while,' Sybil announced, in what Jack called her grand-dame voice.

'But first, we talk,' the count intervened, looking across at the priest for support.

Renzi cleared his throat. 'I have an apology to make to you both. I am embarrassed that I did not speak when we met at the Pietà.'

Flora schooled her expression to neutrality and waited.

'I had a reason,' the priest went on, 'though that does not excuse my discourtesy. But... you see, I had received a most disturbing communication and I did not want to speak of it. I did not want to involve you in more trouble and thought that, if we talked, this would happen. You would ask me how I am and I would have to tell.'

'But Stephano wishes to speak today,' the count put in hastily. 'He has realised he must share his trouble.'

'What trouble would that be?' Jack's tone was not particularly friendly. He'd appeared increasingly irritated from the moment they'd walked into the drawing room. 'What would you have been forced to tell us?'

'I have received a note,' the priest began, his voice a little unsteady. 'I do not know the writer. It was a note that mentioned my dear housekeeper, Filomena. It asked for money.'

'A ransom?' Jack asked swiftly. 'You pay the money and Filomena goes free.'

Renzi nodded, seeming for the moment too overcome to speak.

'But why not tell us the evening we met? You're telling us now.' Flora had begun to share her husband's irritation.

The priest's strange behaviour that evening had disturbed her greatly, leading her – and it was her own fault, she acknowledged – into danger. She had found it difficult, impossible in fact, to forget that frightening pursuit through the alleyways of San Polo.

'I thought I could find the money,' the priest said humbly. 'I thought I could pay and bring my housekeeper home, back where she belongs. No one would be worried. No one would be in danger.'

'But you couldn't,' Jack finished for him.

'A priest is poor and it has not been possible to find all the money this person demands. So... I have had to come to my good friend, Massimo, and beg him for a loan.'

'And his good friend Massimo has counselled that he should not pay the money at all,' the count put in. 'It is blackmail, nothing more, and he should go to the police.'

'And you have been to the police?'

Flora was confused. They had been summoned here to

meet Father Renzi and learn of the ransom demand, it was clear, but why, when the police were already involved?

Stephano shook his head. 'I dare not go to them. The note – it makes plain that Filomena is safe but only for the moment. If I go to the police, what terrible thing might happen to her?'

'So... is this where we come in? A last resort.' Jack's tone verged on the acid.

'You promised to help,' Sybil said, her voice every bit as waspish. 'I thought you should be given the chance.'

'How very good of you.'

'How much money did the note mention?' Flora cut in, impatient with the inevitable sparring between mother and son.

The priest named a sum that was so modest it had her raise her eyebrows. Jack, too, she saw, was taken by surprise. Both had been expecting a very large demand.

'It is not much,' Renzi said, realising what their raised brows might signify, 'for most people, at least. But for me, it is a fortune.'

'And you have no idea who wrote the note?'

It was a forlorn question, she knew, but the priest seemed a man who kept things close to his chest and if he had even the inkling of a suspicion, he should disclose it.

He shook his head. 'It was not written by a hand. The letters were cut from a newspaper.'

'The old trick,' Jack commented. 'But is there anyone you suspect, Father?'

The priest seemed to shrink in his chair.

'You must say.' Sybil stared hard at him. As always, she pulled no punches.

'I wondered... I did wonder if it might be someone from the Tasca family. Probably it is not, but Filomena's nephew is still friendly with Luigi and—'

'You think it could be Luigi Tasca?'

Renzi held up his hands in a despairing gesture. 'I have no

real idea, Signor Carrington. All I know is that I must rescue this poor woman in whatever way I can.'

'And this is where you come in,' Sybil said, smiling brightly. She looked over her shoulder as a black-suited manservant stood in the doorway. 'But first, we eat.'

'What are *we* supposed to do about it?' Jack muttered, walking beside Flora through a spacious hall to the dining room. 'Kidnap Tasca and force the truth out of him? If it *is* him.'

Flora made no response, but stopped to look through one of the floor-length windows at the scene beyond. Through the haze of warmth, a range of gentle hills appeared on the horizon, protective and benign, seeming to hold the winery in their embrace, with acres and acres of vines stretching up the hillside and into the distance. Casa Elena must produce thousands of bottles every year, she thought, a lucrative endeavour if this beautiful house was anything to judge by. Wine, she knew, was growing ever more popular at home, a future challenge to traditional beer. Perhaps she should be selling wine rather than books!

For a moment, Flora was back in the All's Well, walking its aisles, breathing its air, deep in its bookish atmosphere. In an instant, a wave of homesickness had swept her from head to toe, temporarily stunning her. It was the first longing for home that she'd felt on this trip. They had only two days more in Venice, one after this visit, and, though she was sad to leave an entrancing city, suddenly it was books that were calling to her. It was Abbeymead that was waiting.

The dining room she was ushered into proved another masterpiece, aglow with pale peach, and as resplendent as the previous salon, while the stately lunch that followed matched its surroundings: an *antipasto* of caprese salad, a *primo piatto* of ricotta gnocchi with walnut and thyme butter sauce, followed by a main course of braised beef and parmesan polenta, and just in case the count's guests weren't quite full enough, a selection of ice creams and sorbets along with lemon almond cake. Limoncello and *amaro* replaced the several bottles of wine that had been consumed during the main meal.

Conversation had remained muted until the braised beef was under attack, but it was then that Jack, who had been mostly silent, glanced across at the priest. Catching the man's eyes, he fixed him in a steady look.

'When you were the priest in Asolo, you had items stolen from your church, you told us.'

Father Renzi looked guarded. 'That is so,' he agreed cautiously.

'When we asked you before, you seemed unsure, but have you had items stolen from Santa Margherita as well?'

At their first meeting, the priest had mentioned a candelabra that had temporarily gone missing, but nothing else. Yet, according to Daniele, his brother had spoken on the telephone of items stolen from Santa Margherita. Clearly, Franco hadn't been referring to the theft of the painting – his call had been made before the artwork went missing – so to what had he been referring? What exactly had been stolen?

Renzi took a deep breath. 'Small things,' he confessed. 'An embroidered hassock, a jewelled rosary, a gold baptism cup. Filomena told me things had gone missing. Each week, she reported a new disappearance. It worried her greatly.'

'But not you?'

He looked down at his hands. They had become agitated, alternately plucking at and smoothing out his cassock.

'I did not want to accept that the trouble was starting again,' he said finally. 'I had lost my home in Asolo, lost my church, my congregation, all for speaking the truth. I moved to a city I did not know and, at a time I was near to retirement, I had to start again. It has been difficult, very difficult, but I have managed. Filomena, too. And now, this threat had appeared – for us both – that the trouble was beginning all over again.'

'Essentially, you ignored her concerns,' Flora remarked.

The count looked annoyed, holding up his hand as if to ward off further criticism. 'That is unfair,' he said. 'Stephano has made great sacrifices. He deserved a calm life. A gentle life.'

'No, no,' the priest disputed. 'It is perfectly fair. I should have taken notice. I should have reported the thefts to the church authorities, but I covered them up for my own peace of mind. And look where it has led.'

No one chose to answer his question and the remainder of lunch was eaten largely in silence. When the array of desserts arrived on the table, Sybil said rousingly, 'Well, now you both know the score, *can* you help?'

'All we can do is try,' Flora said, earning a deep frown from the husband beside her.

Jack would have his say later, she knew.

21

'Why did you make that promise to my mother?' he demanded, when they were once more alone and driving back to Venice.

'I didn't promise,' Flora pointed out. 'I only said that we'd try to help. And what else could we have said?'

'That there was nothing we could do. That Renzi would be well advised to contact the police and tell them he's being black-mailed. It's a hopeless situation, Flora. We haven't the remotest chance of finding out who sent that note. And it *is* the role of the Venice police, not ours.'

'But the priest won't go to them, and I can see why. They won't even investigate Filomena's disappearance. The woman is kidnapped, or worse, and all they'll say is that she's trotted off for a holiday.'

'Which could be true. What kidnapper packs a bag for his victim?'

'That alone should have given them pause,' she argued. 'Where would she have gone? She doesn't have the money to travel far and she has no relatives where she might stay. But the police have made absolutely no enquiries.'

Jack was silent. He knew she was right, Flora thought, but

wouldn't admit it. 'In any case,' she continued to argue, 'I don't think the situation *is* hopeless – not entirely. When we were at the farm in Asolo and spoke to Matteo Pretelli, and to Enrico Tasca, asking them if they had any idea where Matteo's aunt might be—'

'They said they hadn't,' he interrupted, snappish in a way Flora had rarely experienced. It seemed that today's meeting with his mother had affected him badly, getting beneath his skin when normally he refused to let her bother him.

'They said they hadn't, but they weren't worried, were they? Didn't you find that strange? I would have expected that at least Matteo, a close relative and a boy who must have spent many happy hours with his aunt, would have been extremely concerned at her disappearance. But he wasn't.'

'He also used the present tense,' Jack recalled, his testiness fading.

'How...?'

'When Matteo spoke of his aunt, he used the present tense. I remember noticing. It might simply have been a language issue – or, it might be that, for him, she is still alive. It's not a break-through as such. It takes time for people to accept their nearest and dearest might be dead, but it is a hint that he might know more.'

'If he does, then Luigi Tasca knows as well. And he's the one Father Renzi suspects of blackmail.'

'I'm not convinced it is Tasca. Don't you think he would have demanded more? He's a convicted thief – maybe still a thief if he's been stealing from Santa Margherita – and he must be used to "earning" much larger sums of money.'

'I *was* surprised. The note mentioned a very modest figure. On the other hand, Tasca would know the priest's circum-stances. He'd know that Renzi couldn't pay a great deal and decided it was sensible to settle for less, maybe pitching the demand just above what he thought he could get.'

'Renzi hasn't the money, but the Catholic church does.' Jack's scepticism hadn't gone away. 'It's a very wealthy institution. Filomena has worked for the church most of her life, and the blackmailer could legitimately expect the authorities to dip their hands into what are very capacious pockets.'

'But not if the priest was the target rather than the church,' Flora said musingly. 'Which means that whoever sent the note knows how close Filomena is to her employer, how many years they have been together, and how desperate Father Renzi would be to see the woman back safe and sound. Even if it's not Tasca, it has to be someone close to the priest and his housekeeper. Someone who packed her bag before she disappeared!'

For a mile or two, there was silence in the car until Flora picked up the conversation as though it had never dropped. 'If it was Luigi Tasca who sent that ransom note, he would probably have told his best friend. Which would account for Matteo using the present tense when talking of his aunt.'

'If that's the case, why hasn't the boy rescued her? Why hasn't he called the police himself?'

'He's scared? Luigi has something he can threaten him with? Or...' She paused. 'Matteo is part of the plot.'

'To kidnap his aunt?'

'That might have been accidental.'

'Really?' Jack shifted in his seat to look at her. 'How can kidnapping an old lady be accidental?'

'If she somehow found about the theft. She already knew that items had gone missing from the church and probably had a suspect in mind. Tasca. She could have been a danger to him.'

'But this was an enormous painting,' he protested. 'Not small valuables. Luigi Tasca is a petty criminal, not an art thief.'

'Luigi Tasca is a thief, full stop. He also had a grudge against the priest. Why not steal the painting that provided Renzi's church with the money that keeps it going?'

Jack's shoulders slumped. 'And you think the situation isn't hopeless! It strikes me as so confused, there's no way of untangling it. If you're right and Matteo knows what's going on, knows that Luigi is the villain, there are others who might, too. Tasca senior, for example. They're a solid little group, aren't they? Is Enrico Tasca involved in the thefts – has he set up as a fence as well as a farmer? Or like Matteo might be, is he scared to speak out? Scared of his son? Does Luigi have something he can threaten him with?'

Flora settled back against the leather seat and allowed the breeze filtering through the half-open window to cool her cheeks. She felt overfull from the gigantic lunch, but frustrated, too. Jack was right to point out all the anomalies, all the annoying things that didn't make sense. But that didn't mean they should sigh and turn away. It didn't mean they should give up.

'We need to go back to the restaurant,' she said purposefully. 'Back to La Zucca. That's where the final answer lies.'

'This was not a good idea,' Jack said, several hours later, as the waiter brought aperitifs to their table on the terrace of La Zucca. 'But then I never thought it was.'

'It's not the best I've ever had,' she admitted, 'but coming here is the only thing that makes the slightest sense. In any case, we won't be eating – after that lunch, I don't think I'll eat for a week – and we don't need to stay for long.'

'Just long enough to land ourselves in major trouble. I'm feeling uncomfortable already.'

As always, it was a beautiful evening, the air soft and warm and richly perfumed by the wooden troughs of freesias that bordered the terrace. In the distance, the shouts of gondoliers, hard at their evening's work, and closer by, the gentle swishing of the canal against the quayside.

'Uncomfortable? Really?'

'I feel there are eyes everywhere and all of them trained on us,' he explained.

'I don't see why.'

Flora was feeling chirpy. The evening was beguiling in itself, but it was the dress she'd chosen to wear that was the real boost. A daring red satin – an off-the-shoulder style, too! – that she'd bought on impulse a few days before leaving Abbeymead. She had kept it for their last evening in Venice, except that this was their last but one, but it made her heart sing and she would wear it tomorrow as well. Admiring glances had followed her, she'd noticed, as they'd walked to the restaurant from St Mark's and Jack had been especially complimentary. That was something to hold close.

'I don't see why you think we're being watched,' she repeated. 'All the customers are busy with their food or with each other and the owner is nowhere to be seen. There's a manageress in charge of the restaurant tonight – I glimpsed her as we were shown to the table.'

'And the deadly duo?'

Flora shook her head. 'Neither of them are here. They're probably back in Asolo, skulking. You see – we have a clear run.'

'I'm not sure what that means exactly but I have a premonition that it's bad news.'

'Jack, we came here to discover the truth and that's what we should do.'

'By visiting the ladies' washroom? I'd much rather you didn't. Unless you're fixated on it, I should go instead – not to the Ladies but the Gents.'

'That wouldn't help. The men's washroom is at the rear of the restaurant. It's the women's section that's just above the cellar – along with all those doors.'

'Locked doors,' he reminded her.

'I wasn't able to try every one of them,' she said defensively.

'Not before Matteo and the horrible Luigi appeared. Some of them might have been open.'

'And revealed a stolen artwork worth millions of lire!'

'You can mock, but I could be right.'

She took a sip of the drink Jack had ordered, a negroni, he'd told her, though she wasn't sure she enjoyed it. Looking across the table, she saw how set his face had become and reached out for his hand.

'This isn't like you, Jack. You've been half-hearted about this case from the outset and now you're sounding positively negative.'

'Probably because I am.' His clasp on her hand tightened. 'I'm sorry. I don't want to be a naysayer, but I'm worried for you. These people, if they're the criminals you believe, won't play gently, and I don't want you hurt for the sake of a painting.'

'It's not just a painting, is it? It's a woman, too. And don't say that we don't know Filomena, that we've never even met her, and we should let it go. She's in danger and she needs our help.'

'The trouble with you, Flora, is that you want to help the whole world. Bring you an injustice and you're storming the barricades, no matter how perilous or hopeless. I love you for it, but it scares me.'

'Think of an elderly lady somewhere who's even more scared than you,' she said quietly.

He let go of her hand, resigned, it seemed, to what she'd planned. Flora took a second sip of her negroni, hoping she'd soon like it better, and waited for what seemed the right moment, when her fellow customers were taken up with their drinks and their food, and the waiters busy clearing and setting tables.

Quietly, she got to her feet, kissed Jack lightly on the cheek, and slipped into the restaurant. Checking the manageress was as occupied as her waiters, she walked to the rear of the room and took the stairs she remembered to the basement.

Halfway down the staircase, a customer was emerging from the women's washroom and held the door open for Flora. Thanking her, she pretended to walk through but, as soon as the woman had disappeared up the stairs, allowed the door to slowly close. Down the last few stairs and here they were – six closed doors.

Checking that no one else was about to descend the staircase, she moved swiftly to the first room, trying the handle and finding the door locked. It was, as Jack had predicted. And the same was true of the next door and the one after that.

At the last but one, she thought she heard a noise inside and put her ear to the lock. Surely, she must be mistaken. But no! There was a definite movement of some kind. She could still hear it. A mouse? A rat even? The noise had sounded louder than a small creature would make. Someone or something was in there! She turned the handle as gently as she could, trying not to alarm whoever, or whatever, was there, but was again unlucky. Still... she had a nail file in the handbag she'd left on her seat – maybe that would work. It would certainly be worth risking a return.

Turning to go, Flora felt a hand. Two hands, heavy, and bearing down on her. Then her arms were grabbed from behind and twisted back so fiercely that her shoulders were wrenched almost from their sockets. She was propelled to the end of the passage, a knee in her back, and the final door kicked open. At last, an unlocked room, she thought bitterly. Shoved roughly through the doorway, she lost her balance and fell, hitting the hard earthenware floor with a thud.

The door slammed behind her assailant but not before she'd managed painfully to twist her head to one side and glimpse a face. The face of Luigi Tasca. She'd been right! But what use was knowing for sure that it was Tasca behind these crimes if she was imprisoned? And it *was* a prison she found herself in.

Even spreadeagled on the floor, she could see the plaster

peeling from the walls, the floor dirty and unswept, and the ceiling cracked and flaking. A single light bulb hung from its centre but what illumination there was came from a small slit of a window low down in the wall. It was barred and, when she'd scrambled to her knees, bending her head to peer through the iron railings, it was water she could see, eddying inches below the window. The canal! No escape there.

She pulled herself to her feet, feeling decidedly shaky. Two rickety chairs were the room's sole furniture and she shuffled over to one before collapsing onto the seat. Her arms and shoulders were screaming with pain and her knees stung where she'd landed on the hard floor. But at least her brain was still working and she must use it. Think, Flora, think what best to do.

If she didn't return to their table soon, Jack would be worried. He was already twitchy and her absence would send danger messages flashing in his mind. He'd think her in trouble and come looking for her. That would be the worst thing he could do – he'd be walking into the enemy's hands.

Please don't come, she prayed. Please leave and find help. But do it quickly.

22

Jack was worried. If his watch was correct, Flora had been gone nearly fifteen minutes. How long would it take to try each door, even with six handles to be rattled? A few seconds only if the rooms were locked. But if she'd managed to open a door? Had she found something? The painting? Filomena? It was highly unlikely, but nothing was impossible.

And if the old lady had indeed been locked in La Zucca's cellar all this time, Flora would stay with her. She'd need to calm the poor woman, reassure her, give her the confidence to walk up the stairs and out to freedom. He would wait a while.

But as the minutes ticked by, he knew in his heart there was trouble. What best to do? Go in search of Flora or ring the police for help? What on earth could he say to them? I think my wife is in trouble – she went to the washroom of this restaurant near the Grand Canal and hasn't come back? It would sound ridiculous.

A waiter had glided up to the table, a smile inching its way into his face. 'Signor Carrington?' he asked.

'Yes.' His heart felt a hard squeeze. The man seemed uneasy, his smile pasted on.

'It is your wife, signor. She needs you. Please to come with me.'

Had Flora fallen ill, felt unwell perhaps after the negroni? Or maybe fainted from the heat? He could understand if she had – come the evening, the atmosphere below stairs would be stifling. He would go to her, take her back to the hotel as quickly as possible. Once outside, fresh air should do the trick.

The waiter stood politely to one side as Jack got to his feet and made for the restaurant entrance. 'She is downstairs?' he checked.

'Sì, signor. Please to go quickly.'

The staircase was badly lit and, racing down, he almost missed the bottom step, only to be brought up sharply by two figures jumping from the shadows, their arms reaching out for him. Jack had half turned, meaning to rush back up the stairs and call for help, when an empty sack was thrown over his head, rendering him sightless.

Polenta, he thought, as the sack descended. Even in his confusion, it was the nutty smell that registered. He'd been made blind, but it wouldn't stop him fighting. It couldn't stop him. Flora was down here, somewhere close, he was sure, and depending on him, unless... no, he wouldn't think the very worst. His arms thrashed from right to left, trying to connect with a body, and he sensed that the men were dancing around him in an effort to avoid his blows. As he started to tire, one of them was able to grab his arms while the other was quick to begin tying his wrists together with what felt like twine.

This time he had to use his legs, kicking backwards at his antagonist. The man yelled out with pain – he had scored a hit, it seemed but, in response, the twine was forgotten and a punch to Jack's head landed painfully. It was taking all his resolution now to continue the brawl, but once more he kicked out as furiously as he could. The man must have side-stepped, having learnt his lesson, and Jack was pushed viciously in the back and made to stumble along what, from the brief glance he'd managed, was a narrow passageway. The loud creak of a door opening ahead reached his ears before he was shoved roughly into a room, then heard the door slam shut behind him.

His hands had remained untied, his captors having given up trying – a possibly stupid oversight, he decided. It meant, at least, that he could free himself of this stifling sack. Tearing the hessian covering from his head, his first sight was of Flora, wide-eyed and lodged in the corner of the room, as though the walls on either side could protect her.

He gave a wry smile and walked towards her, holding out his arms. 'Not much of a rescuer, I'm afraid,' he said.

For a startled instant, Flora had continued to huddle in her corner but then realisation dawned and she rushed across the room, kicking the hessian sack aside and throwing her arms around him.

Jack kissed her fiercely. 'You're OK?'

'Yes,' she murmured into his chest.

'Thank the Lord for that!'

'And you?'

'A painful head, a sore back and an itchy nose. Not exactly tragic, but what a mess we've made of things.'

'I suppose.' She stood back. 'One thing we have done is prove our suspicions of La Zucca were right all along.'

'*Your* suspicions, Flora. I couldn't believe anyone owning a restaurant like this would get mixed up in such dirty work. Perhaps Fabbri isn't involved, but there's someone here who doesn't want us exploring too deeply. I didn't see who attacked me. That wretched sack was over my head before I had a chance.'

'Not a good look,' Flora said, finding a smile from some-where. 'I *did* see someone. Tasca – Luigi Tasca. And Fabbri has to be involved. How can he not be? He must know his premises are being used for a criminal purpose. And now we do, too.'

'What good will that do, though? The restaurant is a hotbed of crime, but we can't prove it. We're prisoners. And how the hell do we get out of here?'

He walked to the window and bent down to peer through the bars. 'Not through there, at least.'

'It's the only possible exit, except for the door.'

Jack came away from the window and began pacing the small space. 'Why *are* we prisoners? Have you thought of that? We haven't discovered what they're up to, just vaguely that they're up to something. They could have escorted you back upstairs again, so why lock you up? We've discovered nothing – no painting, no elderly lady.'

'They're not taking any chances,' Flora replied placidly. 'They've seen me down here before, remember.'

'And other women, too, I reckon. The washroom is close by and not well signposted.'

'I heard a noise in one of the rooms and was listening at the door. That's when they grabbed me and pushed me in here. I think there may be someone in the next room.'

Jack frowned. 'Are you sure it was a person?'

'It was only a slight movement. It could have been a rat, I suppose, though I haven't seen any yet, but it sounded like something sweeping the floor rather than tiny feet scurrying.'

'Probably not a rat. The cellar's not damp.'

'So?'

'Rats like water. Buildings in Venice are mostly built from Istria stone and the basements are waterproof. The wood piles that support the buildings are usually oak or larch and they're water resistant, too.'

'Jack!'

'What? Oh, sorry!' He gave an apologetic smile. 'This city, the way it was constructed, has always fascinated me.'

'Could you rather get fascinated by how to get us out of here? Or find out who, if anybody, is in the next room.'

'The last is the easier.' He pointed to a grille at the top of the opposite wall to the gash of window. 'That's for ventilation, not light, but there should be enough space between slats to get a reasonable view.'

'It's really high up. I don't think you'll be able to see. You're tall, I know, but not tall enough.'

'I can stand on that apology for a chair and hope it doesn't collapse beneath me.'

She shook her head. 'You still won't reach it.'

'Hey, you're supposed to be the optimist in this partnership.'

But once Jack had dragged the chair against the wall and climbed on top, holding his breath in case the wood should splinter, it was clear that Flora had been right in her estimation. He could knock on the grille with his hand, but was too far beneath to see through it.

He was about to climb down when there was a shuffling sound on the other side of the wall. It came clearly to them both.

'That's it,' Flora whispered. 'The noise.'

They stood in silence together, waiting.

'*Chi c'è?*' a quavering voice asked.

'Who's there?' he mouthed to Flora.

'*Sono Jack Carrington. Mia mogle è con me. Siamo prigionieri. Parla inglese?*'

'I speak a little but not good. Your wife is there?'

'Yes, we are prisoners,' he repeated. 'And you?'

'*Anche io,*' she said sadly.

Flora had dashed across the room to stand below the grille. 'Filomena?' she asked.

'*Sì, sì,*' the voice said, growing stronger. 'Filomena Pretelli.'

'*Cos'è successo?*' Jack asked. 'What happened?'

Filomena stumbled over words spoken in a foreign language but, within minutes, it was clear what had happened on the night the painting was stolen. She had been arranging flowers in the church, she said, but later that evening realised the ring she'd worn since a young girl was missing. It had fallen into one of the vases of flowers, she'd been sure, and so returned to the church in order to retrieve it.

'*Lui era lì*. Luigi Tasca. *Su una scala*.'

'Luigi Tasca was there on a ladder?'

'*Sì*. He was stealing. I think he steal before. *Mi ricordo... il pouf*.'

'You remembered the hassock?'

'*E la rosario*.'

'And the rosary.'

'*Sì, sì*. Now, our beautiful Rastello. I go, tell Don Stephano. Call police. But the boy too fast. Very strong. He come down... *saltare dalla scala*. He has *corda*.'

'Rope. He tied you up – to a pew?'

'*Sì. Un banco*. I have *fazzoletto*, handkerchief, in the mouth.'

'And your nephew, Matteo?' It was Flora who asked.

'*Mi ha protetto*.'

'He protected you?' Jack sounded sceptical and saw Flora's eyes widen in disbelief.

'Luigi Tasca is thief,' Filomena said severely, 'but Matteo good boy. He sad for me.'

'Did Matteo help him steal the painting?' Someone must have, Jack thought. It was far too heavy to lift from the wall alone and then carry to a waiting boat.

'Luigi make him help.'

'How? *Come?*'

'They are friends. After he work, he drive from Asolo to Santa Margherita. Then Luigi ask him, help me, and Matteo *folle*.'

'Foolish,' Jack translated.

'Matteo say *sì*. But he *scioccato* when he see me. Let Zia Filomena go, he say.'

'And what did Luigi Tasca say?' Flora sounded breathless. It had become a frightening tale.

'He say OK. You help and your aunt go. I do not steal, he say. I take painting. *Sequestro il dipinto.*'

'He was kidnapping the painting!'

'*Sì, sì*. To punish Don Stephano. He want Don Stephano to lose church.'

'To keep paying him back for Father Renzi telling the truth,' Jack said grimly.

'Monsignor will be angry. So much trouble. He tell Don Stephano he must leave.'

'What was Matteo's response? What did your nephew say?'

'He tell Luigi you go to prison. *Ancora*. But Luigi say no one know that he take painting. No one know where painting is. His father has place for it.'

'Enrico Tasca knew what his son was doing?' Jack asked, quietly appalled. He could imagine Filomena nodding her head at this.

'Here, here is the place,' she said.

'In this cellar?'

'*Sì*, I think so.'

'Then Silvio Fabbri must also know.'

'Signor Fabbri not happy. I hear him. But he is friend of Enrico Tasca and Tasca promise the painting go soon.'

'Luigi promised that you could go soon, but didn't keep his promise,' Jack pointed out.

'We must take her, Luigi say. She will tell. But Signor Fabbri not happy when I come. He scared I am here.'

'So he should be,' Flora declared. 'How despicable! All of them. Despicable men!'

'*Anche lui è un amico*. He is friend also.' Filomena was philosophical. 'He help Enrico. But Luigi is very bad man.'

'And that's putting it mildly,' Jack said quietly. 'Filomena, we have to escape and get help for you, but there is only one small window in this room and it has bars.'

'You have room by canal?'

'Well, yes, but—'

'Maybe a door for boats.'

'You mean to deliver goods?'

'Sì. Always. Maybe they no use it now.'

Jack cast his eyes around the room. At first sight, it didn't appear true of this building. But when a beam of light filtered through the window – the sun was on its slow journey to sunset – a shadow fell on the wall beside the window. A shadow that, if he looked closely, showed a faint outline. A rectangular shape. The outline of a door? Could this have been an entrance to the canal?

'I think there *was* a door here,' he said slowly. 'But it's been plastered over.'

'*Non forte?*'

'Not strong? It's possible the plaster is weak if Fabbri thought he might need it in the future.'

'You try,' Filomena suggested.

Jumping down from the chair, he took it with him and walked over to what, on closer inspection, was a definite outline. An experimental thwack of the chair splintered the plaster. Several more blows had further chunks falling to the floor.

'I think it's working,' Flora said, looking up at the grille and hoping Filomena could hear and understand.

Over and over, Jack pounded the chair against the wall, after each blow listening for any sounds above. Flora worked alongside, tearing down whatever loose plaster she could find, her hands soon scarred and bleeding. It wasn't long, however, before first the legs and then the back of the chair came adrift, leaving Jack to wrap his jacket around the seat, all that was now left, in an attempt to muffle the sound. They had been hammering at the wall for at least ten minutes, and it was now a race to find an escape route before anyone above stairs realised what was happening. It was possible that Tasca and his confederates were in another part of the building – probable, he thought, otherwise they would surely have appeared by now.

A last piece of plaster was torn down and a handle in the shape of an iron ring sat glistening in a beam of light.

'Filomena was right,' Flora said. 'The door to the canal is still there.'

But when Jack attempted to turn the ring, there was no movement. He tried again, putting his remaining strength behind it, but the iron ring remained obdurate. Dare they make more noise by pounding the door's wooden planks with the now sorry-looking chair seat? They stood for a moment, waiting in silence. Still no sound from above but...

'I'll try a shoulder,' Jack said. 'It will be quieter.'

And it was, though what damage it was doing to his body, he didn't like to think. On the third heave, there was a creaking, a movement, a slight gap appearing at the top of the door. He grabbed the iron handle once more and thrust with as much force as he could and, slowly and painfully, the door ground open.

'We've found the door,' Flora turned to say to the grille, hoping again that Filomena could hear. A muffled 'Si' came back.

Directly ahead were three stone steps, ridged with green slime, and beyond them the waters of the canal. The door was low, making it necessary to stoop to reach the steps.

'What now?' Flora asked. In the frantic activity of smashing their way through the plaster and finding the door, it was clear she hadn't thought this far ahead.

'Now we swim.'

It seemed so obvious, but so impossible. 'I can't swim, you know that. I'll have to stay, but you must go. You can get help.'

'I'm not leaving you here.' Jack was adamant. 'Anything

could happen in the time it will take me to persuade the police to come. If, indeed, I can. We'll manage – I'll do the swimming and tow you alongside.'

'No, Jack, I can't do it!' She shrank back, staring at the dark expanse ahead, and there was terror in her eyes. 'There's no way I can get into that water.'

23

_____

Suddenly, there were angry voices breaking through their stalemate. Young men quarrelling. The noises came from the floor immediately above.

'Matteo and Luigi?' she asked.

Jack held up a finger. 'Listen!'

He might listen but all Flora heard was a babble of furious Italian.

'What's happening?' she whispered. 'Can you understand any of it?'

'One of them,' he said quietly, 'I think it must be Matteo, seems in a major panic. He says that the police are looking for his aunt. And for the painting. And now that *we're* here, now *we're* prisoners, everything is much worse. Or something like that.'

There was a pause while Jack screwed up his face in concentration. 'He's shouting again about the police coming here. What has Luigi just done? Things get worse and worse.'

Another burst of Italian followed. 'Is that Luigi speaking?'

Jack strained to hear. 'I think it is. He's saying that it was you – he means Matteo – it was you who sent the ransom note. It was a stupid thing to do. It's *you* that's made things worse.'

The voices were now very loud, angry and overlapping, leaving Jack struggling to understand. Another stream of invective and he shook his head. 'I'm not sure... they seem to be shouting insults at each other. Oh!'

Abruptly, the voices had stopped and in their place, the sound of feet thumping across the floor. A crash of china? Of furniture?

'They're fighting?' Flora's anxious eyes met his.

'Sounds like it. Oh!' he exclaimed again.

'What?'

'Someone has a weapon. A knife? It must be Luigi. That was Matteo's voice, telling him to put it down.'

Together, they stood motionless, locked in a kind of paralysis, as loud thumps continued to hammer through the ceiling. A crackle of splintered wood echoed loud and clear. Thudding feet, scuffling limbs, furious yells. But then, the most horrible cry.

The long drawn-out cry of death, Jack knew.

Flora's face was ashen and, without another word, he took hold of her hand and tugged her towards the steps.

'We have to go, Flora. You must trust me. I'll see you safe.'

Pulling her after him, he slipped into the water before she could protest any further.

Holding on to the bottom stair with one hand, Jack held out the other. Mutely, Flora took it. She had tumbled into a nightmare she couldn't escape but, forcing herself not to think, she was coaxed down the slippery stone, step by step. Whatever had happened in the restaurant above was bad, very bad, and she was desperate to get away. Filomena... she hated to leave her, alone and frightened, but there was nothing they could do for her while they were locked in this room. They must, at least, try to escape.

In the darkness, she sensed the water slither slowly up her ankles, then her knees, and now she was waist deep. She felt a rush of intense cold, a creeping penetration, an enemy closing in, and was terrified. She wanted to kick out, to scramble back into the room, but girdling her round the waist, Jack held firm. For a minute, he trod water with her until, satisfied that she had calmed sufficiently, he said, 'Hang on to my shirt and let me do the work.'

Heart thumping, she followed as he launched himself forward, clinging to the clump of linen, a fragile lifeline. Water was splashing at them on either side and blurring what vision she had. Unable to see clearly, she nevertheless sensed that Jack was swimming further out into the canal – into the maelstrom of boats and water traffic. Why was he doing that? She wanted to yell for him to stop. But the water was lapping her ears, lapping her mouth, and she was bereft of breath. All her energy, all her wits, were focused on continuing to clutch the one piece of security she had, the ragged piece of shirt.

It seemed they had been in the water forever and a deadly numbness was taking hold, leaching strength from her limbs and turning arms and legs into pillars of ice. The water was creeping higher, too, then it was bubbling around her mouth and then – she was beneath the surface, floating downwards, her grip slowly loosening as she fell into calmness, into peace. Until... animal instinct, an innate desire to live, had her grab at the lifeline she had almost lost and pull herself closer to Jack. Forcing her head above water, Flora breathed air once more.

Jack was swimming in a different direction now, veering left towards the cobbled quayside. Over his head, Flora caught a glimpse of lights, of people. Her heart exploded with relief. They were only yards from safety.

Five minutes later, he was at the bottom of a flight of steps and reaching down for her.

'We made it,' he gasped, water streaming down his face, his hair plastered to his head. 'And it looks as though we have a reception committee!'

She barely registered what Jack was saying. *We're safe, we're safe,* were the sole words her mind would form and it was not until they stood dripping and cold on the canal side, that Flora realised that the lights she'd glimpsed weren't just those of the street lamps. They were far too bright and far too numerous, and coming from a succession of boats moored close by. Some of the lights were blue and swirling. Police! But how?

A man in uniform was approaching them, a frown on his face. '*Cos'è questo?*' What is this? he'd asked. Then in English, 'You go swimming?'

'Not voluntarily,' Jack replied, too exhausted to speak anything but his native language. 'We have been held prisoners.'

'*Prigionieri?*' The man frowned even more deeply, unsure it seemed if they were making fun of him.

'*Sì,* at La Zucca.' Jack pointed towards the restaurant – far closer than Flora would have imagined. Was it such a short distance that they'd swum? It felt as though they'd taken on the Atlantic Ocean.

'Ah!' the officer exclaimed. Their plight was now making sense. 'You swim from the cellar?' He sounded astonished.

Jack nodded. 'It was the only way to escape,' he said simply. '*Vieni, vieni!*'

The man hustled them forward, and they had no choice but to follow him to the nearest police launch. At the bottom of the polished steps, he spoke rapidly to his colleague at the wheel and in minutes two large blankets were produced. Gratefully, they took one each and swathed themselves in warm wool.

'*Caffè,*' their rescuer ordered. Then turning to them, 'We talk later,' and with that, he strode away.

'I'm not sure these chaps are the Venice police,' Jack said, as he cuddled her close. 'The badge looks different.'

'Is different,' their new acquaintance said when he brought them the coffee. 'We are from Rome.'

Jack's face cleared. He evidently understood what was going on and Flora wished she could, too.

'Art theft,' Jack told her.

The man nodded. 'We come for the Rastello.'

'But how did you know where to find the painting?'

He tapped a finger against his nose and grinned. 'We have ways.' Then laughing, he said, 'A man, he talk.'

'A waiter at the restaurant?' Jack hazarded a guess.

'*Si, il cameriere*.' He handed them two mugs; it was the best coffee Flora had ever tasted.

'What made you think of the waiter?' she asked, when the officer had returned to the helm.

'When the chap came to the table tonight, I sensed he was uneasy. He was asking me to come to your aid but was doing it under orders, I felt, and he didn't like it one bit.'

'But you came still!'

Jack grinned. 'A wife in peril! What else could I do? But that waiter, I've remembered, was the man who came between Franco and the owner when they quarrelled the first night we ate at La Zucca. And he was the same man who served us when you first went searching for the women's washroom. When we left, I reckon he must have seen Luigi Tasca come after us. With a knife.'

'The same knife as tonight's?'

'Who knows, but at least Tasca was only practising on me. Unlike this evening.'

'If the waiter called the art squad, it must have been before the fight. Otherwise they'd never have got here in time.'

'I guess so. Maybe, for him, seeing us locked up, as well as

Filomena and the painting, was the last straw. He'll be in trouble for not calling the police earlier, but far less trouble than if he were caught in the restaurant red-handed. Look, something's happening.'

They stood up, mugs in hand, and watched as Matteo Pretelli appeared on the quayside. He was handcuffed and being marched between two policemen to a second launch.

'He's alive!' Flora looked stunned. 'He wasn't the one to die.'

'Nor was Silvio Fabbri.' The restaurant owner was next to appear, once more handcuffed and pushed none too gently down the steps of the launch.

'He *was* in the restaurant after all,' Flora said. 'Keeping watch, no doubt.'

'And recognised us. Which was why you were forced into that room and I had a sack thrown over my head.'

As they stood watching still, an ambulance pulled up at the quayside and they hadn't long to wait before a stretcher, carried by two orderlies, emerged from the La Zucca entrance. Ominously, a sheet covered the entire body.

Many of the restaurant's customers, already alarmed by the arrival of the police and the sight of handcuffs, were aghast at this latest development, abandoning dinner plates and gathering their belongings for a hasty departure.

'Luigi Tasca?' Flora asked.

'It has to be.'

'Dead,' the policeman confirmed, coming forward and nodding with satisfaction at the scene beyond.

'So, now, Matteo is a murderer as well as a kidnapper. Poor Filomena. She loved her nephew.'

And there *was* poor Filomena, released from captivity and carried in the arms of a burly officer. Very carefully, he lifted her down into the third of the police launches.

Flora's heart went out to her. 'What a dreadful ending to a dreadful experience.'

Jack's hand slipped beneath the blanket to find hers. 'She's going home,' he said. 'Home to Father Renzi. That must count for something.'

24

It was well after midnight, Flora saw from the boat's dashboard, before their rescuer, having left his colleagues still working at La Zucca, dropped them at the Cipriani steps. Disturbed from his doze, the evening porter jumped guiltily to his feet as they walked through the entrance and scurried across to the reception desk to hand them their key.

'A shower and bed, I think,' Jack said, taking her hand.

But their ordeal was not yet over. The policeman who'd brought them to the hotel had followed them into the foyer.

'There are some questions,' he said, stopping them in their tracks. There was a smile on his face which Flora didn't entirely trust. 'We do them now or we do them tomorrow?'

'Now,' Jack said emphatically and she supposed he was right. Better to get this terrible evening finished for ever.

'Please.' He gestured to the comfortable furniture that lined one wall and, obediently, they walked over to a sofa and sat side by side. It was fortunate that, by now, their clothes were a good deal drier.

The officer took out his notebook. 'You were at the restaurant?'

Both of them nodded.

'And you were locked in the cellar?'

They nodded again.

'Why were you at La Zucca?'

'We'd gone for a drink on the terrace,' Jack said calmly. 'It was another beautiful evening and we wanted to make the most of it.'

The policeman looked sceptical. 'Other customers had a drink on the terrace. Why did the owner lock *you* in the cellar? It makes no sense.'

'I'm fairly sure it wasn't the owner who took us prisoner.' Jack remained calm. 'It would have been one of the young men, though I don't know which.'

The man shrugged. 'But still... why?'

Flora had a sudden sinking of the heart. Was the man suspicious of *them*? Thought *they* might have something to do with the theft of the painting? Surely not.

Jack must have decided to come clean, she realised, or at least half clean, because he admitted, 'We were hoping to discover if Filomena Pretelli was being held there. Father Renzi, her employer, asked us for help when she went missing.'

The officer frowned. 'This is a matter for the police in Venice.'

'The police in Venice weren't interested,' Jack said drily, 'and the priest was exceedingly anxious.'

'But why would you think this lady was being held at La Zucca?'

'There had been trouble before between Father Renzi and the young man who died this evening – he seemed to us to have a strong connection to the restaurant. It was a guess on our part, but it turned out to be right. Flora – my wife' – he took her hand – 'went to the washroom and thought she heard noises in one of the locked rooms and was listening at the door when she was swooped on by this individual, pushed into another room and the door locked.'

Flora wasn't sure how much of that the policeman had followed, but he seemed satisfied and passed on to his next question.

'And you, signor?'

'I was tricked into following. Told she needed my help but then bundled into the room beside her.'

'That is quite a story,' their questioner remarked.

'But a true one,' Flora was quick to say. 'And what will happen now?'

The policeman tucked his notebook out of sight and gave another awkward smile. 'The young man who is alive will be *accusato* – with murder, maybe. Or perhaps something not so serious. Signor Fabbri has told us that he saw the fight and does not believe that Pretelli wished to kill. It was an accident, he says, while they were fighting. The boy will be in prison for a very long time. And Signor Fabbri will be joining him. He keeps a painting that was stolen and he knew that a poor lady was *rapita*.'

'Kidnapped?'

The officer nodded, getting to his feet. 'It is possible we ask for a statement from you, Signor Carrington, but also possible that we will not contact you again. Your part this evening has been... unimportant.'

He had turned to go before Flora, unable to contain herself, burst out, 'Unimportant!'

Jack took hold of her hand and pulled her to her feet. 'A shower and bed, I think,' he repeated.

It seemed they would not be talking over the terror they'd just lived through – at least, not yet. In their present state of exhaustion, perhaps it was best. She must banish it from her mind, Flora decided, and behave as though she were simply returning from a late dinner and a delightful evening. Except that tonight, her beautiful red dress was a sodden rag and her best shoes forever unwearable.

Taking her cue from Jack, she went straight to the bathroom and, after a swift shower, wrapped herself in the towelling dressing gown and plumped down on the bed while she waited for him to reappear. Suddenly, out of nowhere, there were tears coursing down her cheeks. A non-stop flow of tears. Flora was crying, without even realising.

'Good to get the canal water out of your hair, isn't it?' Jack had sauntered out of the bathroom and was towelling his head dry.

'Flora?' She'd made no response, and, frowning, he looked across at her. Then walked quickly over to the bed and knelt down, cradling her face between his hands. 'What on earth's happened?'

'I don't know.' She sounded pitiable, she thought, like a small child trying to explain a bad fall. 'I really don't know.'

'Brandy,' he said, 'that's what you need. And a double.'

'Not again, Jack.'

'Yes, again,' he insisted. 'It's exactly what you need and I should have thought of it earlier.' He made for the telephone on the bedside table and gave his order to whoever was awake at that hour.

Flora looked up and managed a watery giggle. 'You'd better put pyjamas on before the waiter arrives.'

'OK, but then we take our drinks out onto the balcony and you tell me just what's going on in that head of yours.'

Within minutes, the brandy had arrived at their door – the service in the hotel was amazing – and they were sitting side by side in the comfort of cushioned wicker. Glasses in hand, they looked across the narrow stretch of water at the spellbinding scene ahead: a shimmering San Giorgio Maggiore, rising like a fairy-tale palace out of the dark waters of the lagoon.

For a long while, Jack was silent, allowing the peace of the night to settle around them, but finally, he said, 'Now tell me.'

Flora wanted very badly to share the jumble of feelings she was battling, but how to make sense of them? She supposed it must be the fear she'd felt, a fear like no other, clutching at her husband – not even her husband, but a fragment of his shirt – as he'd swum them to safety. Then the relief, the hardly believable moment, when somehow, she had no idea how, she had emerged from a watery tomb to climb steps to the quayside. To stand once more upon dry land.

'I don't think I've ever been so scared,' she began. 'Well, maybe once before when I was locked in the priest's hole. That was probably as fearsome. You rescued me from that, too.' Her voice had a wobble she couldn't control. 'It's impossible to describe the terror I felt, Jack. The darkness, the water suffocating me, the sense that I would never see light again.'

He reached across and grasped her arm, stroking it gently. 'You made it, though. *We* made it.' There was a long pause while he sipped his drink. 'I think... I think perhaps... that maybe we should *re*think these adventures. Stop trying to solve the world's problems.'

She pulled a small face. 'You've said that before,' she reminded him. 'More than once. But somehow, we always get involved.'

'Then we need to try harder.'

'It's difficult to refuse when people close to you ask for help. Or you can see there's a wrong that needs putting right.'

'That's the one that always gets you! Somehow, Flora, you have to stop being a warrior for justice.' He clinked his glass against hers. 'Tonight, though, we should celebrate – just a little. Filomena is home where she belongs, the painting will soon be hanging in Santa Margherita once more – as long as the Church deems it safe – and some very bad men are on their way to prison.'

'Will the team from Rome take over the case, do you think? Or will they just deal with the stolen painting? I wasn't clear from what that policeman said – except that at one point I thought he was going to arrest *us*!'

Jack grinned. 'He was wavering! I'm really not sure whether it's the team from Rome or the Venetian police who will do the charging, but Matteo Pretelli is a murderer whatever, though it seems he'd no wish to kill his friend. And the officer this evening acknowledged that.'

'He'll plead self-defence, won't he, and probably escape a life sentence? But whoever takes on the case, it looks as though Fabbri will be charged as well.'

'Which is justice,' Jack said, stretching tired limbs towards the balcony rails. 'He may not have planned the theft or been involved in the fighting, but he kept silent when he should have spoken. He let friendship triumph over doing what was right.'

'So did Enrico Tasca, I'm pretty sure. The policeman tonight said nothing about him, so perhaps it will be the Asolo police who make the arrest.'

'Whether or not he's locked up will depend on how much involvement he actually had. At the very least they'll want to talk to him. Did he know his son had stolen the painting? Was he the one who arranged for Fabbri to store it in his cellar and to imprison Filomena? Or was he completely ignorant?'

Flora shook her head furiously. 'He knew. Filomena said so. And when we spoke to him in Asolo, I'm sure he knew the housekeeper was alive and, if he knew about her, he knew about the painting.'

'Several juicy prison sentences on the way then.' Jack swirled the last of his brandy around the glass and finished the drink with a sigh of satisfaction. 'Feeling any better?' he asked gently.

'A little.' Flora's smile this time was steadier.

'Then if you're ready... we have another busy day ahead of us.'

Jack was right, she supposed. But though the evening's tumultuous events had left her drained, she felt tense, not wanting to give up and go to bed but too tired to do anything sensible. And she didn't want to think of tomorrow. She'd been trying to forget Bianca Benetti, she realised, though that was impossible. They had promised Sally they would visit the girl and offer any help they could, and it's what they must do. But there were sure to be more tears and, at the moment, Flora had endured more than enough.

Before they fell asleep that night, she turned to him, snuggling her head against the pillow.

'Do you realise that we never mentioned Franco tonight? Yet it was his death that started us asking questions.'

'The truth might come out at the trial but, in any case, Franco's murderer is now as dead as he is.'

'You're sure Luigi Tasca killed him?'

'Who else? We know that Franco went to La Zucca and confronted Silvio Fabbri the first night we ate there. You were guessing when you said that something had happened in the time between Franco recommending the restaurant to us and the furious quarrel we witnessed, but I think you were right. I reckon his mother must have telephoned and told him what was being said in Asolo. That their old priest was in trouble again. That Father Renzi had lost a painting and a housekeeper.'

'And Franco immediately suspected that both of them would be at the restaurant?'

'He could have picked up stories, hints, of what was in the offing on one of his many trips home. Then his mother phones and his suspicions become real, so he steams round to La Zucca to have it out with them. Tasca takes fright. His plot has been uncovered and Franco is a danger to him – the man has to go. Luigi seems to have been particularly handy with a knife.'

'But Franco was pushed into the canal, not stabbed.'

He yawned. 'What difference? Tasca is a killer.'

'But—'

'No more thinking, Flora. Stop those wheels of yours turning and let's go to sleep.'

25

Flora hadn't expected to sleep well and so it proved. The large brandies Jack had insisted on made sure that for the first few hours of the night she slept heavily, but then she was awake and with a mind that wouldn't quieten. Beside her, Jack slept peacefully, and she tried hard not to disturb him. In truth, she doubted she could. He had the ability to sleep anywhere or any time.

He was so much stronger than she, Flora recognised. She might have all the feistiness in the world but he had the fortitude. When she thought of the life he'd led, it seemed inevitable. A child of parents who'd fought incessantly, sent to boarding school at far too young an age, then passed between mother and father like an unwanted parcel. As an adolescent, he'd coped with his mother's erratic care – smothered one minute, screamed at the next – or his father's dubious lifestyle of gambling for a living, with a succession of 'friends' filling his mother's place. When, finally, he'd freed himself of these histrionics and landed a much-prized job on a Fleet Street paper, a cruel war had snatched the moment away. His young life, like so many others', had been taken from him. Instead of the journalism he loved, the company of colleagues he admired, he'd been forced to become a soldier. There had been years of fighting – in Italy, on the D-Day beaches, in a liberation march across France – before he'd known any kind of normality.

And herself? No wonder she lacked the fortitude Jack possessed. She had lost her parents as a small child, it was true, but her aunt had rescued her from an orphaned state, loved her as a mother, and brought her to live safely in a small Sussex village. It was a safety she had known all her life – and continued to know. Curling up against her husband's warm body, she was lulled by the thought. While Jack was in her life, she was safe. Her eyelids grew heavy and slowly she surrendered, falling into a deep sleep and knowing no more until the room was lit by bright sunshine and she felt her hair being stroked from her face.

'Eight o'clock,' Jack murmured. 'If we're to seek out Bianca and leave some of the day for ourselves, we'd better get moving.'

If, last night, Flora had been disinclined to 'seek out Bianca', this morning she was even less enthusiastic. What they both needed, she was certain, was a peaceful day. One spent together, sauntering alleys and pottering in shops, followed by a visit to the pool maybe, and a fabulous last dinner – though not at La Zucca! She was still utterly wrung out and, turning to face Jack, saw that he was looking almost as tired.

'The ferry to the Lido will wake us up,' he muttered. 'I think.' And when she didn't reply, added, 'There's always lunch – we mustn't forget the Hotel La Perla!'

Even lunch at a fabulous hotel no longer looked so attractive, but duty called and she pushed back the covers and searched for her slippers.

'I'll feel better when I'm washed and dressed.' It was said hopefully.

Amazingly, she did, choosing to wear her second-best sandals – she had little choice now – and a favourite sundress.

An elegant navy-and-white spotted cotton which, though she didn't like to boast, fitted her perfectly and was a surefire way to brighten her mood. Smiling at her reflection in the bathroom mirror, she enjoyed the luxury of a full ten minutes of hair brushing – the shower might have washed away the canal water, but there had still been a stickiness to her waves – before walking back into the bedroom, only to find her husband had once more fallen asleep.

Gently, she shook the one shoulder that was visible. 'Jack! Wake up! You were the one rallying *me* a minute ago.'

He gave a low groan, burying himself more deeply in the bedclothes.

'No groaning,' she said firmly. 'We've a lovely day ahead. Come and look.'

Through the long windows, she could see a thick haze over-hanging the lagoon. The sun, it seemed, was in hiding today, yet Flora was anything but unhappy. Brilliant sunshine was all very well, but the cooler air brought with it a new energy, a new determination, and, despite yesterday's terrifying experience, she felt ready to make the most of this, her last day in a city she'd begun to love.

'A few more minutes, surely?' he pleaded. 'For being a hero?'

'That was yesterday – and you've already had your few minutes.'

'Such a taskmaster! And so young!'

Reluctantly, he rolled out of bed and stumbled into the bathroom, unaware of a knock on the bedroom door. Flora went to answer, immediately alert. It will be trouble, she thought, always trouble. A hotel bellboy stood in the corridor holding a small slip of paper.

'From England,' he said, handing it to her, his eyes bright with excitement. Evidently, this was an unusual event. 'A telegram, signora.'

The boy had gone before Flora had time to read the message and it was with trepidation that she carried the slip of paper back into the room.

The short message took no more than a second to read. 'Jack,' she shouted to him in the bathroom, 'it's Alice.'

His head appeared around the bathroom door.

'What's Alice?'

'This telegram.' She waved the paper at him and, in an instant, he was at her side.

'Something serious?' He looked worried.

'I wouldn't think so,' she said calmly. 'Although for Alice it is. Look.'

SALLY MISSING. PLEASE HELP. ALICE.

Jack frowned. 'What does she mean, "Sally missing"?'

'Sally can't have arrived home yet – at least, I think that's what it means. She stayed in Venice to be with Bianca, didn't she? I don't think she could have telephoned Alice to tell her she'd be back a day late.'

He grimaced. 'I'm not surprised she forgot to call. As I remember it, she was rushing to catch the later train as it was.'

'Alice will be frantic.' Flora put her hand to her forehead. 'You know how anxious she gets. How she feels about anywhere beyond Dover.'

'You'd better telephone her and put her mind at rest. When I've finished here' – his razor was still in his hand – 'I'll meet you on the terrace. Breakfast still calls!'

At the reception desk, Flora asked if, as an emergency, she could use their telephone. It would be quicker than waiting to be put through from the kiosk they'd used previously. The young man behind the desk seemed uncertain but, as soon as she showed him the telegram, he waved her into the manager's office and left her alone to make her call.

It was the receptionist at the Priory who answered, telling Flora that the kitchen had only an internal phone but that she would fetch Mrs Jenner herself, as long as the cook was at work today. It was a possibility Flora hadn't considered and she made ready to end this call and try Alice's home number instead.

There was a lengthy pause, but then Alice's voice came down the line, breathless and tight with anxiety.

'Flora, is that you?' And without waiting for an answer, Alice was off. 'Thank goodness you've called. I don't know where to turn. It's Sally, you see, she hasn't come back. She's got herself lost, Flora. Or she's had an accident. One of them canals, I'm certain. I knew the girl shouldn't have gone. I knew it. You'll have to look for her. You and Jack. You need to do it straightway. I'm sorry about your honeymoon, I really am, but you'll have to find her. Go to the police, that's the thing to do. The police—'

'Alice,' Flora interrupted her. She was tempted to laugh but tried to keep her voice neutral. 'Please calm down. Sally isn't lost. She had to stay an extra day in Venice and didn't have time to tell you. She was travelling back yesterday and I'm sure she'll be with you any hour now.'

'What did you say?'

'She stayed for an extra day,' Flora said patiently. 'She stayed for Bianca – you remember, the Italian girl who asked her to come to Venice.'

'But why?' Alice sounded bewildered.

'Bianca has lost her father. He died quite suddenly, a heart attack, and Sally didn't like to abandon her.'

'Not why did she stay, but why didn't she tell me? Doesn't she realise? I've been sick with worry.'

'I'm sorry,' she apologised for the absent Sally. 'It was all such a rush. Bianca was dreadfully upset and Sally was trying to comfort her and, at the same time, change her ticket for a later train. We're going to see the girl today – we promised Sally –

and ask if there's anything we can do. There's just been too much going on, I'm afraid.'

'Too much goin' on!' Alice gave an irritated huff. 'Just wait till I see that young lady. Worryin' me like that – not a wink of sleep last night! She'll be gettin' a piece of my mind, that's for sure!' For a moment, she fell silent and, when she spoke again, she sounded cautious.

'Everythin' *is* all right there?'

'Everything,' Flora lied. 'But the Priory?' Adeptly, she turned the conversation. 'Sally mentioned you've had some trouble.'

'More'n I can say, my love. It's been a right picnic here and I can't wait for Sal to get back and sort it out.'

Flora waited to hear more.

'Two of the maids fightin' over some man. I ask you!' she said, disgustedly. 'And now Charlie goin' off the boil just as Hector's gettin' back on his feet.'

'Going off the boil?' That didn't sound like Charlie. 'How, exactly?'

'Gettin' careless is what I mean. Not listenin' to instructions, gettin' a bit cheeky, too. Sal won't have it, I warned him. He'll be out on his ear unless he pulls himself together.'

'What's going on, Alice? Charlie has always been a lively lad, but never rude.'

'It's Brighton,' she said, as though that explained everything. 'Now he's got some money in his pocket – Sal gave him a rise when he started working under Hector – he's off to Brighton every spare hour he has, and you know what that place is like! I met Mrs Teague t'other day at Houseman's and she's worried. Says her lad is spendin' money right, left and centre, goin' to them coffee bars, playin' jukeboxes. No doubt mixin' with all the wrong'uns. And he's no dad, has he, to set him right. It's all down to his poor mother.'

To Flora, it sounded a very mild rebellion, but Alice was

plainly upset and every small problem had assumed large proportions. 'He'll get bored with going to Brighton,' she said knowledgeably, though she had no real idea if Charlie would. Going to coffee bars and playing jukeboxes hadn't featured heavily in her own young life. It had been drinks in the student bar and then a rapid transition into managing the bookshop and caring for a very sick aunt. 'Try not to worry, Alice. Sally is sure to be with you today and you know what a capable girl she is. In no time she'll have sorted out Charlie *and* the maids. And we'll be back in Abbeymead ourselves very soon.'

She felt a touch on her shoulder. 'Breakfast,' Jack said quietly, having overheard much of the conversation.

'I best go now,' she said, 'but Jack sends his love. Me, too. And we'll be sure to see you the day after tomorrow.'

Replacing the receiver, she smiled. 'A storm in a teacup, I'd say.'

'So I gathered from what I heard, though Charlie might need a little advice.'

'When we get back, he's all yours. But at least that's Alice soothed, for the time being. Now all we have to face is a day at the Lido.'

'It could be worse,' he said, sounding philosophical.

26

Despite his earlier reluctance to spring into life, Jack managed to consume a substantial breakfast, and it was a good hour later that they joined a small queue that had formed for the Cipriani launch. The boat would ferry them across the Giudecca Canal to St Mark's Square where they could catch a *vaporetto* direct to the Lido, the island invisible from the quayside this morning.

The *vaporetto*, when it arrived, was already crowded and the absence of seats had them standing at the rail watching the small craft plough its way from stop to stop: San Zaccaria, Arsenale, Giardini, and finally across the long stretch of water to their destination.

Flora was enjoying the journey. A stiff breeze had begun to blow, teasing her hair and making her cheeks tingle, as the small vessel barrelled a path through what had become churning water. Gradually, the sun began to emerge from its earlier haze, the familiar warmth bathing arms and legs that had stayed bare.

Jack had to raise his voice to be heard over the sounds of water and wind. 'The Lido looks a fair distance.' It was a pinprick on the horizon, Flora saw. 'But in reality, it's not that far.'

'I don't mind how far. The views are amazing.'

Interest lay in whichever direction Flora looked. Silent islands were scattered all about them, the shallows littered with shambling palisades; she could just make out small figures hard at work on the nearest sandbank, knee-deep in sludge and prodding in the mud for shellfish.

'I hope you like the Lido as much as the journey,' Jack said in her ear.

'Why wouldn't I?'

'You might find it a trifle dull – there's not a lot happening on the island. The film festival doesn't arrive for several months. There's a *casinò*, though. That's sure to be going great guns.'

'Are we planning a visit?'

He laughed. 'Not unless you fancy losing what lire we have left! I thought we'd make our way directly to the restaurant. We're a bit early but I'm sure Hotel La Perla will cope. I booked a table the day we got back from Asolo, so they're expecting us. And you'll love the place, I know – it's a walk in the past, a relic from when the Lido had its heyday. A bit stuffy perhaps, but the architecture is beautiful.'

Ten minutes later, Flora had her first sighting of Hotel La Perla, standing proud of a wide beach, its parasols and sunbeds arranged in military fashion. Holding on tightly, she leaned over the boat's rail to get a better view.

'It is beautiful, I agree. And... you know it's very much like a picture I once saw. As a young child? A book I found in the mobile library. It was filled with images of paintings... *Bathing in the Lido*, that's what it was called. I remember the name because I loved that picture. All the women were in Edwardian bustles and holding frilled sunshades. It looked amazingly glamorous.'

'The glamour might be a little worn now. The Lido isn't quite as buzzing these days.'

'Maybe not, but it's still very lovely. And very peaceful.'

Once the *vaporetto* had manoeuvred alongside the landing stage, it emptied quickly, its passengers eager to stream ashore. Walking from the floating platform onto dry land, the smell of the sea hit Flora anew, her ears filling with the sound of cicadas.

Jack touched her arm. 'See what we've left behind.' He turned to face the distant city. 'Just look at that view.'

She turned along with him and, together, they gazed across the lagoon at a hazy Venice, its skyline crowded with domes and campaniles and the familiar red rooftops. Here and there a flag fluttered in the breeze.

'It's wonderful!' How many times had she said those words in the last few days? 'And so is the hotel, just as you promised.'

An immense white square of a building lay ahead and, set against the blues of sea and sky, it offered an idyllic picture. Hand in hand, they walked the short distance along the promenade towards the hotel's entrance where a uniformed man stood majestically to attention. Hotel La Perla was very different from the Cipriani, Flora decided quickly. That hotel, despite its luxury, still felt intimate – the modest lobby, the garden, the duck pond even, had made her feel immediately at home. Here, the splendour was more intimidating.

'Rather grand, isn't it?' Jack said quietly, as they climbed the steps and passed between marble pillars into a foyer of art deco magnificence.

The dining room lay straight ahead, the maître d' waiting at the door to escort them to a table nestled between a gigantic potted plant and a pillar of pink marble.

'It's fabulous,' she said in a low voice, 'but so grand that it's making me nervous.'

Jack pulled a face. 'Flora Steele, nervous? Never! Hopefully, our waiter won't be as daunting.' He gestured to the terrace that ran the length of the dining room and, beyond that, to the sand and the sea. 'I wish we'd brought our bathing costumes. The beach looks inviting.'

After her hair-raising experience of the night before, Flora was quite happy to have left bathing costumes behind. She would be happy enough if they were left behind forever. But the mention of water had caused her stomach to knot. Was it water, though, that was making her feel slightly sick? A memory of the danger, of the terror, they'd encountered? Or was it something else, the shadow of unfinished business? Something she couldn't quite grasp but that lay there like a beast in wait. Ridiculous! The danger had passed, the terror was no more, and she could relax. It was over, wasn't it? Over, her inner voice repeated.

'I was thinking we could have paddled,' Jack was reassuring her.

'You don't need a costume to paddle,' she contended, but before he could argue otherwise, the waiter was at their side and, rather than intimidating, eager to conduct a lengthy consultation over what they should order as an *antipasto*, what as the *primo*, as the *secondo*, and which wine should accompany each course.

'We'll never get through this meal,' Flora prophesied, 'let alone find Bianca's house before it's time to catch the *vaporetto* back. But' – she broke off – 'this looks delicious.'

The first course had arrived, beef carpaccio and horseradish, and Flora stopped talking to take up her knife and fork.

'There's a lot of food, but the service seems pretty nippy. We should be OK for time. I looked at the map before we left and, from what I can see, Bianca's street is only a few roads distant from the hotel. It won't take us long to walk there. And you're right, this *is* delicious.' Jack stopped talking, too.

Within minutes of their finishing the *antipasto*, the waiter had removed their empty dishes with a practised swoop and was ready to serve the crab linguine.

'This is a real treat,' Flora said, once they were alone. 'Such beautiful food in beautiful surroundings.' She smiled at her husband across the table. 'Our last day in Venice – it's going to be fabulous! Despite the Bianca visit.' She shook herself free of any lingering doubt. 'And that paddle? Maybe we'll have time after we've eaten.'

'We'll make time.' He smiled back. 'We'll walk down to the beach and you can take off those smart sandals and wriggle your toes in the sand.'

An hour or so later, Flora was doing just that, luxuriating in the silky warmth of sand beneath her feet. She bent to gather up her shoes for a stroll along the hotel beach but Jack was before her, scooping them into one hand and holding her tight with the other. The visit to Bianca, with its inevitable sadness, was temporarily forgotten – right now, the world around them was one of pleasure. A flotilla of little boats puttered by, close to the shore; a rower passed them, taking his daily exercise; and in the distance, Flora could see a horse and rider galloping free across the broad sands.

They had been tracing a path beside the water's edge as they walked and Flora was tempted. 'The breeze has dropped now and the lagoon is quite calm. I think I could paddle.'

'Go ahead,' he urged.

'And you, as well. You have to join me.'

He laughed 'I'd better not. We can't both get soaked – one drowned guest will be more than enough for La Perla.'

She let go of his hand and hitched up her skirt. 'OK, but you'll have to watch me having fun!' And trailing her feet through the wet sand, she skipped and jumped over the small waves that broke on the beach.

When she had thoroughly saturated the skirt of her best sundress, Flora walked back to him and took his hand. 'You were right about getting drowned. I'll have to dry off before the hotel allows me through its doors again.'

'We won't go back. Thinking about it, we don't need to. From here, we can walk up to the promenade and you should be dry by the time we find Bianca's house.'

Jack came to a sudden halt, his gaze intent. 'You know...' he began, '... you do know you look amazing?' He bent to kiss her and, in return, received a very wet embrace.

'Flora...' His voice was not quite even. 'I'm so thankful you're here with me. Last night... I was scared... so very scared for you...' He broke off, as the sound of bells drifted towards them across the lagoon.

She was shocked, realising for the first time how frightened *he* had been. 'I'm safe, Jack,' she said, reaching up to stroke his cheek, 'and I'll be with you – always.'

For a while they walked in silence, the swish of the sea in Flora's ears, the sun on her skin, the smell of oleander in the air and, at this moment, she wished they could stay here for ever.

'We should go?' he asked softly.

From his pocket, he pulled a folded square of paper that somehow he'd managed to purloin from the Cipriani's reception desk.

'Just checking,' he said, peering down at the map. 'And it seems about time to make a move – sadly, your paddle is over, my love. Still, at least we've had a morning to ourselves and there's still an evening ahead.'

Reluctantly, Flora took the sandals he was holding out to her and followed him off the beach and onto the promenade. Here, she was forced to spend several minutes brushing sand from her feet before she could begin to walk comfortably.

'From what this map is telling me, the Benetti house is several streets inland,' Jack murmured, as he steered them into a road that ran directly north from the hotel. The map, it turned out, had told him correctly and Bianca's home was easily found.

From the pavement, they looked up at what was superficially an impressive building. It was only slowly, Flora thought, that you realised the pink brickwork was crumbling, in parts quite badly, the windowsills flaking paint and the roof missing some of its terracotta tiles. A flight of steps led to a thick wooden front door. A door that, worryingly, was standing ajar. Had Bianca forgotten to close it? Left it open for ventilation? Or was she close by and intending to return very shortly?

'Stay here, Flora.' Instinct, she knew, was telling Jack that trouble might lie on the other side.

'But—' she began to protest.

Jack, though, was already climbing the stairs.

27

Even before he reached the top step, he heard the voices. A girl, her voice cracking, seeming to plead with an unknown visitor. Or was it visitors? Then a heavier, harsher voice. An uttered curse, an angry bellow, and the sound of a chair falling to the floor.

Jack slipped through the open doorway, his ears straining to hear more, unaware that Flora had followed him up the flight of steps and into the house.

The narrow hall was empty, but from the room ahead came the unmistakable noise of scuffling bodies, of more chairs being overturned, and finally a girl's frantic cry.

Without waiting to hear more, Jack rushed forward, pushing wide the half-closed door that lay ahead and, abruptly, coming face to face with two hulking men. They were holding a girl between them, both her arms clamped tight to the men's sides. Her head was bowed and her hair a tousled mess, but she was a girl he recognised. Bianca Benetti.

One of the men, still holding firm to his captive, took a step forward so that his breath came hot and nauseous into Jack's face.

'*Uscire!*' he barked.

'I'm sorry.' Jack was at his most urbane. 'But I don't speak Italian.' He had no intention of going anywhere, not until he'd seen these blockheads out of the house and Bianca safe.

'Get out!' the man snarled in English.

'Not yet, I think.' Jack offered them a polite smile. 'We're here to see Signorina Benetti. We're having tea with her.'

Walking past the two men – true gorillas, he thought – Jack pulled out the remaining kitchen chair and sat down at the small, square table, a benign smile on his face. The men appeared nonplussed. Should they let Bianca go and attack this man before throwing him down the front steps, or should they continue to hurt and harass the girl while he looked on? Or would it be best simply to accept defeat and leave? Jack could imagine the various options passing through their minds until a mutual choice was silently agreed upon and option number one became their preference.

Damn it, he thought. Fate was playing games with him. Again. Not content with demanding he escape an underground prison and a watery death, it had now decided that he must take on these two towering brutes in what would be an unfair fight – and somehow triumph.

In unison, the men advanced on Jack, having flung Bianca to one side so roughly that she collapsed against a kitchen cabinet. Grabbing him by the shoulders, they began to heave him from the chair, prior to administering the punishment they had in store. Immediately, he allowed his body to fall limp and, for the moment, that confounded them. But their hold on him faltered only for that moment and, when they rejoined the battle, it was with even more force than before. They had levered him halfway out of his seat when Flora determined enough was enough.

A saucepan was at hand, she saw, usefully abandoned on

the draining board, and, rushing into the room, she snatched it up and aimed it at the head of the man nearest her. It landed with a satisfyingly loud thwack, a second stroke sounding even louder. Once again, the man's hold on Jack slackened, this time very considerably. He slewed around, slightly punch drunk, his face a blob of scarlet, and Flora braced herself for his counter-attack. Bianca, though, having recovered her breath and her feet, had snatched another saucepan hanging from the line of hooks on the cabinet and was busy inflicting a similar injury on the second man.

For an instant, the outcome teetered in the balance but Jack, having staggered upright, broke free of the last restraint and was making for the cabinet himself, plainly in search of a weapon with which to join the saucepan-wielding women. The men, now bereft of their captives, seemed hesitant, unable to process what was happening. There was a panicked exchange of looks that said clearly, 'Let's go.'

And they did, swearing in Italian that they would be back. That Bianca Benetti would pay, in one way or another.

'What did that thug mean,' Jack asked, 'that you'd pay one way or another?'

They were sitting, somewhat uncomfortably, on a circle of wooden-backed chairs in a room opposite the kitchen. The Benettis' living room was narrow with barely space for more than an old and beautiful walnut chest of drawers and the trio of single chairs, their shabby cushions fraying at the edges. A wide picture window, however, brightened the space and looked out onto a pleasant communal garden that was shared by several of the houses in the street.

'I owe them money,' Bianca admitted, her voice dull and defeated. 'And I can't pay.'

'You borrowed money from those men?' Flora frowned at the idea. It seemed extraordinary to Jack, too.

'Not them.' Bianca slowly stirred sugar into the coffee she had just made. 'From their boss. Those men are just his... enforcers... is that what you call them?'

'In American films, perhaps.' Jack gave a half smile. 'So, who *is* their boss?'

'A horrible man. Two horrible men. They stay at the Minerva for two, three weeks and I was their chambermaid. I talked to them many times and I thought they were good people. I told them I was in trouble – that I must have money very quickly – and they said they could help.'

'The help they offered was a cash loan?'

She nodded.

'It must have been a large sum.' That was pretty clear, Jack thought, but why had Bianca been so desperate for money that she was willing to trust a man or men who were so obviously dubious? Had she been in a blind panic and why?

'The money wasn't for you?' Flora hazarded.

'For my father,' the girl said. 'He needed money. Needed it quickly. When *Mirabelle*, the first *Mirabelle*, was smashed to pieces and could not be repaired, he had to pay for a new boat. Or he would not work.'

'But the new boat, the one that took us to Burano – wouldn't your father have already ordered it?' Flora was still frowning, trying, Jack could see, to work out how suddenly it had become imperative to borrow this huge sum.

'The boat had been ordered,' the girl confirmed, 'and built. But not paid for. When it was ready to collect, Papa had not the price, so he asked the boatyard if they would keep it a while until he could find the money. Then the accident happened and he *had* to have the boat. He had to pay. He was desperate, and that is when I arranged the loan.'

'And what exactly were the terms of the loan?' Jack was

unsure there would be anything written down, but it was as well to check.

Bianca confirmed his worst fears. 'It was something we agreed,' she said, trailing off.

'Agreed verbally?'

She nodded again, then burst out, 'It was going to be fine. They were nice people, I thought. They would let Papa repay when he could. But then they asked for interest and Papa managed to pay, but it wasn't enough. They told us that now they want all their money back, plus more interest. That he must sell the boat, sell this house. They come here often, push their way into the house to threaten him, to bully him, until...' She broke off, her voice choked. 'Until they left him dead,' she finished. 'And now they have come for me.'

Her feet beat a muffled tattoo on the polished floorboards. 'I should never have done it. I *would* never have done it if I had known what kind of men they were. Papa had no idea how to get the finance. I thought I was saving him!'

She jumped up, too distressed to continue, and, gathering up their empty cups, rushed back into the kitchen.

'I'm so sorry, Bianca.' Flora had followed her, putting her arm around the girl's shoulder and hugging her close.

'It was my fault that Papa was in trouble.' Bianca blew her nose forcefully. 'And I grabbed the chance to make things right. Or that is what I thought.'

'How could it have been your fault?' Jack heard his wife ask, as he joined them in the kitchen. He shared Flora's puzzlement. There was certainly something odd about the financial pickle Bianca had landed herself in. Any money Piero had lent must have been returned by the time he had to pay for the boat.

'I was getting married,' she said in explanation, her voice lifeless. 'But you know that. We were moving to an apartment in Mestre, a new apartment. It is not the best place to live and the flat was not expensive, but I had saved only a little and Franco had nothing at all, although I did not know it. Not for a long time. We needed to pay a deposit and then we would arrange a loan for the rest of the price, but through a bank. It is the proper way.'

'The deposit, though – you borrowed it from your father?' Flora guessed.

'I didn't,' she said indignantly. 'I knew nothing. It was Franco who asked my father for money, then pretended to me that it was *his* money paying the deposit, but it was not. It was Papa's and when his old boat was destroyed and he had suddenly to pay for the new one, the money he had saved had gone to Franco.'

'Was there a reason that Franco had no savings?' That seemed extraordinary to Jack. 'He was in a very good job. In fact, he'd had a number of very good jobs.'

The question had Bianca grip the back of a chair and look blankly down at the bare wooden table.

'He drank,' she said at last. 'I did not realise how much, not immediately. When I first met him, he would have two, three drinks maybe, in an evening, and that would be it, but then gradually he drank more until he would get through a whole bottle of wine in one evening, all by himself. Spirits, too. When I found out that he had borrowed money from my father, that he had no money of his own, I realised that he'd spent everything he earned in one bar or another.'

She sank down onto the chair, Flora taking the seat opposite. 'I think that deep down Franco was not happy with his life.' She gave a small, bitter laugh. 'To me, it always seemed glamorous. He worked in a luxury hotel. He was an important member of their staff and he met famous people every day, people with money, with influence.' She paused. 'But perhaps his heart was not content.'

That fitted with what Sally had told them, Jack thought, remembering their conversation. Franco hadn't seemed to enjoy the world he'd made for himself. He'd been born into a country family with a life as a small farmer awaiting him once he grew up. But he'd wanted more. Or thought he did. He'd travelled to England seeking his fortune, looking for new opportunities, and found them. But evidently it hadn't made him happy, and he'd decided to return to Italy. With experience of working in a five-star London hotel, he'd won a job at the Cipriani, but contentment still appeared to elude him. There'd been regular visits to his family, long spells spent back in Asolo. Had he missed his earlier life so very much? Thinking about it now, it might well have been why he'd chosen to marry a girl from a very similar background. Bianca's father was a working boatman on the canals of Venice, and how different was that from a farmer tilling a few fields for his living?

'Was it your idea to buy the apartment in Mestre?' Flora broke the long silence.

The girl shook her head, a flat denial. 'It was Franco's. As soon as we got engaged, he said we must buy a flat. He was certain it would be better than renting. His parents had rented their farm all their lives, he said – the house they lived in, the fields they worked – and what had they to show for it? What would they have when they could no longer work?'

'And Mestre?' she asked gently.

Bianca sighed. 'It was not Franco's idea of a good place to live but it was all we could afford. He did not like the small houses, the factories, and he hated how far he would have to travel to get to the Cipriani. What he longed for was an apartment in Venice. Don't we all?' Again, that small bitter laugh. 'One in Dorsoduro perhaps, by the side of a small canal. But you have to be rich to live in Venice and we were not. There was no chance that we could ever afford such a place.'

'If Franco borrowed the deposit from your father, then surely he could have asked the builders for it to be returned – when he broke the engagement and no longer needed the apartment?' Jack felt baffled at the many things that seemed not to add up.

Bianca jumped up abruptly, spilling a few drops of coffee on already stained tiles. 'He could have done, if he had ever paid the deposit,' she said in a strangled voice. 'But he never did.'

28

'What!' Flora exclaimed and Jack shared her amazement. It was a very large sum of money to go missing.

'The deposit went on drink?' he suggested, wondering how anyone could drink that much.

'Some of it, probably. But most of it Franco gambled away.' Bianca must have seen the astonishment on their faces and said quickly, 'He was not a gambler. Not usually. I did not know, but he began to go to the *casinò* – he said later that it was to double the money he had borrowed, so that he could repay my father and we would not have the debt on our shoulders.'

'I'm guessing Franco was a better drinker than a gambler,' Jack said.

The girl nodded, averting her face. 'All the money Papa had saved was wasted.'

'And you knew nothing of this?' Flora got to her feet and walked over to the girl, holding her hands out in sympathy.

'It was when those bad men began to threaten Papa that I learn the whole story. They said they would hurt him, Flora – beat him and worse – if he did not pay the money he owed them, now that they ask for it. I begged Franco "get the deposit back from the building company", but of course he had never paid them. He had thrown away the money. Papa could not pay and was frightened. Very frightened. It put his heart under much stress. It was what killed him.'

There was little in that you could argue with, Jack thought.

'In effect, they were murderers.' Flora was less dispassionate.

The girl turned, her face a cold mask. 'No! Franco was my father's true murderer. His true killer.' Her voice was sheeted in ice.

Flora took a step backwards. 'That's quite an accusation. Did you confront Franco with it? Did you accuse him?'

The same question had sprung to Jack's mind, but he wished that Flora hadn't asked it. Bianca was a cauldron of emotion, none of it good, and his instinct for danger had begun to make itself felt again. He looked across at the two women, holding hands in friendship. No need to worry, he told himself. No need to make mountains where there were only molehills.

Bianca broke away. 'What if I did?' she asked angrily. 'Franco caused hurt, he caused misery, caused death, and you think he should go free?'

'What I think doesn't matter. How did he answer your charge?' Flora asked quietly.

Bianca's expression was disdainful. 'He did not answer. Of course, he did not. He was a weak man. To everyone in the world, he was confident. He looked smart and clever. But in truth, he was weak, weak, weak. He refused to meet me, did you know? After all that had happened and when he knew my father was ill and heavy with debt, he refused to talk to me. Would not give me even a few minutes.'

'Did he say why?'

'He said that he was too busy! A stupid excuse – that bad things were going on in Asolo and that first he must sort this out.'

'So, instead ... you went looking for *him*?' she pursued, staring at Bianca as though she would unearth every secret the girl possessed. The hazel of Flora's eyes was almost black, Jack noticed, a danger signal if ever there was one.

Bianca made no response, her mouth clamped tightly shut.

'And you found him, didn't you, near the Accademia?' Flora continued.

'Why do you say that? What makes you think you know?' Bianca's slight body had stiffened alarmingly and Jack got to his feet. His instinct hadn't lied.

'I believe that when Franco wouldn't come to you, you went looking for him and ran him to ground close to the restaurant where we ate dinner on our first evening in Venice. The restaurant he'd recommended to us a few hours earlier. He came to La Zucca that night to conduct his own confrontation – over the bad things that were going on in Asolo. Not so stupid, after all! We overheard the quarrel he had with the restaurant owner and then we saw him walk away. You were there watching, and that was when you must have followed and confronted him with what he'd done. With what you held him guilty of.'

'So, what if I did?'

'You killed him,' Flora said without expression but with absolute certainty. 'Silvio Fabbri wasn't to blame. Neither was Matteo Pretelli. Nor even Luigi Tasca. It was you who killed him.'

Bianca's figure seemed to collapse inwardly and she covered her face with her hands. 'He wouldn't speak to me,' she gulped. 'Not a word. Me! The girl he had asked to marry. The girl whose father had given every lire of his savings so we could begin a life together.'

'And when he refused to talk to you?'

'He turned his back on me. Walked away, as though I was a piece of rubbish in the street. To be ignored, to be kicked to one side.'

'And you followed him again?'

'I was angry. So angry that I ran after him.'

'And pushed him?'

Jack moved closer, his heartbeat too rapid.

'He fell into the canal,' the girl confessed.

'Hitting his head as he fell,' Flora added.

Bianca turned abruptly, now face to face with her questioner. 'I did not know. I promise, I did not. Franco could swim. I thought he would get wet, that he would look silly, nothing more.'

'Instead, he was knocked unconscious and drowned before ever he could be rescued.'

'I did not know,' Bianca repeated forlornly.

The girl sounded genuinely sad, Jack thought. Remorseful even. He could relax.

'When you heard the news that Franco Massi had drowned,' Flora went on, 'you didn't go to the police and tell them what had happened. Why not?'

'Why would I do that?' The girl was suddenly belligerent.

'The police were looking for a murderer. You could have explained that Franco's death was accidental.'

'But they would not believe me. They would blame me. Lock me up. Say I was guilty.'

'But you *were*, Bianca. You were.'

It was as though a wash of cold air had blown through the stuffy kitchen – that was the only way Jack could describe it – a blast of air laden with ice that froze all three of them into immobility.

'We will have to report the accident, you must know that.' It was Flora, of course, who broke through the ice. 'We really have no choice.'

'No!'

The girl, suddenly freed from her torpor, enraged and larger than life, had whirled around and snatched at something Jack couldn't see. Leaping across the intervening space, she grabbed at Flora, ripping through the polka dot dress to pull her into a brutal clasp. In the light streaming through a window high above, Jack caught the flash of a blade and sprang into action. Lunging at the girl's legs, he brought her crashing to the floor. She kicked out at him, once, twice, the hard leather of her shoe hitting him squarely in the head. For a few seconds, he lost consciousness.

The knife had spun away to land beneath the table and Bianca, inching to her knees, began to crawl towards it. But Flora was there before her, snatching at the knife as she was pulled into a deadly embrace by her opponent.

A loud knocking at the door brought Jack back to consciousness. His head was vibrating with pain and he tried desperately to focus. The front door! That had been the front door. It must still be open, he thought dazedly. Unless the gorillas had closed it behind them. And that seemed unlikely.

A heavy tramp of feet and two officers dressed in the uniform of the Venice police were in the room, the first snatching the knife from Flora and the second whisking her hands behind her back, a pair of handcuffs at the ready.

'You've got the wrong woman,' Jack croaked, *'la donna sbagliata*. Don't let the other one go.' His flailing hand pointed to Bianca, already making for the kitchen door.

The second officer was swift, grabbing the girl from behind before she could slip away, and holding her fast.

'Cosa è successo qui?'

A third man had joined the group, demanding to know what exactly was going on. And well he might – the kitchen had become rather crowded. This one was in plain clothes, a detective, Jack surmised.

'Signorina Benetti' – Jack pointed to a furious Bianca struggling unsuccessfully to free herself from the policeman's grip – 'is responsible for the death of Franco Massi. She admitted as much before she attacked my wife. Massi's *was* an accidental death,' he added.

The detective's head swivelled around, his eyes trained on Bianca. 'This is so?'

The girl said nothing, refusing even to look at the speaker, but it was pointless her denying the charge. Only feet away were two witnesses to her guilt.

'And you did not report this accident?' the officer continued, shaking his head in sorrow. Again, Bianca refused to speak.

He gave an irritated shrug of his shoulders. '*Portala alla questura.*'

The handcuffs went on and the younger of the police officers propelled a still struggling Bianca forward, out of the kitchen, out of the front door, and into a waiting car, the police station their destination.

The detective turned, taking his time to assess them, Jack realised. A smart man in dress and intelligence. But then you didn't get to be an investigator without those qualities.

'I think,' the man said slowly, 'that I may know you. You are the English people my colleagues from Rome found at La Zucca – after you had swum the canal to escape?' He looked severe.

'We are,' Jack admitted, feeling stupidly guilty.

'And now you are here,' the man continued in perfect English, 'with a woman who has killed and with a dangerous knife. How is this? Did you not come to Venice for a holiday?'

'We did.' He must sound even guiltier, he thought. Best not to mention the honeymoon.

'Then I suggest that is what you do. You have the holiday. First, though, you must give your names and your English address to my officer here, but then you may go. It is possible we will contact you when you have returned to England.'

'I understand,' Jack murmured, hoping devoutly that Bianca would have the good sense to confess exactly what had happened on that wretched night, and that the Venice police would have no reason to speak to them ever again.

'But for the rest of your stay in our beautiful city,' the detective allowed himself a smile, 'please – keep out of trouble.'

He strode to the door, signalling to the remaining police officer to record their details in his notebook. The interview was over.

'Before you go...' Flora said bravely.

'Yes?' The man stopped, his hand on the door.

'How is it that you and your colleagues arrived here at just the right moment?'

'*Serendipità, signora*. We came to question Signorina Benetti and look what we found!'

'Question her about Franco Massi?'

'No, no, no. It was a small matter of a disturbance. In England, some time ago.' He consulted his notebook. 'At a hotel called the Old Ship in the town of Brighton. You may know it.'

'We were aware that Bianca attacked someone there. A man who had promised her a job and refused to keep his promise.'

'This I did not know. Only that the young woman is accused of injuring a man who now wishes to see that she is punished. We have been asked by his lawyers to discover everything we can.' He beamed. 'You see, signora, it was Fate that brought us here at the right moment.'

Just occasionally, Jack decided, Fate could work in one's favour.

29

It was a police vessel, anchored off the Lido jetty, that took them back to the Cipriani. No waiting around for the next *vaporetto*, Flora thought gratefully, and feeling as wrung out as she did, that could only be good news. What the hotel would assume when they arrived yet again in a police launch, she refused to think. It was as well they were leaving early the next morning before they could tarnish their names any further. She was sad, though, very sad, to be leaving the city.

A long bath, she was thinking, as she climbed the steps from the hotel landing stage. A warm soak with a glass of something cold maybe, then a swift packing of the suitcases and a delightful dinner together in the floating restaurant with its magnificent view of an illuminated St Mark's and beyond.

Voices from the foyer brought her up sharply. Voices she half recognised. Slowly, the magical ending to what had been by any standards an unusual honeymoon faded into the mist.

'We have come to say thank you. To thank you so very much!' A joyful Father Renzi, jumping to his feet, greeted them as they walked into the lobby.

'Yes, indeed! It is a thank you that comes from our hearts!' It was Massimo Falconi, heaving himself from a deep-cushioned sofa and holding out his hands in welcome.

'You did well.' Sybil, apparently, was here, too, her response typically ungenerous.

But even she had got to her feet and was smiling. The navy blue silk she wore, a strapless, tightly fitted cocktail dress, certainly looked celebratory and Flora could only mourn, wishing she could say the same for herself. The favourite polka dot frock, torn at the neck and with ugly dust stains on the skirt, would take considerable effort to repair, if at all. By her side, Jack had fared little better, looking as though he'd gone several rounds in a boxing ring, his shirt crumpled and sweaty, and a small lump making its appearance on one side of his head, barely hidden by the thick flop of hair.

The count gave a delicate cough. He had walked right up to them now and it was clear that in the dim light of the foyer their ragged appearance had only just struck him.

'We came only to say thank you,' he said quickly. 'For the wonderful help you have given Father Renzi and, of course, given me. But we will not keep you. You will want to...' He tailed off, unsure how to phrase the sentiment politely.

'They'll want to wash,' Sybil said crisply. 'And change. Most definitely change, into something less... less raffish. But we can wait.'

Every pair of eyes were turned on her, expectant and plainly unsure what they were to wait for.

'To have dinner,' she said, impatience soon making an appearance. 'The restaurant is expecting us. I have made a reservation, but we three can have drinks in the garden – while *you* make yourselves a little more respectable. Let's go, shall we?'

With an imperious hand, she gestured to her husband and the priest to follow her out of the lobby and onto the front lawn where lights were being lit amid the scatter of tables.

That was the end of the quiet meal she'd envisaged. Flora sighed inwardly, while a sideways glance at Jack told her that he, too, had resigned himself to a very different evening from the one they'd been planning.

'My mother is hard to ignore,' he muttered, half under his breath. 'But it shouldn't take us long to pack.'

'Let's hope not!' Flora tucked her hand in his and, together, they made for the marble staircase.

Within the hour and looking a great deal more presentable, they had returned to the garden and were sharing a table with their visitors. The packing had been hasty, a matter of emptying the wardrobe and two of the chests en masse, then bundling clothes as best they could into the two new suitcases bought for the occasion.

It was evident, as they took their seats, that the count meant to celebrate this evening. A waiter was standing by, an ice bucket containing two large bottles of champagne perched on his trolley. When the man departed, having poured each of them a full flute, Falconi raised his glass in a toast.

'I cannot tell you how heavy the weight I have carried. Now it has been lifted from my shoulders,' he said. 'Something very bad was happening in Asolo. I knew it but could do nothing. But today, because of you, it is not. Stephano, here, is once more a happy man. He has his dear, sweet housekeeper safely home and a future at Santa Margherita that he can look forward to. We should drink to that.'

Obediently, they raised their glasses and drank.

'The police have told us very little,' Jack said, pouncing on an olive from the selection the waiter had brought. 'Have you learned any more of what's happened to the crew at La Zucca?'

'The painting is still with the team from Rome,' the priest said, the fate of the Rastello evidently at the forefront of his mind. 'It will be with them for some time, I think – an expert must examine it for damage. But, if all is well, it should be restored to Santa Margherita within weeks.'

'And Signora Pretelli?' For Flora, the person rather than the painting was the most important.

'Poor Filomena.' The priest tugged at his beard, seeming to feel his housekeeper's pain. 'She is feeling very bad. For her, this is a tragedy. It is not only that she was made a prisoner, that she was scared and feared she might be harmed by those wicked men, but that her nephew – a boy she loves very much – was part of this dreadful plot.'

'It always felt particularly ugly that Matteo would treat his aunt so shamefully.' Flora took an exploratory sip of the champagne.

It wasn't a drink she was used to, though she'd sampled it once or twice before. The first time, she reminisced, had been at Jack's birthday dinner, the evening they had first kissed. That had been special. She'd thought then that it tasted out of the ordinary – its zesty tang, the bubbles that prickled her nose – and, after a few more sips tonight, decided again that she rather liked champagne.

'I have been to the police cells and spoken to Matteo,' the priest said sadly. 'It seems that he is part of this business against his will. Luigi is his best friend and when he asked Matteo for help, Matteo must give it. The help is to carry the painting to the boat and then to the van they bring from Asolo. It is much too heavy for one man to move. Luigi tells him it is *un rapimento*.'

'A kidnap?' Jack said.

'Sì. The painting is lost for a short time, but nothing more. So, how worried should Matteo be? What he did not know was that Luigi was stealing the Rastello and that his aunt would be in the church to see this. And did not expect that Luigi would make them take Filomena with them.'

'Common decency should have made him braver. He should have stopped the poor woman's imprisonment,' Sybil snapped.

'I think he tried,' Renzi said pacifically. 'But events moved too fast and suddenly he was in deep, deep trouble. When I visit, we talk a long while. He tells me that Luigi made a threat he would get rid of Filomena unless they take her with them – I do not wish to think what he meant – and Matteo was not sure if the threat was serious. I feel that perhaps by then he hardly knew his friend. So, after storing the painting, he helped Luigi carry his aunt to the boat, then walked into her apartment and packed a bag for her – I was not at home, but at the bedside of a dying man – and together they travelled to La Zucca where Silvio Fabbri was waiting. It was the best Matteo could do, he tells me, to make sure Luigi did not harm her.'

'But he did harm her,' Flora burst out. 'Even if it was at a distance. *He* harmed her, not Tasca or Silvio Fabbri. He sent the blackmail note to you, Father. If that's not harm, I don't know what is.'

The priest looked grave. 'It was a wicked thing to do but by then, you must understand, Matteo was desperate. He has become part of a plot to steal a valuable painting; he has kidnapped an elderly lady as well. What might have seemed a silly prank is now very dangerous. He warned Luigi that the police will bring the art team from Rome. Tried to persuade him to return the painting and let Filomena go – he promised that his aunt would not report what she had seen, they would say it was a joke that had gone wrong. But Luigi refused. He would not return the Rastello; instead he would sell it and use the money to live after he has escaped from Italy. He told Matteo that he was determined to stay free – he could not go to prison again.'

'So, Matteo just left the painting and his aunt to moulder in Fabbri's cellar?' Jack was scathing.

The priest nodded. 'I do not think he knew what to do. He was, what you say, out of his depth? He wanted to run away, but he is not like Luigi who has been stealing for months. He has no money. And he knows for certain that the team from Rome will soon be here, especially when they hear someone is trying to sell the painting. So... he writes to me in the hope that I will give him money to escape, in exchange for Filomena's safe return.'

'He was lying. There was no way he could guarantee her safety. And then he went back to Asolo and pretended that everything was normal?' Flora sounded incredulous.

'I do not know how he could pretend.' There was a small shake of the priest's head. 'But this he did, even when the police visit his father to ask if Signor Pretelli knows of his sister's whereabouts.'

Flora took a reviving sip of her champagne. 'I'm sure Signor Pretelli didn't know,' she said, 'but I did wonder about Luigi's father.'

'You were right to wonder,' Massimo said heavily, pushing away the dish of olives. 'Enrico Tasca is another who is now behind bars. The police came for him this morning. I do not think he had any idea that his son has been stealing since he came from prison, but he agreed to Luigi taking the painting from Santa Margherita as a clever way to punish Stephano again. It was his van and his boat – the one he rents for his deliveries in Venice – that Luigi used for the theft.'

There was a long sigh from their priestly companion. 'He has never forgiven me for being the one who sent his son to jail.'

'And the restaurant owner?' Jack asked.

'Silvio Fabbri is in jail, too,' Sybil chimed in. 'And a good job. They should all be in jail, every single one of them.'

Father Renzi cleared his throat. 'Such a muddle. Enrico Tasca asks Silvio for a favour – please store this painting in your cellar for a short while. Of course, he believed the Rastello would be "missing" for only a little time – it is what his son tells him.'

'Long enough for Stephano to fall into grave trouble with the church.' The count's anger suddenly flamed, his voice harsh.

'After that,' the priest continued, 'they will return the artwork to the church. So... this is the muddle. Signor Tasca has no idea that his son is planning to sell the Rastello and Signor Fabbri thinks only that he is helping to store goods for his friend. But then a valuable painting arrives at La Zucca and an older lady with it, and he is expected to lock them both up. Imagine the shock!'

'But he did it still. He is a weak man,' Flora said decisively.

'Sometimes, loyalty to a long friendship triumphs over common sense. Triumphs over self-interest,' Sybil put in unexpectedly.

'Exactly.' The priest was grateful. 'This is the case I believe with Silvio. He had a successful business, a good comfortable life, he had no wish to be involved in such bad things. Particularly when Franco arrived to accuse him of stealing the painting and of kidnapping my housekeeper.'

'That was the quarrel we witnessed,' Jack said. 'It was the quarrel that took us back to the restaurant the evening Luigi Tasca came after us and tried to warn us off.' There were surprised expressions around the table. 'Flora was on one of her expeditions,' he explained. 'She was busy exploring La Zucca's cellar when she was nabbed.'

'But that was most dangerous, Signora Carrington,' the priest said. 'You know that, after that evening, Luigi began to follow you? He was suspicious and waiting, so Matteo tells me, for the chance to hurt you both.'

'I didn't realise how dangerous it would be.' Flora was remembering the man in the blue shirt. 'Not at the time, though I *was* convinced that Franco's death wasn't accidental. In the end, it turned out that I shouldn't have been looking for art thieves to blame for his death, but a jilted lover.'

'That girl, Bianca,' Sybil said, allowing the waiter to fill her glass for the third time. 'What a stupid thing to do. Chasing after a man like that. And for what? There wasn't even a baby involved!'

'The baby is a mystery,' Flora conceded. 'I didn't feel I could ask, after those men had scared her so badly. I suppose she might have been mistaken in thinking she was pregnant.'

Sybil gave a snort. 'Mistaken! She seems to me to be a highly dubious character, allowing herself to get so angry that she attacked the man. And then making it worse by pretending it never happened. She'll be charged with murder, I expect, and deserves to be.'

'I'm not sure how deserving or otherwise she is.' Jack turned to his mother. 'But the charge won't be murder. Franco's death was unintended.'

'If you push someone hard and he's standing by the edge of a canal, I can't see how the consequence *is* unintended.' Sybil gave a disdainful sniff.

'Time to eat, I think.' The count smiled at the waiter who had arrived to tell them their restaurant table was ready. 'I have ordered a *primo* for us – *bigoli in salsa*. You will like it, I am sure.'

Getting to their feet, the small party made their way back into the foyer and through to the floating restaurant. On the way, Count Falconi took Flora's arm.

'I think it has not been the honeymoon you expected, Flora – and I can see that you have both come through difficult times. But I hope that one day you will return to Venice, return to the Veneto, and enjoy a more comfortable stay.'

'I'd love to come back,' she said and meant it, glancing at her husband, walking close by.

'We should,' Jack agreed, 'only next time make sure that murder isn't part of the agenda!'

30

A few days later, on a Sunday morning, the blinds of the Nook remained down, a firm signal that for most of the village the café was closed. Inside, however, was a hive of activity. Tony had been baking most of the previous day as a welcome home to the honeymooners and now the friends, missing only Sally, were gathered around one of the Nook's largest tables enjoying an afternoon tea: sandwiches of ham and mustard and cheese and pickle, and an army of cakes to satisfy even the greediest appetite. A fat Swiss roll filled one plate while cherry and almond tarts, maids of honour and fondant fancies spilled across others.

This was a working day for Alice and, later that afternoon, she was due back at the Priory to supervise the four-course dinner the hotel would be serving its guests. But for now, she was happily making her way through the cake selection.

'Your fancies have come on a lot, Tony,' she said bestowing her blessing on a lemon and lavender fondant. 'You always had a bit of a problem with them, if I remember, but these are good.'

He accepted the praise with a smile. 'Thank you, Alice, nice to know. Though they're never likely to equal yours.'

'True enough, but it's good to keep tryin',' she said graciously, taking another large bite of fondant.

Jack, sitting beside his wife, gave her leg a surreptitious nudge. 'We're home, for sure,' he said under his breath.

Flora's response was a grin. They *were* home and no matter how wonderful Venice had been, she was happy to be back in Abbeymead. Tomorrow, she would walk into the All's Well and once again take charge of her precious bookshop. Rose had done a sterling job in her absence – that had been universally agreed around the table – but nothing, Flora knew, was going to satisfy until she'd wandered through her shop, from latticed windows to the final bookcase, and personally checked that everything was just as it should be.

'Did you know that Finch man is selling up?' Alice asked, pouring them a second round of teas.

'Really?' Flora was surprised. 'But he's only been here a few years.' And was still 'that Finch man' to the natives, she thought, amused.

Ambrose Finch had bought the old schoolhouse and its adjoining cottage from Miss Howden, who for many years had been housekeeper there. Minnie had inherited the large house and garden when her employer, a man Flora had liked enormously, had met a violent death. It had been a surprise legacy and, rather than keeping an expensive house going in Abbeymead, albeit one that had been beautifully modernised, Minnie had decided she'd prefer to move to a cottage in the neighbouring county. Her brother, with a permanent home in Surrey, had been keen that she joined him.

'Village life is probably too quiet,' Kate suggested. 'Wasn't Mr Finch in a high-powered job before he retired?'

Tony nodded. 'He was, worked in the City – in finance,' he said knowledgeably. 'I had a long chat with him once, when he asked the Nook to cater for his sixtieth. You remember, Katie?' he asked his wife. 'Anyways, he said then that he missed the cut and thrust of the world he'd left behind. Maybe he'll go back to it. He still looks pretty sprightly.'

There was a mutter from Alice. 'He must be mad even to think of going back. What I wouldn't give to retire!'

'Nothing,' Flora said, laughing. 'You'd give nothing. You'd be so bored you'd become your own meals on wheels, cooking for the whole village.'

'Do you know how much he's asking for the house?' Jack asked, his tone light.

'Thinking of buying, then?' Tony pulled a face. 'Unless your books are being filmed by a Hollywood studio, Jack, I reckon it will be way too expensive.'

Flora gave her husband a sharp glance. The schoolhouse would certainly be expensive to buy, and why think of moving when they had a perfectly nice home in the cottage Aunt Violet had left her?

'I expect he'll want a fair sum,' Jack said amicably. 'I guess you have to pay for space.'

Which, of course, is what the cottage hasn't, Flora added silently.

'Mebbe you should find out from the Finch chap. You'll be needing more room with all them babies to come!'

Tony was teasing and Alice laughing, but Jack wasn't, Flora noticed, and felt her stomach flip. Though he was godfather to the Faradays' baby daughter, Jack had never expressed any interest in becoming a father himself. She looked hard at him – had he changed his mind?

The possibility of a baby had never really been discussed. On the rare occasion the subject had hovered in the background, it had been brushed aside, passed over for a safer topic. As a small girl, Flora had been left an orphan, her mother's pregnancy indirectly to blame for the loss of both her parents. If her father hadn't urgently needed to get his wife and Flora's unborn sibling to a hospital in what had been dreadful weather, dangerous weather, the car crash would never have happened and she would have grown up in a family of her own. She had never quite managed to lose the fear, the hurt, the sense of abandonment. And Jack knew it.

'Beware babies, whatever you do!' Tony was still in joking mood. 'Sarah might be over her colic but now she's found her throwing arm. Nothing stays in the cot or the pram for more than five minutes and then she bawls because all her toys are gone. The bending I've had to do! I've joints creaking like an eighty-year-old's. But thank the Lord for Ivy – she never seems to tire of the game.'

'Perhaps the chap who's renting Overlay House might be interested,' Flora suggested. 'In buying, I mean. The school-house is right in the middle of the village and if he really is a spy...' It was time for her to do some teasing.

'That's my niece talkin', I suppose,' Alice said crossly. 'I never suggested to Sal that he was a spy, just that there was somethin' odd about him.'

'Because he doesn't work?' Jack helped himself to a second fairy cake.

'Well, that, among other things. He can't be more than fifty and there he is lyin' about all day. By all accounts, he hardly ever comes into the village, has most of his groceries delivered, and does nothin' to the garden either. I walked that way last weekend and I'm sorry to say, Jack, it looked one big mess.'

'Who's the spy now?' Tony asked, then seeing Alice's expression, must have wished he hadn't. 'Perhaps the man has money.'

'That's the point. If you've got money, why would you rent that rundown house?'

'Please, Alice, you're hurting my feelings,' Jack protested.

'You'll see for yourself soon enough. As well as the garden, the house looks a lot worse now than it ever did when you lived there. If the man has money, why doesn't he rent somewhere nicer? Buy a house even? And why come to Abbeymead in the first place? He knows no one in the village, doesn't speak to anyone much, and never seems to have any visitors. He's like you were, Jack, when you first came.'

'And I was suspicious?'

'Well, we all thought so,' Alice said with certainty. There were hoots of laughter around the table.

'But how's that lass Sally was lookin' after?' Alice seemed keen to change the subject.

'Bianca? She's...' He looked towards Flora for help.

'She's coping,' Flora said.

Neither of them fancied explaining more, neither of them willing to reveal exactly how they'd spent their last days in Venice. It was better that way. What they would say to Sally when they saw her, they hadn't decided. If she didn't already know – and, as Bianca's former employer, it was possible the Venice police had already contacted her – they would have to break the news that the girl she'd befriended had been arrested. Sally would be utterly shocked. Saddened, as well. Bianca's was such an unnecessary crime: a violent push in extreme anger, and then a refusal to be truthful. The girl was almost certainly destined for prison, charged with involuntary manslaughter, or its Italian equivalent. Her father's brand new boat would have to be sold, Flora imagined, to pay the debt the Benettis owed those horrible men; and when Bianca came out of prison, she would have nothing.

'I'm glad the lass is OK,' Alice said, happily oblivious. 'And glad the pair of you made it home safe and sound. I had my doubts, but there, I was wrong and I don't mind admittin' it.'

Flora exchanged a guilty look with her co-conspirator. If anything, Alice had understated the danger when she'd prophesied likely disaster from a city built on canals. They had certainly met with disaster, though it was Franco Massi who had paid the ultimate price. But the theft of a valuable painting, a kidnapped housekeeper and their own watery imprisonment would remain a silent story, shared only between them. It was never a good idea to give Alice ammunition for her warnings of doom.

'Any more tea?' Tony had filled the kettle and returned with a newly refreshed pot. Four cups were pushed forward yet again.

'So, when are you due back at the college, Jack?' he asked.

'Not just yet. I've another two months before term starts, a welcome chunk of writing time, and I certainly need it. I've a whole new novel to plan. But I'll drive over to Cleve at the end of August, before the students return, and check what I'm doing in my final term.'

'I was sorry to hear that you're leaving the college,' Kate said. 'You seemed to be happy there.'

'Flora isn't sorry,' he said drily. 'She'll be popping corks the day we lock the college flat for the last time.'

'We'll all be popping corks,' Alice said. 'Abbeymead is where you belong, both of you. I think we should have a toast – to the return of the Carringtons! – but it'll have to be with teacups.'

'Teacups it is.' Jack raised his to clink with Flora's, the others following suit.

'Oh-oh. I hear trouble!' Tony quickly put his cup down, ready to jump to his feet. A small snuffling noise from the rear of the café had gradually been growing louder and now broke into a full-throated yell.

'You sit down. I'll go.' Alice pushed back her chair. 'That child has got a pair of lungs on her, that's for sure!'

Strolling home along Greenway Lane, Flora reached for Jack's hand. 'Are you happy to be back in the village?'

He smiled down at her. 'Very happy. More than I thought. It's good to go travelling but even better to come home to the friends you love.'

'And a cottage you love?' She sounded wistful.

He'd wondered when the sale of the schoolhouse would surface, but hadn't expected it to be quite so soon. When, in the week, he'd met Ambrose Finch in the village bakery and learned the man was seriously thinking of selling up, he'd been interested. Very interested. Percy Milburn's old house was a beauty: large, airy and with every modern convenience Percy could have thought of. It was a house in which a couple could weave a history for themselves, in which over the years a new family could grow. He'd said nothing to Flora at the time and, aware of how very sensitive she could be where children and families were concerned, had tried not to think too much of it. And it *was* only an idea, after all.

'The schoolhouse was only an idea,' he said aloud.

'But one you've been considering.'

'Not seriously. As Tony reminded us, it would be an expensive purchase.'

Still holding his hand, she walked on in silence and Jack felt unable to break it.

'With my inheritance, we could afford it,' she said suddenly.

'Possibly. I'm not sure.' He was deliberately casual. 'I've no real idea of the price – Ambrose Finch might be hoping to make a very large profit. But, in any case, the money is yours and should stay yours.' He stroked her hand as confirmation. 'And there's no reason to move,' he went on. 'We have a perfectly comfortable cottage, one that you and your aunt have lived in for years. And one that you love.'

'But *you* don't. No!' She held up her hand to stop him from speaking. 'Don't pretend you do, Jack. I know you feel cramped. I know that you're uncomfortable with how little space we have. You've said so. And lately you've been saying it more often.'

'Just because I'm a moaner—'

'That's something you aren't. After living at Overlay for years, I can see that it's been difficult for you to adjust.'

'Overlay House was so much bigger, that's all. A great deal scruffier, but bigger!'

They walked on, Jack noticing that in the short time they'd been away, the hedgerows had grown a little dustier, the foxgloves taller and the buttercups spread more widely. It wasn't until he pushed open the cottage gate and they were walking up its red brick path, that Flora spoke again.

'If we *were* to make a move,' she said carefully, 'what would happen to the cottage? I couldn't bear to think of it left alone and unloved.'

He tried not to look surprised. Was this moment a turning point for them both? 'There are always tenants to be had,' he said, trying to sound detached.

'They would be people we don't know. Strangers. I'd hate that. And so would the cottage.'

'They might not be.' He opened the front door and stood back for her to pass. 'I can think of two people who might want to rent here and they're hardly strangers.'

'Really?' She seemed surprised at the idea.

'Hector and Rose? They're getting married this autumn and they'll need somewhere to live. Rose can't share his room at the Priory and Mrs Waterford is unlikely to welcome Hector at Larkspur Cottage.'

Flora had begun to walk to the kitchen but, at this, she came to an abrupt stop, whirling around to look directly into his eyes. 'You *have* been thinking about the schoolhouse, haven't you?' she demanded. 'Seriously thinking about it.'

'It's just an idea, like I said.'

'Jack!'

'OK, I've been thinking about it, ever since I met Finch and heard what he was planning. But I know how precious the cottage is to you, and that's where we'll stay for as long as you want.'

'Is that the truth?'

'It is.' He put his arms around her.

'We have a pact?'

'We have a pact,' he agreed. 'And honestly, does it matter that much where we live, as long as we're together? Now, stop worrying and give me a kiss.'

For once, Flora did as she was told. Then did it again.

A LETTER FROM MERRYN

Dear Reader

I want to say a huge thank you for choosing to read *The Venice Murders*. If you enjoyed the book and want to keep up to date with all my latest releases, just sign up at the following link. Your email address will never be shared, and you can unsubscribe at any time.

www.bookouture.com/merryn-allingham

Venice in the 1950s was very different from the crowded city we know today. Small, parochial and peaceful, with a sense of community and an enjoyment of the simple pleasures of everyday life. The nearby *campo* provided residents with everything they needed: bread, groceries, a vegetable market, a newsagent and, of course, a church. Squares likes this have become much less common with shops converted into holiday accommodation or tourist boutiques—and that change was already on the way at the end of the Fifties. Even so, it's still possible to escape to an older Venice and, by avoiding well-trodden paths, you are gifted an entirely different city. Walking the narrow streets, crossing picturesque bridges, resting at a café in one of the small *campi* or squares, you gain a sense of the city that was, and still is, beyond the tourist trail. I hope a flavour of this comes through in *The Venice Murders*.

If you've enjoyed the mystery Flora and Jack uncover, you

can follow their fortunes in the next Flora Steele or discover their earlier adventures, beginning with *The Bookshop Murder*. And if you really enjoyed the book, I would love a short review! Getting feedback from readers is amazing and it helps new readers to discover one of my books for the first time. Do get in touch, too, on social media or my website – I love to chat.

Thank you for reading,

Merryn x

www.merrynallingham.com

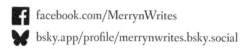

facebook.com/MerrynWrites

bsky.app/profile/merrynwrites.bsky.social

PUBLISHING TEAM

Turning a manuscript into a book requires the efforts of many people. The publishing team at Bookouture would like to acknowledge everyone who contributed to this publication.

Audio
Alba Proko
Melissa Tran
Sinead O'Connor

Commercial
Lauren Morrissette
Hannah Richmond
Imogen Allport

Cover design
The Brewster Project

Data and analysis
Mark Alder
Mohamed Bussuri

Editorial
Ruth Jones
Lizzie Brien